FLIGHT OF THE KING

Also by C. R. Grey

Animas, Book One: Legacy of the Claw

FLIGHT OF THE KING

C. R. GREY

𝒟𝒾𝓈𝓃𝑒𝓎 · HYPERION

LOS ANGELES   NEW YORK

for Aaron, again

 **paper lantern lit**

Text copyright © 2015 by Paper Lantern Lit, LLC
Illustrations copyright © 2015 by Jim Madsen
Map illustration copyright © 2014 by Kayley LeFaiver

First Edition, October 2015
10 9 8 7 6 5 4 3 2 1
FAC-020093-15213

Printed in the United States of America

Library of Congress Cataloging-in-Publication Data
Grey, C. R.
    Flight of the king / C.R. Grey ; illustrations by Jim Madsen.—First edition.
        pages cm.—(Animas ; book 2)
    Summary: Anxious to strengthen the bond that connects him to his Animas, the white tiger Taleth, Bailey must first join his friends in their fight against Viviana Melore and her Dominae movement.
    ISBN 978-1-4231-8343-3 (hardback)
[1. Fantasy.   2. Human-animal relationships—Fiction.]
I. Madsen, Jim, 1964– illustrator.   II. Title.
    PZ7.G8644Fl 2015
    [Fic]—dc23   2014049768

Reinforced binding

Visit www.DisneyBooks.com

A true ruler sees a false one in the mirror;
a false ruler sees only themselves.
The Child of War is the mirror they gaze into:
the Child is both the reflection
and the opposite of evil.

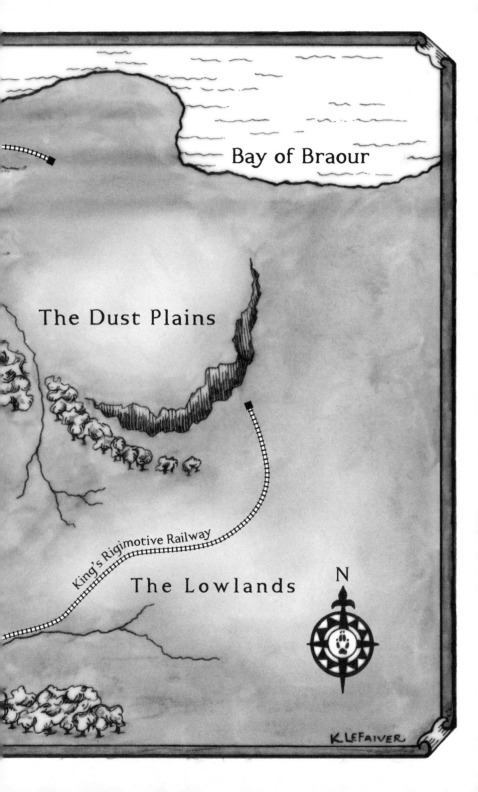

Prologue

A WRETCHED WIND HOWLED across the northern Dust Plains, stirring up brittle blades of dead grass. Barks and yips echoed through a gray stone compound: the sound of ten young jackals, enclosed in a wire cage just outside.

The barking did not bother the man sitting inside the compound. He enjoyed the sounds of chaos.

The Jackal, known only to his intimates and his long-dead mother as Lawrence, sat with his broad back to the window. In front of him stretched a wooden table the length of two lions standing nose-to-nose, littered with gears and scraps of metal. In the middle of the table, like a fresh kill, lay an enormous metal crow. Where its heart would have been was an intricate device with an exposed button. The Jackal pressed it and listened.

The Child of War is here, at the school.... A woman's voice echoed from the bird's flayed mechanical innards. *The tiger must be close by. Don't worry. Tonight the child dies, and your throne is safe....*

The Jackal's snicker filled the room. So, lovely little Viviana Melore was investigating the prophecies—and like him, she would kill to keep her throne. Birds of a metal feather, he thought, tracing his finger along a discarded copper wing on the table. He'd heard about the demise of Ms. Sucrette, however—and not a whisper about a white beast or a dead student. She clearly hadn't succeeded in her task.

"I managed to kill hundreds of white tigers," the Jackal said, laughing, "and Viviana can't even kill one!"

Most everyone in Aldermere believed that the Jackal had been executed—all the better for him, as this allowed his lackeys to gain information that would otherwise be denied him. Parliament had spared his life, exiling him to the Dust Plains. But Parliament had now fallen, and he saw his chance to make some mischief in broad daylight. His Dust Plains agents—thieves and thugs and self-proclaimed "lords" of the outer territories—would be more than happy to plunder the Gray City in his name, for the promise of food and a trunk of snailbacks.

He slipped into the uniform jacket that was draped over the back of his chair and surveyed himself in a small mirror hanging on the stone wall. He was not as strong as he had once been, but his broad figure was still imposing. And the scars—yes, the scars, those certainly helped him maintain a fearsome appearance. He fingered the soft trail of puckered skin that ran from the bridge of his nose down to the underside of his jaw.

Viviana would be a trembling little girl in his presence, no matter how she'd trussed herself up. She'd been a small child when he'd killed her father and ordered his soldiers to set the palace alight. Undoubtedly, she'd grown up with a grudge. But as the Jackal grinned at his own reflection he felt sure that he could easily overwhelm the seemingly impervious new queen. After all, she feared for her throne, and killing the tiger would not help her keep hold of it.

Because I will find it first.

The thought delighted him. The legendary beast of prophecy could actually prove useful, if one was in need of a comeback.

Which the Jackal most certainly was.

One

AS THE RIGIMOTIVE CREAKED into the Fairmount station, Bailey felt a surge of joy. The Midwinter break had only been six weeks, but it felt like months since he'd awakened to his Animas. Being away from his kin had made the days at home seem long and flat—nothing compared to the excitement of his first few months at school. And now being so near to his kin, the great white tiger Taleth, again had him feeling light-headed with anticipation. He couldn't wait to see her, and to continue training with Tremelo, who would teach him how to strengthen and utilize his newly formed bond.

Hal crouched at the rigimotive window, scanning the waiting crowd through his thick glasses. Outside, a fresh layer of snow dusted the station roof and the hedges beyond, and the gaggle of students on the platform were dressed in cozy coats and scarves. Bailey saw his friends Tori and Phi waving, their breath floating up like mist into the air. Phi's falcon, Carin, stood on her usual perch: the protective leather patch strapped to Phi's shoulder.

"It's the girls," Hal said, nudging Bailey excitedly. A pain shot through Bailey's right arm and he flinched. He was still healing from the deep knife wound that ran up his forearm, given to him in the fall by the Dominae spy Ms. Sucrette. Hal sucked in his breath. "Ooh, sorry, Bailey," he said. "I forgot."

"It's okay," said Bailey. He adjusted his sling and pulled his coat over his shoulders.

As soon as he disembarked from the rigimotive, Bailey could sense the presence of Taleth somewhere in the nearby woods. He felt relief to have the tiger so close, though he knew he'd have to keep his Awakening a secret still. The Dominae would be looking for a white tiger and its human kin, and revealing his true Animas would put both him and Taleth directly in their sights. Just as he'd struggled the previous semester to hide the fact that he hadn't Awakened, now he'd have to hide that he actually had.

"Bailey! Hal!" called Phi, hurrying over to them. She and Tori pushed through the throng of students and their kin. A pack of dogs, along with a couple of raccoons and badgers, played happily in the snow as students hustled across the platform to find their trunks. Phi hugged both Bailey and Hal, taking care to avoid Bailey's injured arm. Tori stood back from them, smiling.

"We've been waiting for you," Tori said, with an air of importance. Bailey noticed a small, triangular black face peeking out from her coat sleeve—a snake. It flashed its beadlike yellow eyes at him and retreated. "You're supposed to see Tremelo as soon as you get here, and not talk to anybody about your . . . well, you know."

"My nonexistent kin?" Bailey guessed.

"Right," said Phi, with a finger to her lips. Her dark brown eyes sparkled as she smiled. "He has something for you."

Bailey smiled, hoping that Phi was referring to the Loon's book of prophecies. In addition to training with Tremelo, Bailey was eager to learn more about the strange book that had predicted his Awakening. The book contained a prophecy about the "Child of War," who would herald a new king for Aldermere. It had been written by the Loon, the man who had raised Tremelo. Ever since the discovery that Bailey was, in fact, the Child of War and that Tremelo himself was the True King, Bailey longed to pore over the book's mysterious code. But it could only be read with the Seers' Glass, a prism-like object that deciphered the broken, scratchy letters. Tremelo had promised to study the book over the break, and to tell Bailey what he'd discovered.

With their bags in tow, Hal and Bailey followed the girls away from the crowded rigi platform and onto the main campus. The hedge animals along the path, lovingly sculpted by the groundskeeper, Mrs. Copse, wore white hats of fresh snow. A family of deer darted through the falling flakes on the path ahead of them. A flurry of bats, happy to see Hal again, fluttered out of the Fairmount clock tower in a leathery swarm and surrounded the group, causing Tori and Phi to shriek with laughter.

"They're just saying hello!" said Hal, grinning as the colony circled the clock tower as one, then disappeared under the eaves of its peaked roof.

The Fairmount campus was still decked out for Midwinter— candles shone in every window, and cheery garlands of ivy and cranberry twigs had been draped over all the marble entranceways.

"How was the Gray City?" Hal asked Tori as they passed the library.

"There were lootings," she said. "A printing press near our apartment was ransacked. Papers everywhere, all along the streets, for days. It was a mess! At least the papers looked sort of festive...."

"Who did it? The Dominae?" Bailey asked.

Tori shrugged.

"Who knows? The entire city's gone nuts—whether people support the Dominae or want Parliament back, it doesn't seem to matter. Everyone's just doing whatever they please. I've even seen people trying Dominance for themselves—controlling their kin just for fun. Like a game!"

"That's awful!" said Hal. "There's nothing like that in the Lowlands. Not that we saw, anyway."

Bailey knew that Tori's experience of going home for a few weeks was remarkably different from his own. In the Lowlands, he'd felt very far away from Taleth and his friends, but also far away from the growing power of Viviana and the Dominae. He couldn't imagine what it was like to live in the center of the turmoil.

"No one's able to do what Sucrette did, though," Tori continued, lowering her voice. "I haven't seen anyone able to control someone else's kin, the way she did in the woods that night. I think most people don't even know Dominance is capable of that. If they were, I wonder if they'd be so eager to try it."

The four of them walked on in silence for a moment. Bailey tried to dismiss the grisly images that played across his mind: an advancing troop of bears and wolves and badgers, their eyes cold and murderous. Sucrette, ordering them to kill.

"Did you tell your mom and dad anything about Taleth?" Phi

asked, drawing Bailey back to the chilly commons. He smelled burning logs on the breeze, drifting from the chimneys of the library. Carin the falcon nestled her head in Phi's curly hair, which had somehow grown even wilder over the few weeks they'd been gone.

"I couldn't," said Bailey. He'd wanted to blurt out the whole story as soon as he'd gotten home, especially when he imagined how proud and relieved his parents would be that he had Awakened at last. Instead, he'd pretended that nothing had changed, and had tried to ignore their looks of concern. As far as they knew, he would have an Absence forever.

"It's not that I don't trust them," he explained. "I know they could keep my Awakening a secret, but if I had to explain *why* it's a secret, they'd never let me come back to school! How was I supposed to tell them that the Dominae tried to kill me once already? I can't see my mom taking that in stride."

"No, I guess not," laughed Phi.

"How were things here?" Bailey asked, hoping he hadn't brought up any sore feelings. Phi's family hadn't been able to afford a rigi ticket back to the Dust Plains, and she'd spent the break at Fairmount, in the lonely wing of the Treetop dormitory that the school had kept open for cases like hers.

"It was nice, actually," she said. "I spent a lot of time with Gwen."

"That's great," Bailey said. "I wouldn't mind talking some more to her too." Gwen was only a year older than Bailey and his friends, but she came from an entirely different world. She and her guardian, the Elder, had escaped chaos in Parliament and the Gray City, and had come to Fairmount in search of Tremelo. It was the Elder who had broken the strange and life-changing news that Tremelo was the lost Prince Trent. Now, with the Elder dead, Gwen was also in danger from the Dominae. The safest place for her was at the school.

"She's been a huge help," Phi said, lowering her voice to a whisper. "She's hiding the Seers' Glass for Tremelo."

Bailey felt a twinge of envy. He wished *he'd* been asked to keep the Glass safe, or the Loon's book. But Tremelo hadn't asked for his help.

Bailey and his friends arrived at Tremelo's classroom, which was just as messy, dark, and unorganized as he'd left it the semester before. Worse, even, since Tremelo—a devoted tinkerer—seemed to be at the start of several new projects. In his office, oil-covered gears and ink-blotted papers were piled on the wide, wooden expanse of his desk. This wasn't how kings lived.

"Good, you're here." Tremelo, a tall, lean man with a dark mustache, stood against his desk with his arms crossed. "We need to discuss your plan now that you've Awakened."

"Nice to see you too," Bailey said, shuffling off his winter coat. "Good break?"

"Not enough rootwort rum in the stores," Tremelo replied. Apparently he didn't care how Bailey's break had been as he changed the subject abruptly. "You'll have to be on your guard, Bailey. The school will be watched now that Sucrette's gone."

Bailey nodded, excited to hear what Tremelo had in mind. Six weeks had passed, and Bailey was sure that as king, Tremelo would have reached out to the Melore loyalists by now.

"Of course," Bailey said. "But what else? Have you talked with the RATS? Did you tell them you're the True King? What about the Velyn? Will they fight with us?"

"Focus," Tremelo said.

"But—" Bailey tried again.

Tremelo held his hand up for silence. He looked at Tori, Hal, and Phi, who stood gathered inside the doorway between the class-room and the office, and beckoned them in. He waited for Hal to close the door before going on.

"You're getting ahead of yourself," Tremelo said. "We would need more than the word of an old man and the appearance of an abnormally large cat to spring into the Gray City like vigilantes. I am not running into the heart of the Dominae's operations to get myself assassinated, thank you. Maybe there is a True King, maybe there isn't. Right now, we're *interpreting* a prophecy, not going into battle over it. Understood?"

A silence settled over the room like a thick, suffocating blanket.

"My status as a supposed 'king' is the least of our worries right now," Tremelo continued. "I have urgent news: we're about to be paid a very unwelcome visit by Viviana Melore. She's conducting a goodwill tour of the kingdom's assets: factories, farms ... and schools. Her first stop is none other than Fairmount."

Bailey stiffened. He heard a sharp intake of breath from Phi.

"She's coming *here*?" Bailey said.

"Next Friday." Tremelo nodded. "In less than two weeks."

"Goodwill tour, my eye!" exclaimed Tori. "She'll be asking around about Sucrette!"

"If she even *needs* to ask," Hal pointed out. "What if she already knows we were involved?"

"Don't panic," Tremelo urged. "If she knew that, we'd all be dead already."

"*That's* reassuring," Tori said.

"The tour is a ruse, an excuse for her to find out more about the Child of War. I suspect she'll also try to find the book and the Glass, as it's certain that Sucrette would have mentioned them— but she won't find them," said Tremelo. "Not as long as you all lie low. And that begins *now*. No jaunts off the grounds. No secret meetings, after this one. You will all do your utmost to appear as normal, unaware students."

"But shouldn't we try to stop her?" Bailey asked, though he wasn't sure how. "You're the true ruler of Aldermere, you could challenge her—"

"We'll do absolutely nothing to draw attention," said Tremelo firmly, cutting Bailey off. "If we do, we risk exposing ourselves— and that goes for using the book and Glass while she's here. Working out the Loon's riddles isn't worth the risk."

Bailey looked around at his friends. Hal stood with his arms crossed tightly over his chest, staring at the floor. Tori was shaking her head.

"I don't understand," said Bailey. "We're not going to do *anything*?"

"*I* have a plan," said Tremelo, "if only to gain some information during Viviana's visit. But you must listen to reason, Bailey. Involving you is far too dangerous. Even if I *was* this 'True King,' we're nowhere near ready to challenge Viviana's rule openly. Unless the four of you and Gwen are ready to stand in for an entire army."

Bailey didn't respond. Tremelo was right, though he didn't want to admit it out loud.

"I thought not," said Tremelo. He straightened up. "The Dominae suspect foul play in Sucrette's death. And if Viviana is as intent on stopping the prophecy as I believe she is, then that means she'll be after us. We can't give her any reason to suspect our involvement." He walked to a wire cage hidden behind a pile of newspapers in the corner.

"We must assume that Sucrette sent word to Viviana about the Child of War, even if she didn't name you, Bailey," Tremelo went on as he bent down and unlatched the door of the cage. "So the Dominae will be looking for a white tiger or for anyone who claims to have a White Tiger Animas. Which means you're inviting certain death if you reveal your Awakening. But you can't continue to live with an Absence, either. It will seem too suspicious." Tremelo reached into the cage and pulled something out. When he returned to the desk, he had what looked like a moldy green stocking cap lying along his forearm, with its tail dangling down past the crook of Tremelo's elbow. Tremelo plopped the creature on his desk, where it adjusted a scaly leg over a metal pipe and promptly fell asleep. It was an iguana, and an ancient one at that. Its gray-green skin was flaking off in patches, and the sagging bags under its bulbous eyes were crusted with a growth that reminded Bailey of pictures he'd seen of sea barnacles.

"*Uugh,*" said Tori, and Bailey agreed.

"Say hello to your new kin, Bailey. Many felicitations on your Awakening," said Tremelo. "Tori, I'll need you to pass along a few pointers on how to blend in with the reptilian crowd."

The iguana slowly opened one eye, and then, presumably bored by what it saw, licked its eyeball and went back to sleep.

"It looks like it's dying," Bailey said.

"Its immobility is part of the plan," said Tremelo, sounding tremendously pleased with himself. "No one will notice that you aren't fully interacting with him. And since there are no other Animas Iguana students currently at Fairmount, no one will be the wiser when you carry Bert around."

"Bert?" Tori asked.

Tremelo raised an eyebrow.

"Doesn't he *look* like a Bert?"

"He looks like a handbag," Bailey said.

Tremelo smiled. "He's *your* handbag now, my boy! He'll accompany you to classes, to the dining hall, to Scavage practice..."

Bailey reached out a tentative finger and stroked the ridges on Bert's back. The iguana didn't stir, but a quarter-inch of papery skin lifted off at Bailey's touch. He shook his finger to get it off.

"What about Taleth?" Bailey asked. "Last fall, you were helping me prepare for my Awakening—now that I've Awakened, is the training over? I don't even know how the bond is supposed to work!"

Tremelo's mustache drooped as he frowned, and Bailey saw a glimmer of sincere concern in his eyes.

"It's true, your bond is very fresh," Tremelo said, "which means it'll seem very random to you at first. Moments of insight and shared vision with Taleth will come and go without you being able to control them, usually during times of extreme emotions. These can be jarring, and learning to tap into your kin's mind at will takes time. I wish I could help you ease into it, I really do. But if we were to attract attention to the woods, it's not only you and Taleth who would be in danger. The Velyn would be at risk too."

Bailey breathed deeply, fighting back a lump in his throat. Disappointment filled his chest like a dark cloud.

"Could the Loon's book help?" he asked. "Even if you won't let me see it while Viviana's here, I have to know: what does it *mean* that I'm this Child of War? Could the prophecy help me understand more about my bond? Did you read any of it?"

"I've done what little reading I dare," Tremelo said. "One passage in particular caught my interest: *the reflection and the opposite of evil...*" He seemed to lose himself in thought for a moment, then shook his head. "But the book is hidden away now. I promise, I won't keep it from you forever. But you're in more danger now than you've faced in your entire life. We *must* wait."

"Tremelo's right," Phi said, putting her hand on Bailey's shoulder. "Come on, you haven't even been to your dorm yet."

"I'll see you in homeroom," Tremelo said, turning back to his desk. "Don't forget your iguana."

Bailey picked Bert up and placed him on his good shoulder, where the lizard flopped and settled like a wet towel. He followed his friends from Tremelo's office.

"I don't understand him," Bailey said as they crossed the commons toward the dorms. "The Dominae are coming here, and he *says* he has a plan—but why won't he ask the RATS and the Velyn for help? They'd be here in the blink of an eye if he just told them who he was! And that stuff he said about the prophecy—'maybe there's a True King, maybe there isn't,' as if it weren't clear as day that *he's* the king!" As he spoke, he tried to ignore the humming pull he felt in his chest, urging him toward the woods. Taleth was out there—but he couldn't even build his connection with her. Not yet.

"Tremelo's scared," Hal said.

"And don't forget crazy," murmured Tori.

Bailey sighed. He knew about being scared, and he also knew how overwhelming it felt to learn your true legacy. He was a Velyn—the Child of War—and Tremelo was a king. But even if Bailey's Animas meant he was in danger, his real identity made him feel powerful and important. He couldn't understand why Tremelo didn't feel that same way upon learning he was the son of a king. But Tremelo was right about one thing: with Viviana at the school, Bailey faced his greatest danger yet. He was the herald of the True King and the fulfillment of a prophecy that Viviana would do anything to prevent. If she knew that he was the Child of War, she would have him killed without a second's hesitation. But still—did that really mean that he and his friends could do nothing?

"This will cheer you up," said Phi. "Come see the book's super-secret hiding place!" She smiled, and even Tori seemed pleased, as though she were about to pull the perfect prank. They led the boys across the lawn where the Fairmount clock tower stood, and into the library.

Warm yellow light bathed the entryway, and Bailey smelled the homey aroma of a fire burning in a nearby study room. The girls turned into a large hallway off the main atrium and stopped at an ornate display case. Behind the glass panes of the carved wooden bookshelf stood dozens of books with rich leather bindings and gold decorations on their spines.

"What am I looking at?" asked Bailey.

"If you can't even see it, then Tremelo was right!" whispered Tori. "Look up there." She pointed toward the top shelf, in the left corner.

Bailey followed her gaze. Sitting just as if it belonged there was the Loon's book of prophecies.

"*Hiding in plain sight*, that's what Tremelo said when he put it here," said Phi, looking around to make sure no one was listening. "This is a display of all the first editions that were printed here at Fairmount when there used to be a working printing press."

"Anybody would think that the book belongs here," said Tori. "It's even safer than if we tried to hide it in Tremelo's office."

"Let's hope so," said Bailey, looking around the atrium as a group of Year Two girls walked through, giggling. He hated the idea that only a thin pane of glass stood between the book and anyone who wanted to read it—including him. But Viviana was coming, and being caught with the Loon's book or the Seers' Glass would bring the full force of the Dominae down on them. "Let's hope hiding in plain sight works for all of us."

As they walked back out into the cold winter air, Phi tapped Bailey's shoulder.

"Meet me out by the Scavage fields in half an hour," she whispered. "I have an idea."

Two

GWEN LOOSED AN ARROW from the black walnut longbow Tremelo had given her. It missed the trunk of the tree she'd been aiming for, but snapped several dead, dried leaves off a branch a few inches away. She was improving.

Behind her, three owls sat on the outer windowsill of the tree house where she'd been staying since the battle with Sucrette. The owls ruffled their feathers, swiveling their ghostly heads in the direction of the Fairmount campus. From the trees, Gwen heard footsteps.

She pulled another arrow out of the quiver on her back, nocked it, and lowered the taut bow to her side.

Whit whit whoo—she whistled.

The same whistle echoed back to her, with an added chirp at the end. Gwen eased her grip on the bow as Phi emerged from the trees, leading Bailey. His arm was still in a sling, and he had several broken twigs in his sandy-colored hair. She saw something move under his coat—a scaly face nosed its way out of the top of his collar.

"Hi!" said Phi. She held a haddock sandwich wrapped in paper from the dining hall, which she handed to Gwen. Gwen thanked her, and nodded at Bailey.

"Breaking the rules already?" she asked. "You've only been back a day!" She knew Tremelo had forbidden him to leave campus. He'd demanded that she too stay out of sight.

"I had to say hello, didn't I?" said Bailey. "Besides, I'm technically not off the grounds."

Gwen smiled. She understood his restless energy—she felt it herself.

Bailey shifted the animal inside his coat so that Gwen could see it face-on.

"This is Bert," he said. "My 'kin.'"

"I guess if I had to pick the opposite of a white tiger, that'd be it." Gwen laughed.

"Let's go inside, it's freezing out here," said Phi. Gwen was glad to usher them into the safety of the tree house; it was risky enough having someone bring food, but two of them were practically a parade. She led them up a set of footholds in the trunk of the tree, and through a trapdoor that led into a cozy room, built around the oak. It was used by the Biology and the Bond class in the warmer months, for the students to observe forest life, but during the winter it sat unused. Arched windows lined the hexagonal space.

Bailey passed the iguana to Phi, who held him in the crook of her arm, as he pulled himself through the trapdoor.

"When do you get to take the sling off?" Gwen asked him.

"Next week," he said, "whether it's done healing or not. Can't have a visible injury when Viviana's around."

Gwen set the bow and arrows down next to her pallet, and twisted a lock of her short red hair in her fingers. She too was anxious about Viviana's impending visit. She wondered what the Elder would do if he were here. Try to confront Viviana, maybe, or persuade Tremelo to gather the Velyn and move against her.

"You've been here all alone?" Bailey asked her, taking in the stark tree house.

"I've been visiting her," said Phi. She set Bert on the ground, where he looked around once, and then closed his eyes and seemed to fall asleep.

"Phi's been bringing me food, and books from Tremelo," Gwen said.

"While Tremelo does what?" Bailey asked. "Sit in his office tinkering away?"

Gwen cocked her head like a bird's and looked at him closely. She hadn't seen Bailey since he'd left school for break. He had been excited about his Awakening then, and eager to do more to help the kingdom. Now she saw the way his eyebrows knit close together and the way his eyes cast down to the floor as though pulled there by heavy thoughts. She knew the feeling well. Being cooped up in a tree house, all alone, made her miss the Elder even more. She looked sadly at the leather box that contained Melore's harmonica; it sat on top of the small pile of books Phi had brought her. She hadn't played it for weeks for fear of drawing attention.

"Tremelo's worried," Bailey said, "and there's a lot to be worried about—but that shouldn't mean that we do nothing."

Bailey glanced at Phi, and Gwen saw Phi nod slightly, as though encouraging him.

"Did you two have something in mind?" Gwen asked.

Bailey sat up straighter.

"It's a lot to ask," he said. "But we need someone to trail Viviana while she's here. Tremelo won't do it—"

"And we can't very well leave class to keep an eye on her the whole time," said Phi.

Gwen bit her lip, thinking. She hadn't told Bailey and the others yet about her previous encounter with Viviana, at the Dominae rally where Grimsen the owl was killed. They didn't know that Viviana had seen her, and might recognize her. But did that matter, when she could stay out of sight? Her new friends needed her help.

"You're the only person who can do it," said Phi. "We can't trust anyone else."

"I can try," Gwen said. "Tremelo will be upset."

"I know," said Bailey. "But he's scared. He doesn't want to take any risks—and this might be the only chance we'll have to figure out what Viviana knows."

"That's true," said Gwen. "And we still don't know the extent of Sucrette's influence here in the school. She could have left all kinds of clues for the next spy to come along—or for Viviana herself." This was a dangerous plan, she knew. But she couldn't help feeling that the Elder would be disappointed if he saw how she was hiding. For him, she would take the risk.

"Thank you," said Bailey. "We know it's not going to be easy."

"But be careful. We have no idea what to expect," Phi said solemnly.

I do, thought Gwen. She remembered her heart beating

frantically at the Dominae rally as she watched Viviana command two bears that were not her own kin. And she could still hear the clatter of Grimsen's body, shot through with a metal arrow, hitting the stone floor of that theater. She cast a glance at her own bow and arrows lying on the floor of the tree house. She could never use it to hurt the kin of another person—not out of sheer malice. But Viviana was different. She wouldn't think twice. And for all she knew, Viviana could be looking for her as well as for the Child of War. But that was a risk she'd have to take.

"I'll have to keep the Glass on me," Gwen said. "It wouldn't be safe left here alone."

At her mention of the Glass, Bailey lifted his head and smiled hopefully.

"Do you want to see it?" Gwen asked him. His smile grew wider. Even the iguana stirred, as if he really were sensing Bailey's anticipation. Bert licked his lips.

"If that's okay," Bailey said.

Gwen crossed to the center of the small room, where the ancient oak that supported the tree house sprouted up through the floor. She reached into a hollow knot in the tree's side and drew out a parcel wrapped in a piece of wolf's pelt. The Velyn had given it to her after the Elder's death—they were the only people in the kingdom she knew of who used fur for any purpose. It was a sacred, important thing. She unwrapped the pelt, and there was the Glass. Its many gleaming angles shone in the light from the surrounding windows.

Bailey exhaled as he looked at it, and allowed his tensed shoulders to relax.

"And what if someone comes looking for it here?" he asked.

Gwen held out a tarnished silver coin in her other hand. It was an old beetleback, from Melore's reign, with an embossed image of a spindly-legged bug on both sides.

"Tremelo gave me this," she said. "If I sense danger, I'm to take the Glass and run. I'll leave this in its place as a message I'm safe." She hoped it would never come to that.

Phi gazed over Bailey's shoulder at the Glass, then smiled at Gwen.

"We'd better get back," she said. "Want anything new from the library next time?"

Gwen shook her head.

"Nope," she said. "But if you come across any blueberry tarts, I'd take one of those."

"Consider it done," said Phi.

Bailey eased his way down the footholds first, with Bert riding on his back. Phi paused before following him.

"I'll see you soon," Phi said. "And thank you, again."

"It's nice to feel needed," said Gwen. She felt herself blushing at this confession.

"Be safe," cautioned Phi, and disappeared through the trapdoor, out into the winter cold.

Three

BAILEY WALKED PHI TO Treetop and then doubled back across the snow-covered campus, which glowed in the moonlight. Past the Scavage field, he threaded through the trees that separated the Fairmount grounds from the woods. Bert the iguana nestled underneath Bailey's wool coat, his scaly claws gripping the cables of Bailey's sweater for balance.

When the rigimotive had first pulled into Fairmount that afternoon, Bailey had sensed that Taleth was near. At least, he thought he'd sensed this; he felt a sort of low hum that spread out in all directions from him, like a faint electro-current charge crackling in the air. Was this how it felt all the time to have a bond? He didn't know.

He wondered how different his Awakening would have been if the Velyn, the tribe of his birth, hadn't been nearly wiped out during the Jackal's reign. Did Taleth once have family too? Would he have felt the same strong pull to another white tiger, if they had survived, as he did to Taleth? He had so many questions. He wished that he'd been able to spend more time with the Velyn and their leader, Eneas Fourclaw, before the Midwinter break. Bailey hoped that the Velyn were still in the woods outside Fairmount, and he carried this hope like a lantern, lighting his way through the shadowy trees.

He walked through brambles and over frost-slick stones to the last place where he'd seen Taleth—a small, rocky cliff visible from the highest hill on campus. All around him, he heard the rustling of winter birds and the darting of white-furred rabbits. Then there came another sound, low and gravelly, as familiar as if it had come from his own throat. He saw an enormous white form through the trees ahead. Taleth was waiting for him on the rocks, and she was purring. He wanted to throw his arms around her soft, furry neck—but the truth was he hardly knew her. His first hours with her had been spent fighting for their lives, and he didn't know how she would react to him now. He walked forward slowly, holding his hand out to her.

Taleth waited until he approached, and then she lowered her huge forehead and rubbed it against Bailey's outstretched palm.

When he and Taleth had first come face-to-face, Bailey's Awakening had been undeniable—he'd actually been able to see himself through Taleth's eyes, as clearly as looking into a mirror. Now his connection with her was more like a humming energy inside him, unfocused, chaotic, and untrained. It would take him time, as Tremelo had said, to tap into it at will.

As Taleth purred and sat down on her haunches, Bailey tried

to concentrate on the nature around them, the way that Tremelo had taught him in the fall. He could smell himself, faintly, the way Taleth smelled him: something comforting and foreign about the damp wool of his winter coat, and unmistakably human about his hair and skin. But that was all—as though the humming inside him was set on a low dial.

Bert the iguana shuddered inside Bailey's coat and tried to crawl up onto his neck.

"This is Bert," said Bailey awkwardly as the lizard poked his head out of Bailey's lapel. Bailey couldn't be sure whether speaking to Taleth had any effect on her at all. The tiger leaned forward, sniffing. Clouds of wet breath rose from her nostrils. Her whiskers twitched as Bert craned his scaly head out of Bailey's coat, and touched Taleth's nose with his own.

"Bert's nothing like you," Bailey said—or maybe he only thought it. Taleth stretched and paced past Bailey to sniff him from all sides. She nudged him again, butting her heavy head against his upper back. All at once, Bailey could feel exactly what she felt— her relief at seeing him safe, her delight that she'd found him, her sadness that he couldn't stay here in the woods with her always. It was not like seeing through her eyes, but as if she'd left a trace of her emotions on him.

"I know," he whispered. His own breath rose into the crisp air and dissipated. "I wish I didn't have to stay away. It's not fair."

Bailey tried to hold on to this strange feeling. But the sensation waned, and he was left with only his own sadness, his own relief.

Taleth perked her head and looked over Bailey's shoulder into the trees. She was more worried now; Bailey could tell by her twitching ears. His heart began to beat a little faster as he followed her eyes around the edges of the clearing. Anyone could be watching them at that moment. He put his arms around Taleth's neck, just as he'd wished to when he first saw her.

"I have to go," he said. "It's the only way to keep you safe." He felt the enormous tiger purring—a rumbling that nearly shook his whole body. But if what he'd experienced a moment before could be trusted, he knew that underneath that purr, she was also sad, and that he was the only person in the world who could know that.

Bailey, Phi, and Hal sat together in the dining hall on the first morning of classes, in the company of some other Year One members of the Scavage team. Bailey had left Bert behind in the Towers—the lizard had looked so cozy underneath the heated electro-current bulbs Tremelo had lent him to keep Bert warm. "Basking," Tremelo had called it. Tall windows by their table looked out over the sloping, snow-covered hillside that led down to the Scavage field. Inside the hall, students chatted excitedly about their breaks as they ate egg-and-spinach tarts and bowls of steaming oatmeal with jam made from last year's berries. The morning seemed comfortable and pleasant, but Bailey felt ill as he listened to the group's most prevalent topic of conversation: the unexpected death of Ms. Sucrette.

"I heard she got sick," said Terrence, a boy from Bailey's Scavage squad, who sat a few seats down from Bailey and Hal. "And the school sent her to a specialist in the Gray—but by the time she got there, it was too late."

"She was *murdered*, you idiot—same night that visiting Parliament member died," said Arabella, captain of the Blue Squad, before shoveling a forkful of egg tart into her mouth. Across the table from each other, Hal and Bailey traded worried looks. Arabella was referring to the Elder.

"Parliament, what?" said Alice, a Blue Squad Squat.

"Some old man," Arabella said. "Had a meeting with Finch, and died the same night. Heart attack or something like that. There was a funeral and everything."

"But that had nothing to do with Ms. Sucrette," said Alice.

"Unless the same person was out to get them both!" interjected Terrence.

"But who would want to hurt Ms. Sucrette?" asked Alice. "She was so nice! Phi, you were in her class, weren't you?"

Phi glanced at Bailey before answering.

"We all were," she said, nodding at Bailey and Hal. "She was . . . sweet."

Bailey poked at his breakfast. His appetite had disappeared. He hated thinking of Ms. Sucrette—as a teacher, she certainly had *pretended* to be nice, and done a convincing job of it. But as an agent of the Dominae, she'd been ruthless. As he listened to the others trade theories, he couldn't help picturing her: not only how she'd looked as she advanced on him with a knife in her slender hand, but also how small her broken body had appeared afterward, when the animals she'd dominated had killed her. That image had woken him up at night in the Lowlands, shivering.

The doors to the dining hall opened with a clang, and Headmaster Finch, a skinny, beak-nosed man in a brown plaid suit, entered. He was followed by Mr. Nillow, Bailey's History teacher, who was as round as Finch was tall. Tremelo entered behind them, wearing a thinly masked scowl. He strode over to a corner by the announcements board, and folded his arms in front of his chest. The two other men stood before the rows of tables, and Finch raised his arms in greeting.

"Students, students!" Finch said, though he could barely be heard above the chatter. Mr. Nillow stepped up behind him, put his fingers in his mouth, and whistled harshly. The hall went quiet.

"Thank you, Nillow," Headmaster Finch said, pulling at his plaid waistcoat anxiously. Finch always seemed to Bailey to be both nervous and angry, as though he was afraid of water getting dumped on him, but was ready to punish whoever would do it.

"Many of you may already have heard the whispers about the coming week's exciting events," he began. "And it is my task to make those rumors official—we will be hosting an important guest next Friday: Viviana Melore of the Dominae party, which is making quick work of cleaning up the political system of our fair kingdom."

Bailey fought the urge to snort angrily. It was clear that Finch was a Dominae supporter. From the eager whispers in the hall, it seemed many students were, as well.

"Miss Melore will tour the school during morning classes, and we will host an assembly at three p.m.," Finch said. "Afternoon classes will be canceled that day."

Bailey looked over at Tremelo in his lonely corner. Tremelo glared at Finch. Bailey could only guess at how he felt—even though Viviana was the enemy, she was also Tremelo's sister, and he was about to see her for the first time in twenty-seven years.

"Miss Melore and her accompanying associates from the Dominae party have been invited to stay at Fairmount for a full weekend," Finch continued, "so that they can take in the whole of what the school has to offer—including our very first Scavage scrimmage of the new year!"

A cacophony of cheers erupted around Bailey as his Blue Squad teammates pounded on the table. The Gold Squad, across the room, let out a round of celebratory whoops.

Finch cleared his throat for silence.

"A more serious matter: I know that many of you are still recovering from the loss of Ms. Sucrette," he said. "She was not with us for very long, but she was a much-respected presence while she was here. It's my hope that the news of Miss Melore's visit will shine a ray of light into what seems to be a dark time for our school. And I also hope," he added, with a newly sharpened edge to his voice, "that you will exercise your most sparkling behavior during her stay!"

Finch finished his announcement, and the dining room chatter resumed as students exchanged exclamations about the big news.

"Can you believe that?" Hal said. "Finch was nearly salivating, he was so excited!"

"No wonder Tremelo can't stand him," Bailey agreed.

They turned to look across the dining hall at Tremelo, but he was gone.

As Bailey searched the room, a loud pop broke his concentration, and a bright, blinding light nearly obliterated his vision.

"Ow!" he heard Hal cry out, followed by mocking laughter.

He rubbed his stinging eyes to see Taylor, Hal's older brother, accompanied by his usual gaggle of Year Three Scavage athletes. The semester before, he'd teased Bailey endlessly about his lack of an Animas, and had even stolen his bag, with Tremelo's precious book in it. Taylor didn't know it—but his antics had almost gotten Bailey killed.

"Yes! Point for Gold Squad!" Taylor crowed. A mean-eyed tortoiseshell cat rubbed her arched back against Taylor's shins.

"Those are my stunners!" Hal shouted, pointing at the small pouch in Taylor's hand. They were weapons Tremelo had given Hal to use the semester before, in the battle against Sucrette. "How did you get those?!"

"Let's just say, maybe you shouldn't leave your knapsack lying around on the rigimotive," said Taylor.

He tossed another stunner down onto Bailey and Hal's table, where it exploded with a bang. Students all over the dining hall craned their necks to get a good look at the commotion. Bailey felt his cheeks and ears turning cherry red.

"Give them back to Hal," he said.

"Like *ants*, I will," said Taylor. "Could be useful on the Scavage field."

Taylor deployed another stunner, causing everyone at the table to hide their eyes and shout with irritation. Then he slipped the pouch back in his pocket and stalked off, motioning for his friends to follow. As Taylor and his friends passed through the doors, Bailey saw another teacher standing there, watching them exit—but this was no one Bailey recognized. Bailey felt the skin along his arms prickling at the sight of an unfamiliar face. The man wore a long tweed cape and a scarf bundled around and around his neck. He was very short, with a hooked nose and small eyes. A gray cat stood beside him by the door, where it stopped to touch whiskery noses with Taylor's tortoiseshell. The man met Bailey's stare, and Bailey quickly looked back down at his breakfast, now cold.

"Who's that?" he whispered to Hal. "Over by the door."

"I don't know," said Hal. "Figures there'd be a new teacher, though—to replace Sucrette. He doesn't look very happy to be here."

Bailey turned in his seat to catch another glimpse of the new teacher. The man's nostrils flared as he looked around the room, as though he'd smelled something very unpleasant.

"I guess Finch decided to go with something other than 'sweet' this time," said Hal.

In homeroom, Tremelo had posted a "pop quiz" on the chalkboard that consisted of a series of riddles, such as "What animal keeps the best time?" and "What type of horse only goes out in the dark?" Hal finished his quiz first, and leaned over to see Bailey's paper.

"*Hmm,* that's what I got for the first one too," Hal said. "The 'nightmare' one's the hardest...." Bailey nodded and scribbled down the answer, though he knew Tremelo wouldn't actually be grading the assignment.

When it was time to head to Latin, Tremelo pulled Bailey aside.

"Where's Bert?" he asked.

"Oh, ants!" said Bailey. "I forgot him!"

"It's the first day of classes," chided Tremelo. "The most important time to establish that he's your kin. First impressions are crucial. Go and get him!"

Bailey dashed back to his dorm instead of heading to Latin.

"Some first impression," he mumbled, as he roused the sleepy iguana, and shook another patch of skin off his fingers.

By the time he arrived to class with Bert curled up in his knapsack, he was already late. Hal and Phi were there; Tori had been lucky enough to place out of second-level Latin, and was taking Classics instead. Phi's falcon, Carin, stood calmly on the edge of Phi's desk. Bailey entered just as the teacher at the front of the class—the man he'd spotted in the dining hall earlier—finished writing his name on the chalkboard with a flourish.

"And again, that's *Doctor* Graves, not *Mister*, thank you," the man said in a clipped, businesslike tone.

Bailey took the opportunity of Dr. Graves's turned back to hurry from the door to an empty desk by his friends. But in his rush, he slammed his knee into the chair of a fellow classmate, a curly-haired girl, who shouted in surprise.

Dr. Graves turned around and surveyed the room with a grimace, as though the students in front of him were covered in slug slime. When he saw Bailey, still standing in the aisle, his small eyes narrowed into slits.

"You're late!" Graves snapped.

Bailey felt his ears turning red for the second time that morning. Everyone was looking at him.

"Sorry, sir," he said. He turned to the empty desk.

"Stop right there," ordered Graves. The diminutive man stepped down from the raised teacher's platform before Bailey even got a chance to sit.

"Hardly the example one wants to set on the very first day of a new semester," Graves said, looking Bailey up and down. "I suppose you think you can just wander in whenever you like!"

"No, I don't. I said I'm sorry," said Bailey.

"I heard what you *said*, boy, but I'm not interested in your apology. There are consequences to certain behaviors! Perhaps you'd like a few lines to copy, since you don't feel the need to keep up with what the rest of the class is doing." The gray cat Bailey had seen earlier rubbed against Graves's ankles, then hissed up at Bailey.

Graves's eyes became fixed on Bailey's knapsack. Bailey looked down, and saw Bert wriggling out of the closed flap. He stretched his claws toward the hem of Graves's tweed jacket.

"What is *this*?" Graves asked. Bert clutched Graves's jacket, and before either Graves or Bailey could do anything to stop it, took a hearty bite out of the hem.

"*Gah!*" Graves exclaimed, stepping back quickly and waving his hands to bat Bert away. A thumb-size scrap of brown tweed dangled out of the lizard's mouth as he clutched Bailey's knapsack, chewing.

"Sorry!" said Bailey.

"I could see you were a troublemaker in the dining hall this morning," Graves said. "And I'm never wrong about these things— look at my coat!"

The other students had begun to laugh. Bailey glanced at Hal, whose eyebrows were raised in a mixture of amusement and concern.

"I'll be keeping a very close eye on you," said Graves, wagging a finger at Bailey. "And your revolting kin."

"He's not revolting," said Bailey, before he even knew what he was doing. "He just thinks you should back off."

Out of the corner of his eye, Bailey saw Hal cover his eyes with his hand.

Graves was the type of person whose face became red very easily, Bailey learned. The man was barely taller than him, but he drew himself up into a tweed tower of righteous, sputtering anger.

"You will *take. Your. Seat.* This instant. Insubordination! Cheek! I will have you know, young man, that—"

"Ahem." A quiet but firm voice interjected itself between Graves and Bailey, and they both turned toward the door. Standing there, a wombat rolling at her feet and her glasses slightly askew, was Ms. Shonfield, the dean of students. A young man stood behind her with a clipboard, staring at Bailey and Graves through a slim pair of brass spectacles.

"Good morning, Dr. Graves, Mr. Walker," she said, nodding to each of them. "I see you're settling in."

As she pushed past them, Graves nodded crisply, and Bailey suppressed a small laugh. The spectacled assistant smiled too, and as he crossed to the front of the classroom with Shonfield, he gave Bailey a quick wink.

"I wanted to say a few words to you students about the passing of your dear teacher, Ms. Sucrette." Ms. Shonfield sighed. "Please know that my door is always open for a chat if you're in need of one. My assistant Jerri and I are happy to answer any questions." She gestured to the young man with the clipboard, who nodded. "We're told her death came at the hands of a group of roving bandits in the neighboring woods, and our policy remains firm that no students are allowed in the Dark Woods at any time. Still, I want to assure you that you have nothing to fear. As of now, the school is taking measures to have the bandits cleared out, and our campus borders are as safe as they've ever been."

Bailey felt a tingling at the back of his neck as Ms. Shonfield spoke. The story about Sucrette's death was completely false, but the Velyn were real—were they the bandits Shonfield mentioned? And what did she mean, "cleared out"?

He glanced across the aisle at Hal, who stared straight forward, trying a little too hard to look completely uninterested in this news. Bailey attempted to do the same. Tremelo's advice played in his mind like a song on the gramophone. *Be normal, act normal, don't draw attention.* But he couldn't stop his hands from shaking. The Velyn might be hurt or captured, which meant his kin was in grave danger. Pretending to be normal, when an unread prophecy linked him to the fate of the entire kingdom, was already proving to be a difficult task.

Four

I CAN'T GET OUT—I can't get out!

A child's small hand fumbled with an ornate bronze door-knob, but it wouldn't turn. Across the room, flames licked their way up the sides of the window—the only other means of escape was a gaping maw of fire, and a four-story drop to the gardens below. *Help me,* the child cried. Tears fell down his round cheeks.

Trent! He heard a voice on the other side of the door. *Trent, I'm going to get you out!*

Viv! Please help me!

The doorknob rattled as Trent pressed himself against the carved wood of his nursery door. He wanted to curl up as small he could, like a little mouse, so the fire wouldn't find him.

It's stuck—Trent! The door is stuck! His sister's voice was heavy with fear. *I can't open it!*

Don't leave me, he cried. *Viv, don't go!*

The fire crawled toward him like a beast to its prey. Smoke had begun curling against the ceiling and slipping through the edges of the doorframe in eager wisps.

Don't go away, he sobbed again, but Viv's only reply was the sound of footsteps, growing fainter.

Tremelo awoke. His heart beat wildly. He sat up in bed and lit the oil lamp on his bedside table—so much more reliable than the second-rate electro-current that was allotted for the teachers' quarters. Fennel the fox padded in from the sitting room, where she had been curled on the armchair, dreaming her own dreams.

Since Gwen and the Elder had come to Fairmount and revealed his true name—Trent Melore, the lost prince of Aldermere—Tremelo's dreams had become sharper in focus, and dark memories emerged. Other memories he might have liked to see, happy ones of his childhood, he did not have. He couldn't remember his father, King Melore. If he did, he might feel better prepared to lead an entire kingdom. No one had taught him how. At least, not that he could recall.

And now his sister, the one who had left him to die, was coming to Fairmount. Would he be able to hide his identity? Or would some imprint, something that lived in the dark of her memory as the fire lived in his, force a glimmer of recognition between them? It was best to stay away, though by hiding, he felt more like that small child than a king.

Fennel, sitting on the floor by his bed, sniffed the air.

"I know, I know," he said. The boy, Bailey, needed him. He was in unspeakable danger, and neither of them was safe until Tremelo sussed out Viviana's plans. Nothing else mattered so much, not his longing to piece together childhood memories, not even deciphering the Loon's infuriatingly vague book of prophecies. *A true ruler sees a false one in the mirror; a false ruler sees only themselves . . . the Child is both the reflection and the opposite of evil.*

The prophecy spoke of Bailey—that much seemed clear—but the meaning escaped him. Puzzling over the book had to wait. He needed to concentrate on information now, not riddles. And though he hated putting his kin in danger, Fennel was brave and smart enough to stay hidden. He'd have to rely on her.

As if to respond, Fennel yipped eagerly.

Tremelo groaned and rose from the bed to boil water for a pot of coffee.

On the wooden shelf above his stove were two mugs, a tin of coffee, and an old photograph. He hadn't looked at it for twelve years, not since he'd learned that the Velyn had been wiped out. But since meeting Eneas Fourclaw and his band, he'd unearthed it from his trunk. He glanced at it now: a young woman gazed out at him with a stony, fierce expression. Her stern but delicate face was framed by wild strawberry-blond hair. Elen.

He was certain she hadn't survived the Jackal's massacre. She would've found him otherwise, and Nature knows he'd looked for her relentlessly. When Eneas Fourclaw and the Velyn had reappeared in the autumn, Tremelo had almost allowed himself to hope that they might have known Elen Whitehill or her father. But Tremelo had not mustered the courage to ask, and Eneas and the rest were now gone.

His thoughts turned to the already swirling rumor about "bandits" in the woods. Of course, there were no bandits, but the Velyn, being blamed for Sucrette's death. In the weeks since that rumor had begun circulating through the teachers' quarters,

Tremelo had kept his mouth shut. To set the record straight would put not only the students in danger, but the Velyn too.

"They're not ready for the world to know they're still alive," he'd told Bailey after the first day of classes. "And if they were caught, they'd be blamed for what happened to Sucrette. They had no choice but to leave." At least, that's what he imagined their reasons were. The Velyn hadn't spoken to him. They'd just disappeared. But that was just like them, the Velyn. They always seemed to vanish just when he wanted most to have them near. He wasn't one of them—not like Bailey was—but still, he felt left behind. He could only imagine how lonely the news must have made Bailey.

The water boiled, and he poured it slowly over a paper filter heaped with strong, bitter coffee grounds.

He didn't want to go back to sleep for fear of dreaming again. So many of his friends, and those he considered his family, were dead and gone. But Viviana was real, and she would arrive at the school—at his home—within the day. The little girl behind the door had become a woman blinded by power and greed. And somehow he was expected to stop her. He would need, he suspected, much more than a stout cup of coffee.

Five

THE MORNING AIR WAS cold, and Viviana pulled the fox-fur collar of her winter coat closed. She waved to onlookers as she walked briskly along the platform. The copper spires of Parliament loomed behind her, glinting with frost.

Next to the platform, usually reserved for first-class rigimotives, was the land train. Painted a bright cobalt blue and gilded with gold, it was impressively shiny, with a powerful front engine. Viviana was quite proud; the land train was a special commission for her own engineers, and a symbol of progress for her reign. Meant to use the rigi tracks, it was faster and more powerful than the rigimotive had ever been.

At the threshold of the train entrance, she bid farewell to the gathered crowd. "Thank you for seeing me off on my first tour of Aldermere! Like my father before me, I wish to see innovation again, and—"

"You're nothing like your father! His throne doesn't belong to you!" a red-faced woman shouted.

Viviana refused to be shaken. Another loyalist was nothing new—though they irked her every time. She was forced to employ her greatest skill: her ability to mask her malice behind a dazzling smile.

"*No one* could be the ruler that he was," she said. "My father was a great king, and if I can accomplish only a part of what my father was able to do before his cruel death, then I will have succeeded." She smiled again, waved, and turned to go.

As Viviana stepped into the train, she heard the muffled cries of the woman as her two ferrets, suddenly vicious, began biting at her arms and face. She stifled a laugh—she knew that it was risky to use her power in public, in front of her "less-aware" constituents, but sometimes she simply couldn't help herself. Some citizens needed to learn their places—and Dominance could certainly help them do so.

She settled into one of the velvet booths in the train car and waited impatiently for her staff to board. Fairmount was her first stop on what she had dubbed her Goodwill Tour, during which citizens would proudly show off their schools, factories, and agriculture in the name of progress.

"A wonderful word," Viviana murmured. "*Progress.*" So vague, yet it gave the people of Aldermere something to believe in.

As for her, Viviana was more interested in finding who'd killed Joan Sucrette than she was in entertaining a bunch of schoolchildren. Sucrette's last message described a "Child of War," a student at the school who was part of the Loon's prophecy. Viviana was sure that this Child of War had been responsible, but she still did not know the Child's identity. She reached into the pocket of her fur-trimmed coat and took out a note, delivered just the day before from Fairmount.

Position just as boring as expected, but things will pick up soon—I am on the trail, and have a list of students who may have been involved in Sucrette's death. Looking forward to your arrival, my lady.

Viviana leaned back in her seat as the land train began to pull slowly away from the platform. All the players were in motion—though if she'd learned anything, it was that sometimes matters had to be taken into one's own hands.

Mr. Clarke, the tinkerer, approached with blueprints under his arm.

"I thought we might take the travel time to go over the new plans for the Catalyst," he said. "We have some information back from our testing facility in the Red Hills, outside of Mazelton. Silver has done well, but to increase conductivity, you might consider—"

Viviana cut him off with a wave.

"I defer to you, Clarke. Don't bother me with the details. *You* take care of the tests and the tinkering—*I'll* take care of the rest."

Clarke bowed and left for the next car, where Viviana's staff—a dresser and cook, as well as two messengers and a pair of wide-shouldered guards—would spend their journey.

She missed Joan. Joan Sucrette had been the only one in her complete confidence, who understood the true power of Dominance. These others—they were impressed by what amounted to mere parlor tricks. They did their jobs well enough, and they did seem to believe in her right to the throne, as well as her talent.

But Joan had been different. She'd shared Viviana's hunger, her drive to see the limits of the bond tested far beyond what anyone had attempted before. Even clever Clarke, who completed each task he was given with utmost ingenuity, was urged on more by vanity than anything else. Well. It would not be too much longer before all of Aldermere would see what Dominance could truly accomplish—and then the kingdom would have no choice but to accept her as queen.

As the land train sped toward Fairmount Academy, Viviana watched as the city became smaller and smaller in her view. Small enough, she thought, to crush completely. Her dominion over the city was certain; her followers there were drunk on their own empowerment, but still under her complete control. She was traveling now to the one place that was still, to her, a mystery—but not for long.

Six

BAILEY LAY WIDE AWAKE in his bed, feeling terrified and anxious for Viviana's imminent arrival. If it were up to him, he'd be preparing to fight Viviana and her Dominae. But Tremelo was keeping secrets, and the Velyn had retreated farther into the Peaks.

All that week, in classes and at meals, his mind had drifted to thoughts of the Velyn. He'd had so much to ask them—about himself and his bond and maybe even his real family. But they were gone. He thought about the map he'd found that fall, which charted their yearly route on the Unreachable Road in the mountains, and wondered if he'd ever be able to join them on that journey.

Pulled out of his thoughts, Bailey snapped his eyes open. The map—Sucrette had been studying it in a small, secret room in the library before Bailey had found it. What else might be in there?

He sat up in bed, and saw that Hal was also awake, reading.

"Uh-oh," said Hal.

"What?"

"You're awake long before homeroom," Hal answered. "And you have that 'I'm about to do something risky' look."

Bailey swung his feet out from under the covers and began dressing.

"Gwen said something to me last week, about Sucrette leaving messages for Viviana," he said. "And I didn't even think—we never searched the bookbinding room in the library. We know Sucrette used that room. What if she left something in there? Viviana's going to be here in just a few hours!"

A few minutes later, the two boys passed the dining hall, where the custodial staff was finishing their morning rounds. Bert rode on Bailey's shoulder as they entered the library and slipped past a pair of technicians adjusting a burned-out electro-current bulb in the atrium. Then they hurried up the echoing stairs to the hidden repairs room.

"Why do you suppose this room has a hidden entrance?" Hal asked as Bailey ran his fingers over the camouflaged wood to find the seam. "It's just full of old books."

"Maybe that wasn't always the case," Bailey said. "Some of the rarest books in the kingdom are here at Fairmount. Tremelo may like to hide his things in plain sight, but think about all the projects that got started here during the Age of Invention—like the rigimotive! Some of this may have been top secret stuff."

"So, if we don't find anything of Sucrette's, we could get rich off of some old coot's plans for a flying bus," Hal said.

"That's the spirit," said Bailey. He found the seam in the wood and pushed the door open.

The room looked just as he remembered it—dusty and cob-webbed, with a table in the center where a map noting the Velyn's migration once lay. The map was gone now; Tremelo had taken it for safekeeping. Bailey felt a familiar tingling on the skin of his arms as he recalled the moment he made the connection—that he was a descendant of the Velyn.

Books were piled everywhere, crumbling into disrepair, and seemed to have been waiting for their time to be restored for many years.

"Wow, you weren't kidding. Nature knows what's stashed in here," Hal said, eyeing the shelves. "What's with the floor?" he then asked, taking a step into the center of the room.

Bailey looked down. He didn't notice anything unordinary—except the dust.

"What do you mean?"

Hal stomped his foot down on one of the floorboards.

"It's not very sturdy." He bent down to tap on the floor with his knuckles. "Do you hear an echo?" he asked.

"No," said Bailey, "but you do. . . ." Of course Hal would be able to sense something was off better than he or Tremelo could—it was his sensitivity to sound, like a bat's. Bailey stood behind Hal as he continued to tap different spots on the floor.

"Right here," Hal said, pointing to a spot just underneath the large repairing table. "There's a hollow space under the floor."

Bailey got down on his hands and knees next to Hal, who ran his right palm against the grain of the floorboard. He pressed down hard on the end of a worn-looking board, and like a seesaw, the opposite end lifted up. Bailey let out a low whistle.

The hole underneath the floorboard was dark, but Bailey saw

the shadowy outline of an object, about as big as his History textbook. He reached underneath all the way up to his shoulder.

"Careful," Hal said. "You don't know what's crawling down there."

Bailey felt around for the object. Finally, his fingers came in contact with cool metal. He grasped the object and pulled it into the light.

It looked like a typewriter, with a full set of letters embossed on the delicate keys but no place to put a piece of paper. Shaking it slightly, Bailey could hear the rattle of small bits of machinery inside the contraption's main compartment. On top of the machine was a metal dais that supported a kind of lever, with two buttons at one end, and a fine point at the other.

"What is it?" Bailey asked.

Hal crouched closer. His mouth hung slightly open as he peered at the thing.

"I haven't the tiniest idea," Hal said.

"What would happen if—" Bailey reached out to tap one of the keys. Hal sucked in his breath.

Nothing happened. The key barely moved under the pressure of Bailey's finger, and every other part of the machine stayed completely still.

"It's broken," said Hal.

"Maybe," said Bailey, turning the machine around to look at it from every angle. "Tremelo might know what it is."

Hal stood and walked to the small, round window, from which the boys could see the Fairmount clock tower.

"Homeroom will be starting soon," Hal said. "If we're going to keep searching for anything of Sucrette's, we'd better hurry."

Bailey lifted the heavy machine off the ground and tucked it under his arm. "We don't need to," he said. "I think we already found it."

Together, they closed the solid wooden door of the repairing room behind them, and set off for the Applied Sciences building. The path leading there was already crowded with students. Bailey hid the machine under his coat, and walked closely behind Hal until they reached their homeroom classroom.

Tremelo was already in his office. Bailey wondered, upon seeing the dark circles under his eyes, whether the teacher had been up all night, the same as he had.

"We have a surprise for you, sir," said Hal.

Bailey set it down carefully on Tremelo's desk and explained where they'd found it.

"It's a pretty thing," he said, peering at the machine, and tapping its sides with a wrench. "Though I'll be an ant's uncle if I know what it's for."

The door to Tremelo's classroom opened, and all three of them jumped to attention.

It was Tori and Phi, arriving for homeroom. They set their bags on their desks and peered through the open office door at them.

"It's a party, is it? I guess we weren't invited," Tori said.

"Bailey and I found something in the secret room of the library," Hal blurted out.

The girls entered the office and looked at the box.

"So, what does it do?" Phi asked.

"That's what we're trying to figure out," Bailey said.

Tremelo, who'd silently been running his hands over the sides of the machine, carefully pressed down on one of the keys. Everyone held their breath.

As before, nothing happened.

Tremelo sat back and shook his head.

"I'll have to take it apart," he said. "See what's inside."

Tori sighed and leaned her elbow on the desk. Bailey noticed something move under her sleeve, and when she shook her wrist to let it free, he saw that it was a tiny green snake—just a baby, no bigger around than a twig. It slithered toward the machine.

"Tori, your kin, see that it doesn't—" Tremelo mumbled, but not before the snake found a hole in the side of the machine, like a coin slot, and crept in. "Wonderful," Tremelo said, throwing up his hands. "It's a reptile house. We've figured it out."

Suddenly, all four humans heard a click, and the whir of small metal parts stirring into action.

"Oh, ants!" said Tori. "Don't let it get hurt!"

They leaned in closer, and Tori gasped when the machine let off a rapid-fire series of clicks. Thankfully, the snake emerged out the other side of the wooden base of the machine, unharmed, and looking several shades darker.

"There's something on it," Bailey said as he ran a finger down the snake's scaly back. It came up black. "It's ink!"

"We need a piece of paper!" said Tori. She picked up a sheet of notes from Tremelo's desk and ripped a slim piece from the top.

"Phi, close the office, will you?" asked Tremelo. Outside, the sounds of students milling around in the halls before class had become louder. Phi shut the office door with a thud.

Tori handed the paper over the desk to Hal, who fed it through the same slot the snake had used to enter the machine.

The same clicks and metal whirring tapped out from the inside of the gadget, and the paper curled out the other side of the machine with finely printed words on it. Some letters were missing, but they could make out:

The Reckon in is set for t e Spr g q n x. Joan, I count ng on you

"Joan—that's Ms. Sucrette," said Phi.

"I knew it!" said Bailey.

"This wasn't left for Viviana to find; it was sent here *by* Viviana," said Hal.

"Reckon . . . reckoning?" Bailey whispered. "What does it mean?"

"A calculation of something, or something coming to light," Tremelo answered.

"She plans to . . . reveal something, then?" Hal took another piece of paper from Tremelo's desk and hurriedly jotted down an exact copy of the note, which he folded into his pocket.

"Fascinating," said Tremelo, looking carefully at the machine. "The machine somehow receives a message, stores the sequence of letters, and prints it. Looks like the ink has dried quite a bit since the fall, though. I wish we could make out the whole note."

"A 'Reckoning,'" said Tori. "Sounds big."

Tremelo nodded. Then his eyes settled on Bert, who was dozing on Bailey's shoulder.

"You're doing pretty well with him," Tremelo said. "After homeroom it's straight to the assembly to hear our illustrious guest. If there's any day on which you need to appear to be Animas

Iguana, today would be it. Lest you forget what Viviana was 'counting on' Joan to do."

Bailey shuddered. Tremelo was right. If he was exposed as the Animas White Tiger of the Loon's prophecy, Viviana would succeed where Sucrette had failed—she would kill him.

"I'll keep this safe," Tremelo said, nodding to the machine. "Better get your day started. It's going to be an interesting one."

The students filed out of the office and into the classroom, where other students had begun arriving slowly for homeroom.

Just as Bailey reached his desk, Bert took a daring leap off his shoulder and onto the floor.

"Hey, look who's awake!" laughed Tori.

Bert scurried left and right, bumping his nose into more than one desk leg.

"Come *on*," said Bailey. He went to retrieve the confused Bert from the floor, but the lizard kept crawling away; he was surprisingly fast. "Hey, come back!" Bailey called, as Bert scuttled to the classroom door—but someone else's hands closed around him before Bailey could grab him.

"Here you are," said Dr. Graves. He held Bert, who squirmed in his grip. "Not quite on the same page with this wretched thing yet, are you?"

Bailey took Bert and stepped back.

"I heard that you had a late Awakening. I imagine you must still be getting used to interacting with your ... kin," Graves continued. His left eyebrow was raised in either amusement or suspicion. Bailey held Bert still, his mouth dry and cottony.

"Sure. I guess," he said.

"I'm certain you'll get the hang of it," Graves said, looking Bailey up and down. Bailey stood a bit straighter and fought the urge to brush off a fine layer of dust on his clothes. Bert had a bit of cobweb hanging off his pointy-scaled back ridge.

"Just takes a little practice and an inquisitive mind," said Graves. "Which, no doubt, you have."

Bailey didn't answer—he was too nervous.

Graves nodded a farewell and continued down the hall.

Bailey returned to his homeroom desk and sat down with a thud.

"Just try to tell me that wasn't a little creepy," he said, meeting his friends' stares. "Graves knows something's off about me, for sure."

"Nature's tentacles," said Tori. "Is *every*one a spy?"

Seven

THE SMELLS OF A delicious breakfast—with the rare, strange scent of cooked meats—wafted through the train car. A small creature entered, then darted behind the upholstered seats and crept under the polished tables. She stayed low to ground, which was covered with an odd red fur that felt soft under her paws. A scrap of sausage caught her attention, and she chomped down on it quickly, though food was not her mission today.

Fennel wrinkled her pointy black nose. The woman had sat here, the one Tremelo feared. The scent of perfume hung in the air—she had only just now stepped away into a small room at the back of the train car. On the seat, a stack of papers had been left out. Fennel bit the corner of a folded piece of paper and dragged it from the top of the pile, nudging it open with her nose.

Careful! she felt her kin, Tremelo, urging her. *She can't know we've been here.*

Fennel kept her eyes trained on the sheet of paper before her—a confusing, geometric crisscrossing of lines and curves, with numbers jotted all over. She felt building waves of understanding from Tremelo, who was safe in his office. He was deciphering what she'd unfolded, even if she could not. The sight of it had shaken him, and she felt a hum of activity from him—he was begging her to keep looking. She whimpered softly, her tiny heart fluttering.

The smell of perfume grew stronger as the woman's shadow appeared behind the cloudy glass of the door. The door handle turned. Fennel nudged the paper back into place, and crouched under the seat. She kept her eyes trained on the heels of the woman who walked past. The woman stopped to adjust her jacket and skirt, and then she left the train car. Fennel, as silent as a ghost, followed.

Back in the Applied Sciences building, Tremelo lurched from his trancelike state back into his own mind. Emerging from Fennel's consciousness was jarring, especially when she was upset or anxious. He steadied his breath, which had become shallow and quick during his bond with Fennel. He stared down at the charcoal pencil in his hand and the paper on his desk in front of him—it had been blank when he'd first sent Fennel into Viviana's land train. Now he saw shapes and angles, measurements and notes copied by his own messy hand. He understood what Fennel could not—it was a blueprint for some kind of machine. Boxlike and ornate, with a chamber in its center for a separate power source, it confounded him. He did not know what it was for or what it would do, but finding this out had just become his most important task.

Eight

BAILEY, PHI, AND HAL sat together in silence in the back row of the Fairmount meeting hall. In front of them were rows of laughing, gossiping students, waiting eagerly for Viviana to appear. The land train had arrived on campus that morning during homeroom, which meant that Viviana, the woman who wanted to kill Bailey—who had already tried—was close by. He could almost picture her sniffing the air for him like a predatory beast, and he pulsed with fear.

"She doesn't know who you are," Phi whispered, reminding him. "Just be calm."

"Have you heard from Gwen today?" Bailey whispered back.

Phi shook her head. "I saw her yesterday, though, and she said she hadn't changed her mind about helping us."

Bailey was worried about Gwen getting caught, but also he felt a sort of comfort, imagining her close by. Tremelo was nowhere to be seen, and Bailey hoped he was busying himself with the plan—whatever it was.

Tori was another matter entirely, however. Hal had saved her a seat, but as Bailey scanned the crowd, he saw her several rows ahead, talking with a boy he didn't recognize.

"Who's that Tori's with?" Bailey asked.

"His name's Lyle," Hal said, as if it were the name of a disgusting food. "And I don't trust anyone whose name rhymes with *bile*."

"How did they meet?" Bailey asked.

"He's from the Gray too," said Phi. "They met on the rigimotive back from Midwinter break, and they're in Tremelo's afternoon Tinkering class together."

"Tori's in Tinkering?" Bailey asked. "I never would have guessed that. She thinks Tremelo's a crackpot—as a teacher, anyway."

Phi just shrugged.

"Maybe she has interests you two don't know about," she said. "Or maybe you just never asked."

The chatter in the meeting hall died to a murmur as Headmaster Finch and Ms. Shonfield appeared on the stage. Finch, in a mustard plaid three-piece suit, radiated pride. For once, he was actually smiling. Bailey's skin prickled into gooseflesh as the dean took his place behind a slender wooden podium.

"Students of Fairmount!" Finch called, gesturing for silence. "We are honored to be the first stop on Miss Viviana Melore's tour of the kingdom!" He was met with a smattering of applause. Bailey reminded himself that these students didn't know the evil Viviana was actually capable of; it was only because of Sucrette's attempt to murder him that he'd become fully aware of the Dominae at all.

Viviana entered then, but did not take the stage. Instead, she was led to a seat in the front row of the auditorium as she waved cheerfully at the students and teachers. She wore a purple dress with gold buttons down the front, and a dark mauve traveling hat with matching gloves. Bailey could see already how much she resembled Tremelo—the same dark hair, and the way her eyebrows raised just slightly. It was a sly look, the same one that Tremelo made when Bailey would ask a question that he didn't care to answer. He stared at her as she took her seat.

A group of student dancers came onstage, along with five deer and two antelopes. They performed a choreographed routine in which the human dancers leapt alongside their animal kin, forming undulating patterns of movement across the stage. After the final pose and the following applause, a thirty-member student chorus took to the stage to perform "I Place My Paw with the Kingdom," a rousing battle song, accompanied by the howls of several breeds of dog, several strains of birdsong, and the chittering of a pair of raccoons. With each performance, Bailey became more restless, and even irritated. Everyone at Fairmount was falling over themselves to impress the daughter of King Melore, when none of them knew how unlike that king she really was.

Finally, Headmaster Finch took to the stage again, and introduced Viviana.

"A woman of values, and the daughter of our most-beloved king—we couldn't be prouder to have you grace our halls!" Finch said. Bailey held his breath as Viviana rose from her seat and climbed the three small steps to the platform. Finch stretched out his hands to clasp Viviana's. They kissed very formally on the cheek, and she took his place at the podium.

"My goodness, what a wonderful sight!" she said, looking out at the students. "You students are a treat to these eyes after all the stuffy politicians in the capital. Thank you for having me!"

More applause. It turned Bailey's stomach.

"I've come here with an express purpose," Viviana began.

Bailey breathed in. He suddenly imagined her saying his name, pointing him out in front of the entire school, and ordering his death.

"An invitation!" Viviana said. "It was my father's dream to encourage great advances in the kingdom. But he was cut down, at the very event that sought to showcase the most exciting new inventions of the age. Now I plan to continue his work by holding the Progress Fair once more—just as he would have done!"

Bailey and Hal looked at each other nervously.

"Two months from today, the second Progress Fair will unite the kingdom! And you students must be a part of this celebration. We will feature a student Scientific Competition, as well as a Scavage tournament, at which your Fairmount team is sure to excel!"

A burst of cheers and applause erupted. Viviana smiled, and then began speaking about the upgrades she planned for the rigimotive system.

"I don't get it," said Bailey, leaning close to Hal. "A Progress Fair? Our evil queen's evil plan is . . . a festival?"

Hal dug in his pocket and pulled out his copy of the note that the mysterious machine had printed that morning.

"No, look," he whispered. "She said 'two months from today'—that's not just any day, that's the Spring Equinox—and fits the missing letters from the note exactly! This Progress Fair is where 'the Reckoning' will take place!"

"But 'the Reckoning'—what could it mean?" Bailey asked.

Viviana's speech ended, and the students applauded. Finch returned to the stage.

"As headmaster of Fairmount, allow me to express our thanks to Viviana Melore for including us on her grand tour! Students, you are dismissed!"

An excited chatter broke out in the auditorium, echoing against the high ceilings.

"We have to talk to Tremelo," said Bailey. The three of them stood with the rest of the students, shuffling out of the rows.

Bailey felt a tug on his sleeve, and turned to see Tori falling into line behind him. Lyle, the boy from her Tinkering class, stood close by.

"This is Lyle, everybody," Tori said. "Lyle, this is Bailey, Hal, and Phi."

"How's it going?" Lyle asked, without waiting for an answer. "She's something, huh?"

"Who, Tori?" said Hal.

"No, no—that too, though," Lyle laughed and looked down shyly. "I meant Viviana. Anyway, I've got to catch up with my dad. See you all later!" He waved good-bye to the group and nudged Tori's shoulder affectionately, then pushed ahead through the herd of students.

"His dad?" Bailey asked.

"What are you doing sitting with him, anyway?" interrupted Hal.

"None of your business," Tori said. "I *can* have other friends, you know."

In the atrium, students gathered in excited groups, buzzing about the Fair. Bailey edged close to the outside of the room, holding Bert to his chest. Phi stuck close to him, though the others lagged behind. Just as Bailey was about to reach the exit, someone grabbed his arm.

"Hey," he said, looking up. "Gwen!"

"*Shh!*" Gwen whispered. "Don't draw attention!" She wore a Fairmount blazer, at least two sizes too small, over a plain maroon dress that Bailey recognized as Phi's.

"What are you doing?" Bailey asked. He swiveled his gaze, to see if anyone was looking at them strangely. This had been a terrible idea—Gwen stood out like a flame-haired sore thumb.

"You asked me to be here," Gwen said. "You asked me to watch!"

"The clothes were my idea," said Phi. "To help her blend in!"

"You could have asked me," said Tori, catching up to them. "At least my sleeves are longer."

"We shouldn't be talking about this here," Hal broke in.

"But I have to tell you," Gwen began, "I did see something. On my way here—"

"*Shhh!*" said Hal, through gritted teeth. "*Turn around.*"

Bailey turned and saw Dr. Graves, Headmaster Finch, Ms. Shonfield, and Viviana standing a mere four feet away, right in front of the case of antique volumes where the Loon's book was hidden.

"I confess I have little use for books," Viviana said to Graves. "Machines, inventions—that's where a kingdom's true power lies. In progress, not in dusty pages."

When Bailey turned back to Gwen, he saw that she had gone deathly pale.

"Just act natural," Bailey whispered. "She won't know you're not a student."

"But *Shonfield* will," said Hal. "You've got to hide!"

The five of them continued toward the main doors. But as they pushed their way through, a man with an armload of papers crossed their path and collided with Hal. It was Jerri, Shonfield's assistant. He fumbled, and a stack of papers slipped from his arms and scattered on the atrium floor.

"Sorry! So sorry," sputtered Jerri as he bent to collect them. His brass spectacles dangled helplessly from his thin nose. "A bit nervous, I guess..."

As Bailey stopped to help gather the last of the papers, he caught Phi's eyes and nodded to Gwen. The two girls locked arms and hurried out of the atrium together, followed closely by Tori.

Standing, Bailey glanced at the bookcase again: Viviana was still speaking with Finch, Shonfield, and Graves. Graves was hardly listening to her, however. He was staring at Bailey, Jerri, and Hal. Bailey couldn't be sure whether he'd taken note of Gwen or not.

Finch and Shonfield turned to follow his gaze.

"Oh, dear," said Ms. Shonfield, at the sight of Jerri's papers scattered on the floor. Jerri grimaced apologetically at her, shuffling them into a neat pile.

"What in Nature has happened here?!" said Graves. And then,

in a quieter, harsher tone: "You should be more careful in front of *our guest.*"

"Yes, sir," Bailey said softly. He was surprised he could get the words out at all, given the immense lump in his throat.

"Hello, students," Viviana said.

Bailey and Hal stared. On Bailey's shoulder, Bert blinked.

"Students! Say hello," chastised Graves.

Bailey felt as though someone had suddenly turned him to stone. He couldn't speak or move as Viviana Melore, the woman who had sent an assassin to kill him and Taleth, locked eyes with him for the first time. Her eyes, Bailey noticed, were a delicate shade of purple. He had no clue what his own face looked like in that moment, but he hoped that he didn't look as terrified as he felt.

It was Hal who finally spoke.

"Welcome to Fairmount, Miss Melore," Hal said, and Bailey was so grateful he nearly melted away from relief.

"Hello, welcome," he said, following suit.

Viviana placed a hand on Graves's arm, but did not take her eyes off Bailey. He couldn't help but let a frightening thought pass through his mind—did she *know*? And just as quickly as that thought entered his mind, another followed. His eyes passed to Graves, who was looking at him with pure contempt. What had been a sneaking suspicion now seemed clear—Graves and Viviana were working together.

"Such polite students, Dr. Graves," Viviana said. Finally, she looked away from Bailey and Hal. Still as motionless as stone, Bailey felt his heart begin to beat like a tympani drum. "You were going to show me the classrooms next, I believe?"

Graves, Finch, and Viviana moved down the hall as Bailey

exhaled. Only Ms. Shonfield stayed behind. A wombat waddled beside her, eyeing Bailey suspiciously. Bailey wondered whether the wombat, if not Shonfield herself, had noticed the strange, red-haired student in the atrium a moment before.

"Good day, boys. May I speak to Mr. Walker privately?" she asked, looking to Hal.

Hal pushed up his glasses and stepped away. Jerri gazed down the hall in Graves and Viviana's direction. Bailey was having trouble focusing on anything but Viviana's retreating back.

"I was very concerned with the scene I witnessed in Dr. Graves's classroom the other day," she continued. It took Bailey a second to realize that she was referring to his argument with Graves.

"About that, Ms.—"

"Let me finish, please." She held her hand up in a firm gesture. "I know your history of acting out, and I want to caution you: You are still on academic probation, as of this past autumn. I had hoped that your Awakening"—she glanced at Bert, asleep, on Bailey's shoulder—"would guide you toward an inner focus, and am sorry to see that perhaps I'm wrong. Do you have anything to say for yourself?"

Bailey said nothing. Of all the teachers and administrators, he trusted Ms. Shonfield the most. He would've liked to tell her the truth, but too many people were already in danger. *Act normal, focus, stay quiet.* He was bursting inside with fear and anxiety, but he had to look calm. He shook his head.

"Perhaps Awakening requires more of an adjustment than we'd originally thought. . . ." Shonfield said quietly. "Which reminds me, now that you've revealed yourself to be reptile in your affiliations, perhaps you'd be more comfortable in Treetop, rather than the Towers?"

Both Shonfield and her assistant cocked their heads to hear Bailey's answer. He glanced over at Hal, who squinched up his nose in a look of sour disagreement.

"No, I'm happy where I am, thanks," Bailey said.

"Well, just checking," said Shonfield. "Cross that off my list, Jerri? I will be keeping an eye on you, Mr. Walker. Don't disappoint me!" She squared her shoulders. "Back into the fray," she said to Jerri. "To think we have three whole days to entertain this Dominae woman . . . With Finch and Graves falling all over themselves for a pretty face . . ."

Jerri smiled, a little mischievously, and followed her down the hall to join the others. Bailey waited until they were out of sight before he dared to look at the bookcase. To his relief, the Loon's book was still there, hidden. But relief was quickly replaced by fear, suddenly ballooning bigger and bigger inside his chest: Graves, with Viviana's fingers resting so formally on his arm, was surely the next person to try to kill him.

Nine

"YOU OKAY?" ASKED HAL, as soon as the group of teachers were out of earshot.

"Yeah," Bailey lied. He'd just looked into the eyes of the person who wanted him dead, and he felt as if small insects were crawling all over his skin. "I just wish Tremelo had actually turned up," he said.

"He's Viviana's *brother*," whispered Hal. "What if she recognized him?"

Suddenly, Hal seemed far away. His voice became muddled and Bailey's vision blurred. Instead of standing within Fairmount's library atrium, he had his nose pressed up to a gnarled tree branch. Bailey recognized the landscape just beyond the school—it was the woods near the Scavage fields.

Oh, no, thought Bailey. Taleth, sensing his distress, was doing exactly what she shouldn't: she was edging closer to the school.

Feeling dizzy, Bailey steadied himself and concentrated on his own consciousness: Hal standing before him, and the cold stone marble floor under his feet.

"I have to go," he said quickly, shaking off the last remnants of Taleth's vision. The smell of snow-damp leaves lingered in his nostrils.

"Where?" said Hal. "Bailey?"

But Bailey was already out the tall double doors and running down the front steps of the library two at a time. He had to find Taleth and persuade her, somehow, to stay away before it was too late.

He ran past the classroom buildings and down the hill from the cliff, barely aware of the cold that stung his exposed ears and cheeks. His breath billowed out of him in a mist. Finally, he reached the expanse of trees and undergrowth at the base of the hill that led to the Dark Woods. He paused and looked around wildly for any sign of Taleth. But all was still.

His heart still pounded. After a few deep breaths, he plunged into the bushes. He scrambled over a raised root just in time to see Taleth emerge from behind an oak. She regarded him calmly, her whiskers twitching. Bailey stayed still as the tiger approached him. Carefully, she rubbed his still-healing arm with the side of her furry face.

"What are you doing here?" Bailey said softly. He felt a surge of worry emanating from Taleth. When they touched, an image flashed before Bailey's eyes: a small, grayish-brown animal pursuing the tiger.

"Who's watching you?" Bailey asked. "Is it Graves?"

Bailey tried to focus, but he couldn't connect strongly enough to get a clear answer. Instead, he just felt the longing that Taleth experienced. She wanted to stay close to the school, close to Bailey. Bailey wanted that too, but it was impossible.

"Go, get out of here," he said, and his voice tightened. "You can't stay here; it's not safe."

Bailey pushed at Taleth's flank, urging her to turn away. The tiger padded away a few paces from Bailey, then she stopped and looked out toward the dark. She turned back to him and blinked.

Just as if he had blinked too, all of a sudden, everything was darkness around Bailey. A cloth was thrown over his face and he was being lifted off the ground, away from Taleth. He instinctively lifted his arms to rip the cloth away, but a strong hand grabbed his wrists. They'd been seen.

"Taleth," he cried out. "Run!"

Part of him feared that she would stay and help him—but to his bittersweet relief, he heard a crashing in the bushes, and he knew that she had gone away to safety. He thrashed, trying to break free. A fresh, throbbing pain broke out on his injured arm.

Bailey was dragged, half standing, half stumbling, several yards away by someone who kept their arm locked around his middle.

"Who are you?" Bailey yelled through the dusty cloth. It smelled like old potatoes. "What do you want?"

"For you to stop being such a nincompoop," said a familiar voice. Bailey was thrown down on a soft patch of grass, and the brown potato sack was yanked off his head. Tremelo stood over him.

Bailey sat up. Gwen stood a few feet away, watching them. She was still wearing Phi's too-small clothes, as well as a remorseful frown.

"I told him it was a little extreme," she said.

"Extreme? That's the best lesson plan I've put into action all year," Tremelo said, tossing the sack aside to light his pipe. "You deliberately ignored everything I told you when you returned to school. Running off into the woods with the Dominae just steps away—and asking Gwen to take part in a half-cooked, dangerous plan."

Bailey smoothed out his sandy hair, which had gotten mussed every which way by Tremelo's clumsy kidnapping attempt. Of course Taleth had left him alone back there—she had sensed Tremelo being *Tremelo*, and not any immediate danger to Bailey. Unless you counted severe annoyance as danger.

"You could have been killed if anyone else had found you first tonight!" Tremelo continued. "You're lucky the girls brought Gwen to me; she may have just saved your life!"

"What do you mean?" Bailey asked, looking from Tremelo to Gwen.

"I tried to tell you outside the assembly," Gwen began. "I watched Viviana during her tour of the school this morning, from across the commons. I saw her send some men into the forest, all spread out. They've been combing the woods all day."

Tremelo shook his head, and blew out a puff of smoke.

"You haven't learned a thing since autumn," he said.

Bailey got to his feet, fighting the urge to mention that it was his idea for Gwen to spy, and that what she'd seen had proved useful. But only useful, he then realized, because he'd disobeyed Tremelo's orders.

"I'm sorry," he said instead.

"Come on," said Tremelo. "Quickly now, we can't be seen. The others are waiting in my office. We have much to discuss."

Tori, Phi, and Hal jumped as Bailey, Gwen, and Tremelo entered. Outside in the halls, the sounds of whoops and laughter echoed as students made their way to dinner after an afternoon of no classes. Tremelo locked both the classroom and office doors.

"Now," Tremelo said. "Tell me what was said in the assembly."

Hal spoke up first, unfolding the note with the missing letters.

"This 'Reckoning' thing, she has it set for the Equinox," he began. "And it's going to be big—she's planning to hold a giant Fair in the city, and she's invited the whole school. There's going to be a Scavage game, vendors, and a Science Competition."

"Just like the one King Melore held, when he was killed," Tori said, nodding.

Tremelo was silent for a moment as he brushed his mustache nervously with his thumb and forefinger.

"I too made a discovery this morning," he said finally. He gestured to Fennel the fox, who sat upright and alert next to Tremelo's desk. "With Fennel's help, I was able to find some plans—blueprints—for a very advanced machine Viviana is commissioning." He cleared away some books on his desk and smoothed out a large sheet of paper with a messy conglomeration of shapes and curves drawn on it. Bailey and the others crowded around the desk to get a better look.

"This casing here is engineered to hold something very powerful," said Tremelo, tracing his finger around the outer border of shapes. "Given the construction, the piece in the middle is likely volatile, whatever it is. One thing I *can* tell, it doesn't run on electro-current—it's got some sort of other source. . . ." He trailed off. "Some of this is familiar—the shape of the casing is conducive for amplification, but of what?" He tapped his finger against the blueprint, lost in thought.

"Sir?" said Tori.

"Yes. Anyway," said Tremelo, shaking his head. "It's impossible, at this point, to decipher what this machine is meant to *do*, but it's very likely involved in her plans for this big event."

"So, if we can figure out what the machine is for, then we can stop her from using it?" Bailey said.

Tremelo nodded.

"And there's only one way to find out what it does, though it involves some serious risk," Tremelo said. Bailey sat up a little straighter. "We have to make our own."

Ten

"CONSTRUCTING THE CASING should be simple," Tremelo continued. "I have all the supplies we'll need in my workshop. The middle part—this orblike object—that's what we'll need to research."

He began to name parts they'd need to collect as Tori wrote down the list. Gwen tried to pay attention, but she was still somewhat lost in the shock of the day. The sight of Viviana on the campus today had triggered a panic that had nearly paralyzed her. She'd had fun dressing up in Phi's clothes—almost enough to feel normal again. But as soon as she'd seen the gray uniforms of Viviana's guards, and then Viviana herself, her hands had begun to shake. And when those guards then edged closer to the woods, she'd felt dizzy.

Tremelo had been furious.

"You're not my student—I can't tell you what to do," he'd said after Phi and Tori had shuffled her through the halls to his office.

"But I feel responsible for you. And you've proved yourself just as foolhardy, just as obstinate as—" Gwen was sure he was about to say *Bailey*, but he stopped himself. "If you had been seen by anyone who knows you're not a student, how would you have explained yourself?" She, Bailey, and Phi had not even thought that far ahead.

As the group walked from the Applied Sciences building to Tremelo's garage workshop, Tremelo kept close to Gwen.

"Once we're done here tonight, you'll return to the tree house. If anyone sees you in the meantime, I'll say . . . I'll tell them you're a visiting cousin." He sighed. "Not that that wouldn't raise suspicion on its own, given what the administration knows of my past."

Gwen nodded, and continued the rest of the way in silence.

In the workshop, they split into makeshift teams, scouring through Tremelo's hoard of metal parts, wires, gears, and bolts. Gwen, Phi, and Bailey worked over a table piled high with tangled wires, while Hal and Tori fought at the other end of the musty garage.

"I'd saved you a seat at the assembly," Hal said.

"No one asked you to do that," said Tori.

Gwen locked eyes with Phi, who made a face.

"Look for anything copper first," said Tremelo, shuffling through a wooden crate of metal parts. "Most conductive—that *I* can afford, anyway."

"Like this?" asked Gwen, spotting a few flat sheets of copper tucked behind the workbench.

"Yes, exactly!" said Tremelo. He grabbed them from her and started a pile in the center of the room. "Let's collect it all here," he said. "We're looking for electrical wiring, thin, conductive metal like that copper, and anything that could be used to construct the frame."

Invigorated, the kids dug in. Every minute or so, one of them held up an object for Tremelo's approval or tossed it straight onto the pile. Phi untangled several feet of frayed, cloth-covered wire as Bailey and Gwen sorted the rest of the metal sheets. Hal picked through a tub of nuts and bolts, matching them according to size, while Tori and Tremelo overturned a barrel of discarded motorcar parts to search for framing pieces. The pile in the center of the workshop grew.

"What happens when we figure out what the machine does?" asked Hal. "What's next?"

"We stop it from happening, of course," said Bailey. "Right?"

"Yes, but how?" Hal asked.

"That's obvious," said Tremelo. This pronouncement was followed by confused silence from the students. "Once we know what the machine does, we'll know how to counteract it. And once we know that, we'll build a modified version that Tori will enter into the Science Competition."

Tori looked at them all with a satisfied smirk.

"I wouldn't exactly call that 'obvious,'" said Hal. "Why Tori?"

"Because I'm the only one of us taking Tinkering," Tori said. "And I get it—we enter the competition so that no one will look twice at us lugging some huge machine—"

"Don't assume it will be huge!" Tremelo interrupted.

"Okay, some mystery machine into the Fair," Tori finished. "And then once the time is right, we flip the 'on' switch and—"

"Bam," said Hal. "Whatever 'bam' will be."

"That's right," said Tremelo. "Getting our machine into the Science Competition will mean better access to Viviana, and whatever her 'Reckoning' will be."

Gwen glanced at Bailey as they found another sheet of gleaming copper. He was smiling, his blue eyes glittering with purpose.

"You seem happier," she said.

"Nice to have a plan," he said.

"Ah! And if I'm not mistaken, there should be some silver shavings in my kitchen," Tremelo called out. "Be right back!" Tremelo rushed out of the workshop, nearly skipping.

"King Trent Melore, everyone," said Hal. "The rightful ruler of Aldermere, off to fetch silver shavings . . ."

"He's younger, though," said Tori. "I mean, if you want to get technical about it, Viviana *is* the rightful ruler."

Bailey and Phi stared at her.

"But she's evil," Bailey said.

"Obviously," sighed Tori. "And that's why we have to stop her, and so on. *I* know that. But if you think about it, the Loon's prophecy could just as well be talking about her as it was about Tremelo. Except for the fact that Viviana's a crazy person, there's no real reason that he's the True King."

"That's not true," Bailey said.

"It is," Gwen said, surprising even herself. The others turned to her with curious expressions—eyebrows raised, mouths half-open in anticipation of what she would say next. "I despise her—I know what she's capable of. But if Melore had lived, Viviana would have eventually taken over the throne as the eldest. That's one reason Parliament was so divided when she returned to the Gray." She thought about the men and women of Parliament, arguing deep into many nights about exactly this.

"Right," said Tori. "My parents knew plenty of Melore loyalists at home who thought she ought to be queen."

"It was the same in Parliament," said Gwen. "Though some could see what the years in the Plains had done to her—like the Elder. Others wanted to keep her out because a new ruler would take Parliament's power away." She pulled at her hair. Everyone's attention was on her. She hadn't spoken very much about Parliament, and the dark days before it disbanded. When she considered everything that had happened to her, those days seemed like a lifetime ago.

"But this isn't about who has the right to rule," said Bailey.

"Of course," said Gwen. "The Elder taught me no one has the *right* to rule anything, only the ability to prove that they can. But not everyone in the kingdom thinks that way. And they'll hear the name *Melore,* and think she's what they've been waiting for. They don't know. And by the time they do, it might be too late to stop her. It makes our task harder."

"Sadder too," said Phi. "Viviana must have gone through some terrible things in the Dust Plains."

"You're a very forgiving person," Gwen said, trying to catch the edge in her voice. She couldn't shake the memory of Viviana pointing up at Grimsen the owl and shouting the order to end his life.

"I've seen what it's like out there," Phi said. "It wasn't fair, what happened to her. But that doesn't change what she is now."

"No, it doesn't," Gwen said. She stared at the wood grain of the workbench in front of her, her vision blurred with anger or sadness—or both. A moment passed before she realized that Phi was looking at her, her eyes soft and full of concern.

"You saw her, didn't you? Before today, I mean," Phi said.

Gwen nodded. The others slowed their movements, turning ever so slightly toward her to listen better. She felt a knot begin to tighten in her chest.

"Yes," she said. "I've seen her and Sucrette. There was a *demonstration*...." She said the last word harshly. Gwen put down the wires she was untangling, and took a deep breath. She had witnessed the Dominae's cruel exercises of control, and watched Viviana take the life of an animal Gwen loved. But she wasn't sure she could bring herself to tell them that. To say the words made her think of how she'd failed the Elder.

"She uses machines that look like animals," she said, thinking of the Clamoribus. "They're not alive, made of metal and wire."

"Oh, sure, we've seen those," said Tori. "They were all around the city during break."

Gwen shook her head. "But she thinks of living animals the same way—easy to control. Easy to kill." She paused, and took another deep breath. "She murdered the Elder's life-bonded kin, Grimsen, right in front of me." She broke off.

"I could never forgive that," murmured Phi.

"No," said Gwen, her heart aching at the memory. "Me neither."

As twilight crept over the campus, Gwen hurried silently around the school buildings, back to her tree house. The lamps flickered on along the campus pathways, but Gwen stuck to the shadows. As she passed the guesthouse, a grand brick structure near the teachers' quarters, she glanced up at the lit windows. Viviana was in there—so close. Gwen wondered how difficult it would be to sneak through a window and into the guest rooms, how easy it might be to end Viviana's short reign with a vial of poison or a slash of a quick knife. Easy for someone else, perhaps—and not how the Elder would have wanted this fight to end. Gwen shuddered and scurried on her way.

As she left the lights of the main campus behind, Gwen began to feel a mounting anxiety the deeper she moved into the forest. She sensed the owls of the woods, especially those close to the tree house, hopping and tittering with concern. She quickened her pace.

Entering the clearing where the tree house stood, she felt the eyes of dozens of owls watching her. The windows of the structure were dark, and something told Gwen that she should be careful. She felt in the pocket of Phi's jacket for the Glass. Certain that it was safe, she began to climb the footholds nailed into the trunk.

She paused a few rungs from the trapdoor. No sounds came from inside the little house except for the nervous fluttering of owls' wings. Carefully, she lifted the door and climbed up.

Her pallet bed was overturned, and her books were scattered across the room. With a cry, Gwen noticed the piece of wolf pelt that had protected the Glass was on the floor, rather than tucked safely in the trunk of the tree. Whoever had been here had found her hiding place—she thanked Nature she'd brought the Glass with her. She picked up the pelt, wrapped it around the Glass again, and tucked both into her rucksack.

Next, Gwen looked around for Melore's harmonica. Righting the bed, she found it tucked underneath. The leather box that housed it was scratched, but to her relief, the instrument was unharmed. She held it to her heart, thinking about the Elder. Only then did she notice how loudly her heart seemed to be pounding, and how her hands shook.

Whoever had been here tonight hadn't found what they'd wanted—but Gwen knew that they'd be back. She and Tremelo had spoken about this moment—the moment the Glass was no longer safe at Fairmount. She knew what she had to do.

She did not have much to pack. She changed out of Phi's school clothes and back into her own pants, boots, shirt, and traveling cloak. Leaving the books and the bedroll, she shouldered her rucksack and took up the bow and arrows Tremelo had lent her. She paused, looking at the cozy little tree house that had been her home since the Elder's death. She felt another tug of grief, just as she had gazing at Fairmount earlier. She didn't truly belong here, no matter how kind Phi and Tremelo had been. With the Elder gone, her mission was solitary. She'd been chosen by him, and now by Tremelo, to do what the others could not: to disappear.

For one small, terrible moment, it seemed unfair. She wished she were just a regular student, with no long journey ahead of her except the one across the commons to get an egg tart for breakfast. But the moment passed.

Owls perched on the rafters, watching her. One of them, a scruffy brown owl—young, like her—sounded a low hoot. She felt a seed of encouragement bloom inside her. She fished the beetle-back coin out of her pocket, and dropped it in the knot of the tree in the Glass's place. She began to walk away, but then something pulled her back. She fished the harmonica out of her cloak, and left it too in the hollow trunk for her friends to find.

She climbed down out of the tree house and made her way in the darkness, across campus to Tremelo's garage. She whipped the cover off the motorbike he'd only just finished building, and cranked the starter—once, twice, three times before it sputtered to life. As she wheeled it out of the workshop, she thought she saw a light come on in the teachers' quarters. She sped away, before she was caught—or before Tremelo could come find her, and she'd have to say another good-bye.

Eleven

"FIRST OF ALL, DON'T just grab him like a dinner roll; let him come onto your arm in his own time, like this."

Bailey watched as Tori demonstrated the proper way to hold Bert by reaching out her arm and letting the iguana crawl sluggishly to the nook of her elbow. The two sat alone on a pair of overturned crates in Tremelo's workshop, away from the weekend energy of the rest of the campus. Hal, Phi, Tremelo, and Gwen were due to join them at any moment to continue working on the machine. Tori tried to impart some wisdom about bonding with reptiles, but Bert wouldn't so much as crawl a centimeter toward Bailey, even when he held a fresh bite of broccoli in his fingers. Tomorrow would be the first Scavage scrimmage of the new year, and they'd need to convince everyone that Bert was his kin.

"See how he settles right in?" Tori asked, feeding Bert a nugget of broccoli. "He'll be most comfortable like this, resting along your arm, with his tail at your elbow."

"I see," said Bailey. "Let me try again."

Tori set Bert down gently on the ground between them, and Bailey reached out his arm.

"You have to sort of 'think' an invitation," Tori suggested, "like I do with my snakes. Let him know he's welcome."

"But he isn't actually my kin," Bailey said as Bert relaxed his scaly limbs and closed his eyes. He felt frustrated, and his nerves were still raw from his interaction with Viviana the day before. "Even if we could communicate, he'd rather just nap."

"He *is* sluggish. Maybe he's not getting enough sun?" asked Tori. "You set up those special lamps Tremelo gave you, right?"

Bailey nodded.

"Those lights are on all night, and through the morning too. The humming from the bulbs is driving Hal crazy," Bailey answered. "And people talking about Bert is driving *me* crazy. I can't even count how many people have said, 'I didn't know you were Animas Iguana! Why didn't you ever say so?' Bert was supposed to help me blend in, not stand out more."

Bert flicked his pink tongue between his lips, dreaming.

"At least the other students think you're normal now," said Tori. "I mean—not that you weren't *nor*mal before, but there were rumors...."

Bailey leaned his head on his hand and studied the way Bert's scales surrounded his perpetually closed lizard eyes.

"Yeah, but if anyone's paying attention, it's obvious Bert isn't really my kin. Viviana will be observing the scrimmage tomorrow. What if I mess up? What if Taleth gets curious again, and wanders onto the field? I don't have anything except an iguana who won't even crawl onto my arm!"

Tori shrugged. "You have us," she said. "And if I hear anyone gossiping about you and Bert, I'll set them straight. You're Animas Iguana, always have been."

She glanced down and began to laugh. Bailey saw that Bert had crept toward him across the desk, and was gripping his shirt sleeve with an unsteady claw. It almost seemed affectionate.

"I don't know everything," said Tori. "But *that's* a good sign."

The workshop door swung open with a loud creak, and Phi entered. She was out of breath, and she rushed to them without bothering to close the door behind her.

"Gwen is *gone*," she whispered. "The tree house is empty!"

"What?" asked Tori. "Where did she go?"

"I don't know," said Phi. "But at least she got away safely. Look!" She held out her hand. In her palm was the beetleback that Gwen had shown them. "She left this too," Phi said, revealing the harmonica in her other hand.

"What's that?" Tremelo entered the workshop, with Hal following right behind him. He must have seen the unease on their faces, because he slowly closed the workshop door behind him.

"Gwen's left," said Phi.

Tremelo inspected the beetleback, then handed it back to Phi before glancing around the workshop. "*Hmm.* On my favorite motorbike too, it looks like." He pointed to an empty space between his motorbuggy and a mounted bike frame that seemed to be missing several key components, like an engine and tires.

"I walked out there this morning with a week's worth of food," said Phi, "and when I saw . . . I thought she might be dead! How do we know no one followed her? We've got to look for her. We don't even know what happened!"

"Calm down," said Tremelo. "We can't know until she sends word back to us. But we must trust that she can take care of herself."

Phi's chin crumpled as she looked down at her shoes.

"She knows what to do," Bailey said. "She and Tremelo had a plan. I'm sure she's already safe with the RATS." He wasn't so certain this was the truth. If anyone had followed Gwen to get to the Glass, then she could lead them straight to the RATS or be captured on her own, with no way to let anyone know. "Maybe we can try sending a message, to be sure."

"I can't believe she left the harmonica," Phi said. "It stopped Sucrette's Dominance of those animals last fall—what if she needs it for protection?"

"Maybe she thought we needed it more," said Hal, who held out his hand. "Can I see it?"

Phi handed the harmonica over to Hal, who squinted at the embossed images of a boy and a fox on the instrument's leather case. Opening the case, he shook out the rusty instrument.

"I still don't know how it works," Hal wondered aloud.

"Vibrations—a positive frequency," said Tremelo. "Music is a lot like the bond itself, an energy that can be projected outward as well as felt inwardly. It can even intensify the bond." Tremelo paused and pursed his lips in thought.

"We know that music stopped Sucrette's Dominance before," he continued, plucking the harmonica from Hal's open palm. Hal shrugged. "But what if Viviana was using the same principles to make her Dominance stronger—projecting it outward on a higher frequency. . . ." Tremelo began stroking the ends of his dark brown mustache, and Bailey knew that the teacher was developing an idea.

"May I hold on to this?" Tremelo asked, looking at Phi.

"Of course," said Phi. "For all I know, you're the one Gwen meant to leave it for."

"I'll tell you one thing," said Tori. "I'd love to be Gwen right now—at least she gets to miss the Scavage game."

That afternoon, the Scavage team met on the snowy field to practice for the big scrimmage the next day.

Coach Banter clapped a huge hand on Bailey's shoulder as he entered the warm-up area. Bailey winced a little at the soreness that remained in his arm. Coach was accompanied by his usual stocky bulldogs, who jumped and pawed at Bailey's legs, barking excitedly at Bert.

"You'll be warming up with your kin today," Coach said. "Take some time to let him get used to the field."

Bert was lying along Bailey's arm the way Tori had instructed, doing his best impression of a lifeless stick. Bailey saw Taylor Quindley and the other Year Three players out of the corner of his eye, straining to get a better look at Bert.

"Sure, we're ready," said Bailey, hoping no one could hear the nervous crack in his voice. He had to figure out a way to play alongside Bert—his life depended on it.

"What *is* that thing?" one of the Third Years shouted, pointing at Bert.

"You mean that weird little creature with the lizard?" laughed Taylor. "That's Walker!"

"Get in gear, Quindley!" Coach shouted back, before thumping Bailey on the shoulder and walking off.

After gearing up into his kneesocks and pads—royal blue to signify his squad—Bailey took Bert out to the edge of the field. He knelt and tried to concentrate on how the field must look from the lizard's point of view. Much of the snow had been shoveled away, leaving a slick, muddy terrain underneath. It would be a messy game the next day.

Bert opened his eyes and stretched out a scaly claw. He sniffed at a piece of mud. Bailey leaned down and sniffed it too. Even if Bert wasn't his kin, maybe everything he'd learned in the last few months would help him feel something. Bailey closed his eyes and focused.

And for one overwhelming moment, an aroma of pine filled his nostrils, and he felt crunching snow beneath a heavy paw. His ears were perked, alert—someone was looking for him. Hunting him.

Bailey opened his eyes, his heart pounding. He'd been inside Taleth's head, an experience so much more intense than the low humming he normally felt. It was like Tremelo had said—jarring. Jarring, but wonderful.

Bert gnawed at the piece of mud, which crumbled in his mouth. Bailey grimaced. He wished he could be with Taleth right now, exploring the mountains and growing more powerful together. School and Scavage seemed very small in comparison—and with a giant white tiger, away from Fairmount and Viviana, he'd no doubt be safer.

With Bert in tow, he found it difficult to run and jump the

way he used to. Halfway through practice, he tucked Bert inside a hollow log near the forested end of the field.

"Stay there," he said to the lizard, who immediately fell asleep. Bailey took off, in pursuit of a Gold Squadron Sneak who'd just spotted the Blue Squad's flag. He aimed his Flick and lobbed a glob of paint. It struck the Sneak's left knee, coating her leg in bright blue, but she kept running.

The power Bailey had felt through his brief connection with Taleth had stayed with him. As he ducked under branches and barreled over the wooded terrain in pursuit of the Gold Sneak, he realized how much he'd missed playing. He tackled her just yards from where the flag hung, suspended from the limb of a huge oak tree.

"Good tackle, Bailey!" called Arabella, captain of the Blue Squadron, who was guarding the flag.

"End of play!" Coach called.

"Good practice," Phi said to him, as they found each other near Bert's napping spot. "You can't show off tomorrow, not with Viviana watching."

"You're probably right," Bailey said. "But it sure is fun today."

Bailey grabbed Bert, and together they went to run drills with the rest of the team, who were gathered near the stands. Taylor approached with a smirk.

"Ants' antennae, that thing stinks!" Taylor said, pointing at Bert. "*This* is your kin? What in Nature is it?"

"He's an iguana," Bailey said.

Taylor lifted Bert up by his tail straight out of Bailey's grip. He held the iguana at arm's length.

"Creaking frogs, it looks like a giant insect. Is it dead?" He shook Bert slightly.

Bailey took a step forward and reached for Bert, but Taylor stepped backward and swept him out of Bailey's reach.

"Watch it, Walker," he said. "Or I punt this dumb piece of leather so hard, you'll feel it in your own gut."

As if to respond, Bert twisted himself up and nipped at Taylor's finger. Taylor let out a high-pitched shriek and dropped Bert onto the ground.

"Ants! Oh, anting *roach*-ants! Creaking *frogs*!" he cursed, sucking at his finger. A trickle of blood ran down his hand.

Bailey couldn't help but smile.

"This 'piece of leather' goes by Bert." For the first time, he was proud of being "Animas Iguana." Even if it was a lie.

The next afternoon, Bailey and Phi returned to the Scavage pitch in nervous silence. Bert slept in the crook of Bailey's arm, completely unaware of the frantic worry that Bailey felt. They were about to be put on display before Viviana, in the first Scavage scrimmage of the semester. Bailey was tempted to reach out and grab Phi's hand as they trudged through the snowy campus, just to calm his buzzing nerves. As for Phi, she was steel-eyed, staring straight ahead. Only once did she glance up to watch the skies, and then she shook her head, as though remembering something she'd forgotten.

Bailey followed her gaze, and realized: Carin, Phi's falcon, was nowhere to be seen.

"Where is she?" he asked as they trod down the hill to the field.

"Hunting," Phi answered.

"Are you nervous about playing without her?" he asked.

She shook her head. "Nope."

Bailey smiled. "I wish I felt that confident."

Phi matched his stride and moved closer as they walked. She bumped his shoulder with her own, and Bailey felt his heart leap in his chest.

"It'll be okay," she said.

Bailey wished he could be as certain, though it felt good to hear her say it.

As they approached the pitch, Bailey's heart began to beat faster. The entire school—students, teachers, and even Mrs. Copse and the kitchen staff—was lined up outside the gates to get in and watch the scrimmage. Bailey heard shouts of "Let's go, Fairmount!" The teachers wore blue-and-gold neckties and scarves in support of what wasn't even a real game.

"Oh, ants," Bailey sighed as they made their way to the locker rooms. Viviana was already seated in the dean's box, high in the stands. Her slim maroon coat was buttoned all the way up to a high collar that hid her chin, and the large, round hat she wore looked like beaver fur. Graves, Finch, Shonfield, and a few other teachers sat bundled against the cold, chatting dutifully. As Bailey watched, Graves stopped talking to Finch and peered over the bundled folds of his massive scarf, directly at Bailey. Viviana, sitting next to him, followed his gaze. Bailey's skin prickled all over as their eyes met, just for a second, before he ducked into the locker room.

"She's watching me," he whispered to Phi. "Graves too."

"It'll be okay," said Phi again, though her voice sounded a bit higher this time.

The team changed in the warmth of the locker room before lining up at the edge of the chilly field in two squads, Gold and

Blue. Both Bailey and Phi wore blue-striped uniforms. The players' animal kin, too undisciplined to fall into line, explored the edges of the field and, in some cases, darted out into the terrain ahead of the starting whistle. Bailey wondered what Viviana thought of the display—if she actually cared about the game at all, or whether she was carefully taking note of each and every student at Fairmount who could be the Child of War. As Coach Banter lifted the starting whistle to his lips, Bailey snuck one last look toward the stands. Viviana gazed down at the team, her eyes skipping along the line of athletes. Bailey ducked his head and looked away.

Coach Banter blew the whistle, and the players barreled out onto the field, scattering like leaves caught in a strong gust of winter wind. Cheers echoed across the pitch.

Bailey ran headlong into the trees with Bert in tow. He jogged until he came across an outcrop of rocks, several yards from the Blue Squad's flag and partially obscured from view from the stands by long pine branches overhead. With his Flick in his right hand and Bert on his shoulder, he waited.

It didn't take long: not even five minutes passed before Bailey heard a rustling in the dry, leafless underbrush nearby, and saw a flash of a gold kneesock. He readied his Flick, prepared to send a glob of bright blue paint at the player as soon as he had a clear view. But the Sneak must have heard him, and veered away. Bailey followed the sound of footsteps on the dead leaves, keeping his pace steady. A small movement in the corner of his vision caused him to stop—a tiny stoat, kin to one of the Gold Squad's Squats, dashed away, presumably to warn its human kin that Bailey was on the hunt.

"Ants," Bailey muttered. He'd have to speed up.

Applause sounded from the stands—somewhere on the terrain, a Sneak had been taken out.

Just then, the low-burning embers of his Animas bond seemed to ignite like the flame of a gas lamp. Bailey's breath halted in his lungs. He knew that Taleth was edging the field, drawn by him to the most dangerous place she could possibly be.

"No," he said, though no one could hear him.

"Bailey!"

He looked around—it was Phi's voice calling him, but he couldn't see her.

"I'm up here!"

Bailey craned his neck upward. Phi waved at him from halfway up a tall, spindly birch tree.

"Are you okay?" she half whispered.

The stands loomed at the other end of the field. They were out of earshot.

"It's Taleth," he said, keeping his voice as low as possible. "She's going to get herself seen."

Phi's eyes widened in understanding. She stood on tiptoe and looked around.

"Hide," she said.

"What?"

"Trust me. Hide!"

Bailey ran with Bert behind a flank of pine branches. He heard the sound of an approaching player, and understood—if he engaged, he'd be watched. Instead, he had to stay hidden and out of the game, so he could get to the edge of the field. He tried sending his intentions to Taleth, as he had near Gwen's tree house. *Get away,* he thought. *It's too dangerous here.* But he felt no clarity with the connection, just a jumble of emotions and sensations. He didn't know whether she could possibly understand him.

The Gold Sneak ran past him, so close that Bailey could easily have tagged him—but he didn't dare. The Sneak, a slim, brown-haired Year Two boy, paused and listened. Bailey held his breath, thanking Nature that Bert seemed completely uninterested in moving a muscle.

The Sneak peered in his direction, blinking.

Then Bailey heard a cry and a gasp from the stands: Phi had leapt from the branch above, her arms spread and her legs kicking. She landed just behind the Sneak and tumbled forward, catching him by his ankle.

Bailey froze. He wanted to cheer at Phi's gutsy move, but she looked in his direction, just for the briefest moment, and her gaze told him to run. She'd made sure no one would be looking at him.

Still, Bailey's legs felt like they were glued in place. He shivered, feeling a familiar sensation of gooseflesh. Turning to the stands, he saw a gleaming reflection on the lenses of a pair of opera glasses. Viviana Melore was holding them up to her eyes, and they were pointed right in Bailey's direction. His ducked into the trees and ran. He stayed as close to the pines as he could, hoping that his blue uniform didn't show through the veil of branches between him and the observers.

As soon as he was within a few yards of the edge of the field, he stopped and took cover behind a boulder. Closing his eyes, he frantically tried to get a sense of where Taleth was. "Get away; you can't be here," he whispered over and over.

He heard the snap of a twig to his left. Behind the trees, a flash of white appeared, then vanished.

"Taleth!" He barreled forward—he had to lead her away from the pitch, away from Viviana. He couldn't see her, but the twinging in his chest, the perking of his own ears, told him that she was anxious, and had been pacing the edge of the pitch all morning, desperate for a glimpse of him, to know he was all right.

Bailey heard a scattering of leaves next to him. Looking down, he saw Fennel the fox running in the same direction. She narrowed her black-and-yellow eyes at him and darted ahead. Then, just beyond the next boulder, Bailey saw Taleth. She stood waiting for him between a pair of straight, tall pines. Her whiskers were flattened against her cheeks and her teeth were slightly bared. At the sight of her, Bailey felt his blood grow even warmer in his veins. Fennel rushed at Taleth, who stepped back, apprehensive.

"Go," said Bailey, though every part him wanted to cry out *Wait* instead. *Wait for me.*

Fennel slowed and began to pace in front of Taleth. She barked, then jumped at Taleth again, never going so near as to attack her—only to force her back, blocking her from Bailey. Bailey watched, heartbroken, as Taleth padded backward into the trees, away from him. Her dazzling blue cat eyes met his own, and he felt a tug, as strong as if he had a rope tied around his chest, pulling him to the woods. Then she broke the gaze, and sauntered into the shadows. Fennel stayed sitting on a snow-dusted rock. She gazed at him with unblinking eyes.

"Walker, what are you *doing*?" Taylor ran up behind him. "Looking for ghosts again? You missed the end of the match!"

The scrimmage had ended in a tie, with the final Gold and Blue Sneaks getting eliminated at exactly the same moment—a record, Coach Banter said, amused. Bailey shook hands with his fellow players, and Viviana finally left her seat as the players congratulated Phi on her daring tackle. He watched as Graves and Finch led their illustrious visitor down the steep steps of the Scavage stands, and he could not be sure, from where he stood, whether she was watching him in return.

Twelve

GWEN'S JOURNEY TO THE Gray City took several days, by way of the icy back roads. The motorbike was clunky and slow to start, but it was better than making the journey on foot in the snow. She'd made many stops to assess whether she was being followed. It had been a stressful ride—owls circled nervously overhead, since they could feel the Dominae's presence growing stronger as they got closer to the city.

By the time Gwen reached the outskirts of the Gray City, several frightened owls had peeled off and flown back toward the woods. Gwen felt like a pauper again, her coat soaked, torn, and dirty. She'd lived as a pickpocket in the Gudgeons, the nastiest area of the city, before she'd been apprenticed to the Elder. Now she felt just as bedraggled as she had then. She parked Tremelo's motorbike in a hidden alcove near the dockside marketplace where she used to steal pocket watches. Knowing the thieves who populated those alleyways, the risk that the bike would be stolen before she returned was high. But she couldn't ride it through the bumpy streets and cobblestone steps of the Gudgeons without attracting attention. She slipped her knife into her right boot, and tied the longbow and arrows to the motorbike. She wheeled the bike behind a pile of garbage bags, hoping that no one would come along to collect them.

She'd received a letter from Digby Barnes just after the Elder's death, telling her in coded terms how to find him and the RATS. *We've had to get a little cat to help find the vermin,* the note had said. It might have seemed harmless to any other eyes, but to Gwen and Tremelo it had been a clear hint at how to find the RATS. *Her tail twitches quite smartly, especially when she plays in the old papers.* Neither Digby nor the other RATS knew that the Elder had been killed—and more important, they didn't know Tremelo was the True King. Gwen was eager to tell the RATS the news. Would they believe her? Would they fight for Tremelo, the man they only knew as the myrgwood-smoking son of their former leader, the Loon? There was only one way to find out.

Gwen began her search in the market, where the walls were thick with dated political posters and flyers: "old papers." Once, the market had been teeming with merchants and vendors, but now many of the shops surrounding it were shuttered and closed, abandoned by people who had fled the city. The only shop that remained was a bakery. In its front window sat a heaping basket of raisin bread, fogging up the glass with its oven-fresh warmth. Gwen's stomach grumbled as she gazed through the window. She hadn't realized how hungry she was—she had grabbed everything she owned the night before in the tree house, but she'd already eaten the tarts Phi had brought from the Fairmount dining hall.

"What do you want? Get away from there!" An angry woman with a flour-spattered apron stood in the doorway of the bakery. "Unless you're buying, bark off!"

"I—I'm sorry," Gwen sputtered, backing quickly away. But she wasn't watching where she was going, and she tripped over someone's foot. That someone glared down at her.

"Disrupting the peace, are you?" grunted the man who stood over her. "Can't have that." He didn't wear the uniform of a kingdom guard, the officers who'd kept order under Parliament's regime. Instead, he wore plainclothes, and a wide red sash that crossed his middle. Gwen couldn't be certain who he worked for—but she was willing to bet that he was Dominae.

The baker woman disappeared, slamming the door behind her.

The man looked at Gwen's muddy traveling boots, and the rucksack on her shoulders.

"Where you coming from?" he asked.

Gwen heard a growl by the man's knees, coming from a skinny black dog with bared teeth, tethered to the man by a long chain.

"Who wants to know?" she asked him.

He grinned at her.

"This is the Dominae's city now. It's our job to know everyone's comings and goings."

Gwen heard a jittery hoot from above her—three owls watched her, clustered together on a window ledge.

"I . . ." She struggled to think of a story. "I'm going to visit my uncle," she said. "He's . . . been ill."

One of the owls hopped down from the windowsill and came closer to Gwen. *Don't,* she tried to tell it. *Can't you see you're in danger?* Gwen pushed herself up to stand and dusted off her pants.

"And by the looks of you, you crossed some nasty terrain to get there. I find that *very* sweet. And very interesting." He winked at her, a gesture that was not at all comforting. Then he snapped his fingers.

The dog bolted on its chain at the man's command, its teeth flashing. It leapt on the poor owl. Gwen cried out; she felt the owl's fear behind her own eyes, and a wrenching pain in her side.

The man snapped his fingers again, and the dog let go of the frightened owl and trotted back to its kin.

"Since you're new here, let that be a lesson to you," laughed the man. He sauntered away down the market street.

Gwen leaned back against the stone wall. The pain ebbed.

"I'm sorry," she said to the little owl. Its wing was clearly broken, and it had a bite on the side of its head. It hopped away. "Maybe I can help you," Gwen called after it. But it was no use. The other owls flew away, hooting sadly. They knew it hadn't been her fault, she could sense that. But they also knew that being around her meant being in danger. This is what Dominance does, Gwen thought mournfully. It eats away at the bond until it's not just your own that's broken—it's everyone's.

She limped toward an alley wall where the layers of outdated posters were thick. It didn't take her long to find a white chalk drawing of a cat, no bigger than her hand, on an old poster supporting Parliament's tax on fish. The tail of the cat in the drawing was crooked, pointing to the end of the alley. She walked in that direction, looking out for more white cats along the way. At the end of the alley, she saw one drawn on a flyer for Viviana herself, its tail pointing in the opposite direction of its head, to a curving stone stair behind a tenement building.

Gwen followed the signs, hugging the stone walls along the empty Gudgeons streets—only a few citizens, as bedraggled as she was, hurried past. Finally, Gwen found a drawing of a white cat curled up sleeping on an advertisement for a long-past concert. The advert was pasted onto a sagging wooden house the length of half a city block, with a sign over the door that said THE ALLEY CAT. She knocked anxiously. No one answered, but she could hear voices inside. She knocked again, and was sure that she saw someone looking at her from behind the shutters of a window on the main floor.

Through the door, Gwen heard a muffled voice.

"Did they have fruit at the market?" the voice asked.

Confused, Gwen stepped back. It was either a mistake, or the RATS were testing her. Digby hadn't said anything in his cable about a password or secret question—but then, his message had been so vague, she wasn't sure. It was best, she decided, to simply be honest.

"I don't know," she began. "But Digby Barnes would know who I am, and maybe he could help me . . . find the fruit?"

"No fruit, no admittance," the voice said.

"Wait, please," Gwen asked, her voice shaking. "I don't know the answer to your question, but I want to help—I have some news—not from the market, but from—"

"Not interested!" the voice said.

"Please just tell Digby I'm here!" Gwen pleaded, but she received no answer.

She refused to be shut out, not after everything she'd been

through. She began pounding on the door, hardly caring if anyone else heard. Luckily, the street was shuttered and barred. Everyone was afraid, just like her.

Finally, the door opened. Someone grabbed her arm, and pulled her forcefully inside.

"You trying to wake the dead?" a woman said as the door shut behind her. "Who are you? What do you want here?"

All around the room, mistrustful eyes worked her over. She didn't recognize anyone from the previous fall, when she'd hid with the RATS and the Elder in The White Tiger bar or the underground tunnels below the city.

"Please, I've come from Fairmount. I'm looking for Digby," she said, trying not to let her voice tremble.

"That's right, you are!" bellowed a familiar voice. Digby Barnes, the massive bartender from The White Tiger pub, pushed his way through the crowd toward her. He put a meaty hand on her shoulder and squeezed it reassuringly.

"All, this here's Gwen, and she's the Elder's main girl," Digby said, turning to the room.

"What if someone followed her here?" asked one of the onlookers, a woman with a scratchy voice and dirty apron. "How do we know she hasn't brought them right to our door?"

"There was no one else outside," Gwen said quietly.

"And they'd have taken her off straightaway," interjected Digby. "She's smarter than that. Now, she gets whatever she needs, no questions."

"Thank you," Gwen said in little more than a whisper. "Can I have something to eat?"

A few minutes later, she was bundled in an armchair, with a

bowl of hot soup in her hands and a blanket around her shoulders. The citizens of the Alley Cat had warmed to her after Digby's welcome, especially when she'd recounted the run-in with the Dominae guard.

"They're all over the place, like cockroaches," Digby said. "Viviana set them up just before the Midwinter holiday, in the name of 'public safety.' Public bullies is what they are."

"How have you been getting on here, with them around?" she asked. "Are they spying for her?"

Digby laughed.

"You have to have a brain before you can report intelligence, don't you? No, they're just the lowest rung on Viviana's ladder. Give the nastiest bunch the easiest job to do, and make them think they're important. Their only job is to remind everyone that Viviana's taken power."

Gwen thought about the way the man had just snapped his fingers to make the dog attack, and shuddered.

"Still, can't be too careful. We've had to keep moving each week to stay ahead of them. Someone's always having to go 'round and change the tails on our little drawin's. But we want to hear about you, lass," said Digby. "And the Elder. Did you make it to Fairmount? What did Tremelo have to say for himself?"

Gwen's heart began beating wildly, something she hadn't expected. She took a deep breath.

"The Elder is dead," she said.

It was the first time she'd had to say those words out loud. They sounded so final, so horrible, coming out of her mouth that she wanted to take them back and apologize. But it was the truth. He'd been a link between the RATS and the old king who they loved.

What's more, he had been the only person in the world who cared for Gwen herself. And he was gone.

She heard a gasp and many whispers from the RATS assembled in the room after she spoke. Digby's ruddy face went pale, and he looked down at his hands. For a long moment, everyone was silent. Then:

"How did it happen? Was it the Dominae?" asked the old woman in the dirty apron.

"Did Tremelo have something to do with it? Was it at the school?" asked Digby.

"Did you see whoever did it? Did you kill them?" shouted a younger man with dark, angry eyes.

More questions from the gathered revolutionaries seemed to crowd around Gwen like beggar children in the market asking for a snailback or a piece of bread. She shrank back and set the bowl of soup onto the bar with trembling hands. She wished for sleep—but more than that, she needed to tell the RATS everything.

"He died at Fairmount," she said, feeling the sting of the words as they left her mouth. "We went there to find Tremelo— you thought he'd be able to help you, but we realized that he..." She paused. Looking around the room, she wondered whether she could truly trust each and every person there. As for the RATS, they were hanging on her words, mouths agape and eyes staring.

"The journey was too much for the Elder," she said instead. "And Tremelo will help, but . . . but you'll need to wait for his word." She would tell Digby later—alone—about Tremelo's true identity. He would know who to trust.

Tiredness washed over her, and her shoulders slumped. She looked to Digby.

"All right, that's enough," he said, reading the pleading look in her eyes. "Time for all that later."

He waved the RATS away and guided her out of the main room and down a hallway. He stood aside an open door at the end of the hall, and let Gwen into a small bedroom. It was clear to her from the folded pallets and piled rucksacks that at least three people were sleeping there, and she wondered how many RATS had come forward and joined the movement in the few weeks since she'd left the city.

"Not much in the way of room," he said. "But it's yours if you need it."

"Thank you," Gwen said. Eagerly she unrolled a pallet and lay down. Despite the rising wave of voices from down the hall, she quickly fell into a deep sleep. For the first time in many days, she felt safe.

The next morning, she had to tiptoe over the snoring bodies of several other inhabitants of the Alley Cat to get down the hall to the main room. There she found Digby sitting with a mug of hot sap milk.

"Glad you're an early riser," he said. "I've got something for you, and it's best the others don't see it just yet."

Digby took a wrapped package out of his pocket, and handed it to Gwen.

"He told me that if something was to happen to him, this needed to go to you."

Gwen sat next to Digby on a stool and held the package in both hands. It was heavy, the size of a fist. She unfolded the bits of muslin tied with twine around the object.

She recognized it as soon as the first piece of muslin fell away.

It was the bit of the Statue of the Twins that the Elder had brought back to Parliament with him, those many months ago. She could still make out the fox's paw—the girl twin who'd transformed, while her brother had remained a human. The first Animas bond.

Underneath the piece of stone was a note. Her fingers shook as she lifted the slip of parchment to read.

> *My dearest Gwen,*
> *If Digby has given you this token, then it means I am gone and must rely on you—I have utter faith. The stone should tell you where to begin your journey. From where the statue once stood, look for the tallest peak and travel to it. There, you will find the Instrument of Change. Without its help, our True King cannot find the strength in his heart to lead. For remember, true sight is a light that grows—the physical world is a limited thing, strengthened and made clear by what is stronger and unseen.*

Gwen had always wanted to journey to the Seers' Valley with the Elder. Now he was asking her to go without him, tasked with ensuring the fate of Aldermere. Tremelo would not become a king without her help—she felt at once important and all alone.

Digby put a heavy hand on her shoulder.

"No need to tell me what it says, girl. That's just for you to know."

Gwen smiled.

"Thank you for keeping this safe," she said. "I have something for only you to know, as well."

Digby turned on his stool, his eyebrows rising in curiosity.

"When we left for Fairmount, it was because the Elder wanted to find Tremelo," Gwen began.

"I remember," said Digby. "The Elder was interested in him being the Loon's son."

"But that wasn't quite it," Gwen said. "We weren't going to find the son of the Loon—we went because we believed we'd find the True King there."

Digby set his mug of sap milk down on the counter.

"What's that now?" he said. "The Elder believed in the prophecy?"

Gwen shook her head.

"Not exactly," she said. "But he knew to recognize certain signs." She breathed in deeply and kept her eyes trained on Digby's ruddy face.

"It's Tremelo," she said. "*He* is Trent Melore. The Loon was so sure about his prophecies, because he was the one raising the True King in safety, away from Parliament. He saved him from the fire."

A smile as wide as the Fluvian broke out on Digby's face. He threw his head back and laughed loudly.

"Go on," he said, playfully hitting Gwen's shoulder. "Tremelo? A king? Naw, I don't believe it." He laughed again. "But I do! I *do* believe it! Ha! That old Thelonious. Old Loony." Digby wiped a tear from one eye and laughed again. "I've heard stranger stories—this one, it's strange enough to be true. The Elder had proof?"

Gwen nodded again.

"Well, here's to King Myrgwood, then," said Digby, lifting his mug of sap milk into the air and taking a long swig. After slamming the mug back down, he smiled at Gwen. "Well, now that we have a king, what do we do?"

Gwen laughed.

"I...I don't know!" she said. "But please—you can't tell anyone else. Tremelo isn't even sure whether he wants the throne—"

"*Wants* it?" Digby said. "He sees what's going on, don't he?"

"He'll come around," Gwen said quickly. "And he'll need you and the RATS to be ready when he does. Will you fight for him when the time comes?"

Digby looked to his lap.

"It'll be hard convincing this lot that that oaf is their king," he said. "But if he comes around like you say, I'll do what I can."

"Thank you. And for this too," Gwen said, touching the stone the Elder had left for her. She reached out her hand to shake his.

"None of that, now," said Digby, waving away her hand and squeezing her in a tight hug instead. He eased up, and once she could breathe again, she rose and returned to the crowded bedroom. She set the stone carefully in her own rucksack, alongside the Seers' Glass. As she gathered her things, she heard more and more voices rising over freshly poured mugs of sap milk and coffee.

When she returned, the main parlor was once again bustling, and the RATS were in the midst of a debate.

"What have I missed?" Gwen asked Digby.

Digby waved a frustrated hand at the group.

"We're not the only one interested in the Loon's prophecy," he said. "Talk about the white tiger has been all over the city. Used to be, us RATS were the ones spreadin' that around. But *now* the talk's not just coming from us."

"It means people are excited, and want to stop Viviana just like we do," said a white-bearded man across the room.

"But we can't rely on that," said a young, dark-skinned man named Enoch, whom Gwen was happy to see again. He'd helped her escape the Dominae once before, and in the tunnels he'd taught her to play the Elder's old harmonica. "Just look at how Viviana's been using the same prophecy to her own ends—she's got that mechanical tiger that she parades around with. She's laughing at the prophecy with that piece of clockwork. *She* might be the one spreading the rumors around, so she can claim they're about her." A chameleon named Bill was wrapped around Enoch's neck, blending in with his blue plaid scarf.

"If she's trying to use the prophecy as some kind of political move, she ought to think twice," said Digby. He glanced at Gwen, and gave her a quick wink.

"I say, best to forget about prophecies," said a younger woman standing next to Enoch, "and concentrate on the task at hand—stopping the Dominae ourselves!"

"Someone's outside!"

A cry from the front of the parlor hushed the entire room, and Gwen heard a sickening sound—boots on the pavement, and the barking of dogs in the street.

Digby shot up from his seat and hurried down the hallway with Gwen's hand in his own.

He opened the door to a bedroom and threw open the window. Behind them, Gwen heard the sound of broken glass and shouting. The barking of several dogs echoed down the hallway, as well as rushing footsteps, of people trying to escape.

"Go, girl!"

Gwen grabbed her rucksack and lifted herself up onto the windowsill. She looked back at Digby's round red face, full of fear. A terrible thought occurred to her, that she might never see him again.

"I'm sorry," she said to Digby, before ducking beneath the opened window.

A harsh voice echoed down the hallway. "Halt, in the name of the queen!"

"You have to get out!" she whispered.

"Don't worry about me!" he said. "Go, go!"

She slid away down the alley behind the house. Terrified, she ran through back alleys to the marketplace to find the motorbike. She thanked Nature it was still there, started its engine, and fled the city, away from the crowded Gudgeons and out toward the open valley of the Seers' Land.

Thirteen

THE BELLS IN THE Fairmount clock tower clanged: four o'clock. Hal and Bailey stood by the columns of the library building, waiting for Phi and Tori, who were both, as of that minute, late.

"So now that we've got the casing soldered and the wires connected, what's left?" asked Hal, who was ticking off a list on his fingers.

"The centerpiece—the orb," said Bailey. He watched the lawn for their friends.

"Right, but we don't know what that's made of," said Hal. "I meant the part we *do* know how to make."

In the days following both Gwen's and Viviana's departures, Bailey had finally begun to feel the tight knot of worry in his stomach unraveling. Viviana was gone, and he was still alive—as were all his friends and Taleth. But that worry had been replaced by seemingly endless questions about the Reckoning machine: What was it for? What was it made of? How would it work? The group had met every afternoon during that week, constructing an object that, despite Tremelo's eager experiments, remained a mystery. On top of that, they still had not received word from Gwen. Tremelo had sent a note to Digby Barnes, the leader of the Gray City RATS, but the RATS moved around the city so often there was no certainty that it would reach him.

"There's Phi," said Hal, pointing. She was hurrying across the lawn from the direction of the dormitories, carrying a packed rucksack. Bailey and Hal walked down the front steps of the library to meet her.

"Where's Tori?" Hal asked. "I thought you'd be coming together."

"I don't know," said Phi. "I thought she'd be here."

"Let's go without her," said Bailey. "I'm sure she'll catch up." He turned to walk up the path that would lead out to the teachers' quarters.

"Actually," said Phi, "I'm going to the Dust Plains. . . . I'm not coming with you."

Bailey stopped short and turned to face her.

"What? Why? Is everything okay?" Hal asked.

"Yes—well, I mean no," she said. "My aunt—she was sick for several weeks, and now she's passed."

"I'm sorry, Phi," Bailey said. He didn't want her to go—he felt like he'd hardly seen her since he'd returned from break. "When are you coming back?"

"A week or two," she said. "I'm catching a rigi now. Want to walk with me?"

Bailey nodded. "Of course."

"I'll go let Tremelo know that everyone's late," said Hal. "Not that he's ever on time, either…"

Together, Bailey and Phi walked past the clock tower and between the animal-shaped hedges toward the rigimotive platform.

"Did you tell Coach Banter about missing Scavage practice?" he asked her.

"Ms. Shonfield let all my instructors know that I'd be gone—and the coach too," said Phi.

The wind was very strong near the rigi platform, near the edge of the cliff. Bert nestled inside Bailey's coat, sluggish from the cold. The breeze plucked at their lapels and Bailey saw something glisten inside Phi's jacket—a blue brooch in the shape of a flower, pinned to the inside lining. It was fancier than anything he'd ever seen Phi wearing, and it reminded him of something. But the rigimotive appeared at the edge, and clanked into place on the horizontal tracks. Phi yelled over the squealing brakes as it entered the station.

"I know this is terrible timing," she said.

Bailey shook his head.

"Your family is important." In truth, he was concerned to see her go. First Gwen's disappearance, and now Phi leaving—he couldn't keep track of all the people he wanted to keep safe.

"Is there a way we can reach you? You know, to let you know when we hear from Gwen?"

Phi bit her lip nervously.

"I'd be back before the post even reached me in the Plains," she said. "I am worried about her, though."

"I'm sure she's okay," Bailey said, even though he wasn't.

The rigi shuddered to a stop, and the door at the rear of the car opened.

Phi set her rucksack down on the platform and gave Bailey a quick hug, taking care not to squish Bert.

"Listen," she said, "Graves, Viviana, the machine . . . it's part of a bigger picture."

"What do you mean?"

" 'Part of a bigger picture'—it's what my mom told me when I left for Fairmount. She said not to be scared or anxious, just to figure out my place and then go from there. And maybe it's the same with all of this. That we need to figure out how *we* fit into it—like who we are and who we're going to be when the prophecy unfolds."

Bailey smiled.

"*Who* I'm going to be? Just Bailey, I hope."

Phi shook her head and smiled back. Her brown eyes shone.

"I don't think that's true," she said, picking up her rucksack. "At least, I hope not. Because I don't want to come out the other side as 'just Phi.' "

Out of the corner of his eye, Bailey saw Ms. Shonfield hurrying down the path toward them, with her assistant, Jerri, following.

"Miss Castling!" Shonfield cried. "Wait just a moment!"

Phi glanced at the waiting rigi and waited for Shonfield to climb the platform steps.

"I wanted to see you off personally. Do you have everything you need for the journey?"

Phi nodded, and Shonfield patted her on the shoulder. Bailey realized, seeing the unoccupied leather patch Phi wore, that Carin was still away, hunting. No wonder Phi had been especially moody lately.

"Ahem." Shonfield's assistant coughed, holding out a sheaf of papers.

"Oh, Nature, I'd almost forgotten. One last-minute assignment, my dear—from Dr. Graves." Shonfield gestured to Jerri, who handed over a packet of worksheets. "Can't have you falling behind. Safe journey, Miss Castling! Mr. Walker—behave yourself."

Bailey smiled, and noticed that Jerri was smiling too.

"And the post?" Jerri said, holding up the envelope.

"Oh, yes, of course. 'Urgent' post going out from—who was it?"

"Oh. Um, Graves," said Jerri.

"I should have guessed," said Shonfield with a hint of irritation. She glanced down at her wristwatch. "Jerri, hand that to the conductor yourself? I must meet with Finch." With that she turned on her heel and strode down the platform.

"Tough as nails, that one," Jerri said admiringly. "Real old guard."

Bailey saw a pair of squirrels wrestling playfully on the platform. It made him think of his first day at Fairmount, disembarking from this same rigi, and the chaos of animals that had crowded the platform. Today was colder, and the platform was nearly deserted.

"She doesn't care for Graves much, does she?" asked Bailey. Shonfield, he knew, was a staunch loyalist. And if she didn't like Graves, it was one more strike against him as far as Bailey was concerned.

"He *is* a little demanding. And odd," Jerri said. "I have to make sure this is given directly to the conductor, apparently."

Bailey looked down at the envelope in Jerri's hand—inside could very well be a message for the Dominae.

"I'd best be off! Good-bye, Miss Castling. Mr. Walker," Jerri said, bowing. He walked off to the front of the next car.

Phi touched Bailey's arm before stepping up into the rigi.

"It might be nothing, anyway," she whispered. "But I'll check and see if the conductor meets with anyone in the Gray," she said.

"Good idea," he said as the rigi car began to creak forward. The dirigible balloon whooshed upward, casting a yellow shadow over the platform. Phi waved from the doorway, and then was gone.

Bailey felt empty watching the rigi pull away. With Taleth out of reach in the woods, Gwen gone, and now Phi too, Fairmount didn't seem like home anymore. As he left the platform, Bailey regretted not wishing her a safe journey. He looked around, hoping to cross paths once more with Jerri, but the assistant had disappeared. Instead, he walked across campus to Tremelo's garage workshop. Tremelo and Hal stood side by side, bent over the machine spread across the workbench. Fennel the fox sat upright on a wooden chair, watching Tremelo with intent yellow eyes.

"Where's Tori?" Bailey asked.

"Not coming," said Hal.

"What do you mean, 'not coming'?" asked Bailey.

"Phi catch the rigi on time, then?" asked Tremelo. "Shonfield asked if I wanted to send along some homework, but I'm not that cruel. . . ."

"But what about Tori?" Bailey asked again.

Hal put down the wrench he was holding.

"I was on my way here, and I saw her—with Lyle!" he said.

"And you didn't stop her?" Bailey asked. "Maybe she forgot we were meeting."

"Would that make it any better?" asked Hal. "If she just 'forgot' that we're trying to do something important like, I don't know, save the kingdom?" He paused and took a deep breath. "I didn't talk to her, no. But..."

Tremelo raised an eyebrow.

"But what?" he asked.

"I might have followed them," Hal said. "Just for a minute! Just to listen."

"Hal!" said Bailey. "That's *weird*."

"Listen? Or eavesdrop?" asked Tremelo, a mischievous smile breaking out from underneath his mustache.

"It wasn't like that! And anyway, I think Lyle's got his own Science Competition entry in the works," Hal said. "Tori's helping him! They're going to 'try it out' at the end of the week, after some part they're missing gets delivered."

"Aha, so it's not that you're jealous of Tori's wayward affections—you're worried about your standing in the Fairmount scientific community," Tremelo said, laughing.

"Neither," said Hal, a little too forcefully. "I just dislike when people don't keep appointments."

Bailey studied the machine taking shape on the desk. Since the weekend of the Dominae's visit, he and Tremelo and the others had built an almost exact replica of the casing of the machine according to the specifications of the blueprint. The result was a boxlike structure with an apparatus in the center that would hold what Tremelo referred to as the "orb," the missing piece. The casing had been relatively easy to build, with an assemblage of wires that mimicked the blueprint. But the orb remained a mystery.

"I wanted to show you all something I'm trying out," Tremelo said, gesturing to the machine. "It's a shame the girls will miss it...."

It was clear that Tremelo had been busy since the boys' last visit to the workshop. He'd added three gramophone earpieces to the machine's top, as well as a system of wires and metal cuffs protruding from the machine's side.

"Those weren't on the blueprint," Hal observed.

"I admit, I've struck out on my own," said Tremelo. "But this is something that's been buzzing around in here"—he pointed to his noggin—"for ages. And I think that maybe, just maybe, it might help us understand Viviana's project.

"You see, this casing has been built to hold something volatile—something that's meant to be a conduit of a very large amount of energy. And so from what I can tell, this machine is meant to be an amplifier of that energy. It harnesses that energy and then directs it outward."

He whistled, and Fennel left her chair and hopped dutifully up to the desk. Tremelo picked up what looked like a metal bracelet and fastened it around the fox's neck like a collar. It was connected to the machine's base by three thin wires.

"When Gwen left her harmonica behind, it got me thinking of an experiment. We still don't know what this orb does, but what we can use now is the amplifying system...." Tremelo trailed off as he clamped a wired cuff onto his wrist. "Tell me what you hear," he said to Bailey and Hal. Then he leaned back in the chair and closed his eyes tightly.

Bailey couldn't know what passed between Tremelo and Fennel then. He didn't know what memory they were reliving together, or whether they were just having a wordless conversation. But it didn't matter—what mattered was the unearthly, beautiful sound that flowed out of the gramophone horns. It was like nothing he'd ever heard, a humming that rose and fell in volume and tone until it sounded like many notes at once.

He felt a vibration in his own chest, like the strings of an instrument being strummed. It was the same feeling he'd had when he'd walked into the woods to see Taleth, the feeling of energy thrumming inside him. As he listened to the sounds Tremelo and Fennel were producing, that thrumming in his chest grew until he was sure he wasn't listening alone: somewhere in the nearby woods, Taleth was hearing it too. He could almost feel her ears perking up as though they were *his* ears, and *he* was the one standing on a mountainside, watching the school in the dying light of day. Just the thought of her—this small connection—made Bailey feel more at ease than he'd been in weeks.

Tremelo took off the wrist piece, and the music stopped. Bailey's connection with Taleth faded away.

"Incredible," said Hal. Bailey nodded, speechless.

"It's just an experiment," Tremelo answered. "Still some kinks to fix. I call it the Halcyon."

"How does it work?" Bailey managed to ask.

Tremelo pointed to the metal cuffs.

"When Fennel and I are connected by those," he began, "our bond creates an energy that I can channel into the machine, sort of in place of the missing orb. The sound you hear is that energy becoming magnified, and released into the air around us."

Bailey nodded again. "I was sure that Taleth could hear what I was hearing too."

"I felt the same," said Hal. "Like I was whirling around the clock tower with the bats."

"Wonderful!" crowed Tremelo. "So you see, the Animas bond is an interconnected web. When I magnify my bond, it in turn magnifies yours. It affects everyone, all the time!"

Tremelo's enthusiasm was contagious. Bailey broke into a grin.

"Which means, you could make everyone in the kingdom feel it too," he guessed. "They could become more closely bonded; everyone could."

"This machine, as it is now, is nowhere near *that* powerful," said Tremelo. "But still, it's a start, isn't it?"

"Yeah," Bailey said. He had been so focused on the fight against Viviana that he hadn't thought about what he and his friends were fighting *for*—it was this, the bond and its goodness. It had the power to connect him to another living creature, to *all* living creatures. For just a minute, he forgot about the danger they faced. He felt nothing but gratitude that he'd Awakened, and could take part in this.

As Bailey stood in awe, Tremelo's face changed. A darkness crossed over it.

"But Viviana is using some of this same technology."

"For what, though?" asked Bailey.

"That's precisely what I'm afraid of," said Tremelo.

Fourteen

VIVIANA STOOD IN A snowy field, concentrating intently on the woods in front of her.

She held a long brass blunderbuss decorated with a golden stag and crow, which Clarke had fashioned for her. She enjoyed the weight of it, its solidness, compared to a smaller pistol. Behind her in the land train, her staff busied themselves in the kitchen in preparation for dinner. Clarke, meanwhile, stood by politely and watched her hunt.

Once as a child, she'd traveled to the Golden Lowlands with her father, King Melore. Just as it did then, the Lowlands struck her as the most boring landscape she could imagine. Rolling fields and small towns with dusty main streets. She was in need of a distraction, after the message was delivered that morning.

The girl has fled. Have arranged for a tracker.

She wanted to crumple it up and discard it. Instead, she tucked it into the inside pocket of her embroidered coat.

"Clarke," she said, calling her chief tinkerer to her. "I've had an idea, regarding the Catalyst. Discard the prototypes you've been working on—we'll be using a new casing for it." With the Child of War still unlocated, she could take no risks: the Catalyst needed to remain as inconspicuous as possible.

She heard the rustling of dead leaves, and from out of the woods walked a male deer. Viviana focused her gaze on it. The stag came toward her as if it were being pulled by a heavy, invisible rope. Even hunting was boring, Viviana decided, when you could simply summon your kill to you.

"An excellent specimen, my lady," said Clarke.

Viviana braced her shoulders to steady her aim with the cumbersome blunderbuss, but she could not so easily steady her mind. Not since her illuminating visit to Fairmount. The memory of that one child—one of the students, she learned, who had been missing from campus at the time of Joan's death—leaping through the air so powerfully, so brazenly. And without her kin in sight. Now she'd fled the school. Was it possible, Viviana wondered, that she'd found the Child of War so soon?

"Sophia Castling," Viviana whispered. "Who are you, and what do you know?"

She breathed out once more, readying herself for the kick of the gun. She aimed at the stag and pulled the trigger.

Fifteen

AFTER A DAY'S RIDE from the Gray to the rocky western mountains, a heavy layer of mud and snow caked the bottom of Gwen's coat and boots. She abandoned Tremelo's motorbike when it ran out of gas, and continued on foot. The valley that separated the Seers' Land from the northernmost edge of the Velyn mountains was full of cliffs that slowed her progress, and what had been a thin layer of melting snow outside the city had become thick white heaps that she had to slog through. Once she'd left the city, the flock of owls who had accompanied her from Fairmount reconvened to follow her again. Crossing the valley took her another day, but the presence of the owls encouraged her.

Heavy clouds hung overhead in the afternoon sky when she finally reached the Statue of the Twins. It had been built by the first rulers of Aldermere, who, the Elder had told her, had direct communication with the Seers of the western mountains. Situated at the entrance to the valley, the statue marked the division between civilized, settled Aldermere, and the Seers' Land. Nature herself had once lived here, where she had given birth to the Twins of legend. Those like the Elder—people who believed that the Seers still existed—often came here, only a short distance from the city, for reflection. But for Gwen, it was entirely new. In all her years as the Elder's apprentice, she had never been allowed to come with him to the Seers' Land. She'd imagined the grandeur of the statue, but now the sight of the tumbled stones in its place filled her with profound sadness. This had once been a symbol of the Animas bond, but now it was little more than a stone slab.

The feet of the boy and three paws of the fox remained intact. Gwen ran her hand along the base where the Elder had taken the fourth stone paw. Something in her belly quivered, and Gwen felt herself transported to that day at Fairmount, when she'd stood with the others around the Elder's funeral pyre. She sat down on the cold stone slab and wiped her watering eyes. She pulled her rucksack onto her lap and fished inside it for the stone paw.

"This belongs here," she said as she placed the paw back onto its crumbled niche like a piece of a puzzle that the Elder had left for her to put back together.

From the statue, the highest peak lay to the southwest. She could see white patches of snow dotting the rocks of its side, many miles away. Shouldering her pack once more, she crossed the valley and began the climb up the rocky ridge.

For days, she scrambled over rocks and behind trees. Still, she was nowhere near the highest peak, and she was exhausted. Sleep wasn't easy on the mountainside, where there was no shelter from the cold winds. She made small campfires, despite her worry of being seen—freezing was more of a concern to her. The owls accompanying her had become more agitated as well. Gwen could see it in their shuffling talons, and she could feel their anxiety in her own chest.

The owls sensed a new presence in the mountains, watching and tracking them from the air. Someone's kin, another bird, was pursuing them, and Gwen knew that an animal pursuer meant a human one as well. She was being followed. Gwen climbed faster, and tried to stay hidden behind the thin trees of the mountain as best she could.

After many days, she reached a cliff that cut off the clearest path up the mountainside. Far below, a rogue tributary of the Fluvian river burbled. She needed to keep moving southwest; in the distance, she could see the cliff she was meant to reach, just past another row of mountains before her. But to her dismay, the ravine was impassable.

Desperate, she scanned the edge of the cliff, looking for a place to climb down—but steep sides loomed up from the river like smooth glass. The owls swooped around her. She hadn't stopped to think of what she might need before she'd left Fairmount. If she had rope . . . but that didn't matter. She needed another way.

"Help," she said. It was a whispered hope, one that no human could hear and surely no owl could understand. She walked quickly along the edge of the cliff, searching for a path down or a fallen branch—anything that could help her cross the ravine.

The birds did not come with her. In fact, they stayed at the tip of the cliff, hopping and flying in small, nervous spurts of energy.

"Come on," she called. "There's nothing there." She kept moving forward.

Behind her, she heard a series of excited hoots. The owls still hadn't moved. She searched the sky for signs of the other bird—for signs of their pursuer—but there was nothing.

One of the smallest owls hooted loudly and flew forward off the edge of the cliff. Puzzled and frustrated, Gwen watched as it swooped away into the middle of the ravine—and then perched in midair. The ground was hundreds of feet below, but the owl seemed to be sitting on something solid, and its wings were still. As Gwen watched, the entire flock of owls left their branches and perched between the cliffs, seeming to sit and float on nothing but air.

"What in Nature . . . ?" she breathed. She hurried back to the spot where the owls had taken off. "What have you found?!"

The clouds overhead thinned for a moment, and an orange ray of early-evening sunlight spread over the ridge. Gwen saw a shimmery outline of a bridge hanging all the way between the cliffs. She bent down, crawled forward to the edge of the cliff, and put out her hand to touch it. It was made entirely of ropes: silvery, transparent threads that were almost sticky to the touch. *They're spiderwebs*, Gwen realized with astonishment. As she pulled back her hand, a few small fibers of the iridescent material stuck to her fingers. She rubbed them together, and the fibers fell away. Carefully, she stood and placed one foot on the closest point to the cliff. She heard the ropes creak beneath her, but the bridge felt solid, and she took another step forward. The owls watched her, hooting in encouragement.

Looking down, she saw nothing but empty air and the white river flowing. She almost turned back in fear and panic. But the ropes underneath her held firm, and she was able to grip two ropes on either side for balance. Carefully, she began to inch her way along the bridge. The words of the Elder's letter came back to her: *true sight is a light that grows—the physical world is a limited thing, strengthened and made clear by what is stronger and unseen . . .* If the owls hadn't helped her, her journey would be at an end. All she needed to do was have more faith, just as the Elder had said.

Below, rough rocks poked their heads through the rushing waters of the river; it was a long, long way to fall. But the height also made her wonder if this was akin to flying—the thrill she felt being so high above the ground was intoxicating. She walked faster, and once she'd felt the courage build inside her chest, she began to run.

Suddenly, though, Gwen faltered. She grasped for the ropes near her hand but felt nothing at all—they must have torn. The bridge swayed and she lost her footing. She slipped, but held fast to her pack while she grabbed desperately for the bridge with her other hand. She couldn't see it, but she felt the silky thread move across her slick palms. Clawing for her life, her left hand finally tightened around the invisible thread, and she dangled over the side. Above her, the bridge swayed. The owls who had perched along the transparent bridge fluttered to her and flew in helpless circles around her as she kicked her feet in the air. Sweat pasted her short hair to her forehead, even through the chill of the mountain air. She felt as though she were being torn in two; with one hand she clung to the bridge, and with the other she gripped her pack. It was so heavy, and it kept her from pulling herself up. She tried to lift it over her head and swing it onto the bridge, but she wasn't strong enough, and the bow and quiver of arrows she wore made maneuvering her arm next to impossible. She had to drop the pack, with the Seers' Glass inside, or she would fall and be killed.

The owls clustered around her, beating their wings as they tried to take the pack from her. They were too small, though, and the pack was too heavy. Gwen couldn't hold on anymore, and with a cry that echoed through the deep ravine, she let the bag fall.

The owls, not giving up, dove after it. One by one they tried grabbing at it with their talons, but they weren't strong enough. The bag plummeted toward the river as Gwen watched, sorrowful but safe, with both hands holding tightly on to the rope bridge. Two small owls fell with the bag, still trying to lift it. Gwen begged them, without saying a word, to come back. Let it go, she thought. No more deaths, I can't bear it.

Suddenly, another bird swooped underneath the bag and caught it with its beak. The bird began beating its wings, bringing the bag up the side of the far cliff. With a groan, Gwen swung her right leg up onto the ropes, and pulled with all her might until she was back on the bridge. From here, she watched as the bird disappeared over the treetops at the other side of the cliff with the bag.

"Wait!" she called in dismay. "Come back!"

She stood at the edge of the cliff, watching the darkening sky for a form that would not return. Her mind raced, calculating the supplies that she still had—matches in her pocket, a metal bowl and spoon tied with cords to her belt, and a blanket, as well as the bow and arrows, on her back. But the Glass was gone. The thing she'd needed to keep safe was now gone, and the presence of the unknown bird confirmed that someone was watching her. And now, the Glass could be in the hands of the Dominae and his or her well-trained kin. Either way, she couldn't be sure of anything—except that she had failed.

Sixteen

BAILEY AND HAL SAT in their common room in the Towers, where a pleasant candle glow lit the room. A half-dozen other nocturnal students were crowded around a table, finishing their last hand of Rabbit Flash. Their good-natured jeers and shouts made the space seem homey and safe, although Bailey's thoughts were still on Gwen and Phi—if Gwen was safe, and when Phi would come back. Without them around, Phi especially, Fairmount seemed to give in to the winter dreariness.

Hal, on the other hand, seemed oddly energized.

"That part that Lyle was waiting for came in today," he told Bailey. "Just look!" He took a folded piece of paper out of his vest pocket and thrust it toward Bailey. "I saw him drop this during class today."

Bailey unfolded it. It was a note, written in sloppy handwriting.

We'll try it out in the small study room by the Science section tonight. Tell Nicolette and Simon too. —Lyle

"Was this for Tori?" Bailey asked.

"I don't think so, or he'd have just given it to her right there in class," said Hal, staring out a window where a lone bat was flapping its wings against the glass. "There's clearly a whole group of them. But whatever they're 'trying out,' I bet Tori's in on it too. She and Lyle have barely been apart!"

"You would know," teased Bailey. In truth, Bailey was worried about Tori as well—or at least disappointed. That afternoon had marked the third time in as many days that she had failed to show up at Tremelo's workshop.

Hal poked his glasses into place.

"I've taken an interest," he said, "and I think we should investigate."

Bailey looked out the window, where the bat still hovered. He got up to open the transom and it flew in. It fluttered onto Hal's leg.

"Investigate?" Bailey asked. "It's a science experiment, not some top secret operation." He folded the note and handed it back to Hal. The bat hopped up to Hal's shoulder, hooked the top of its wings into Hal's collar, and settled itself comfortably there. With a careful finger, Hal petted the little bat's nose.

"*Our* science experiment is a top secret operation," Hal whispered, looking around the common room. "Look, *you're* the one always raring to go poking around. Aren't you the least bit suspicious?"

"It's interesting, I guess," said Bailey. "But I'm not sure why you're so obsessed."

"Lyle's no good for Tori," Hal said. "In Biology and the Bond last semester, he didn't do any work, just sat there with his feet up all the time, cracking jokes."

"That *does* sound like Tori's type," Bailey admitted.

"Exactly!" said Hal, exasperated. "That's the whole problem. She needs balance!" Hal threw out his arms, upsetting the frazzled little bat.

"I think if you ever tried to tell Tori what she 'needs,' she'd punch you," said Bailey. "But I'll go with you." Spying on Tori's new boyfriend was hardly the kind of adventure he'd been looking for. But the longer he sat still, the more his anxiety grew.

"Perfect," said Hal, clapping his hands.

Bailey nabbed Bert from his slumber under the heat lamps, and the boys walked from the Towers to Treetop, the dormitory where students with bird and reptile Animas lived. Bert rode inside Bailey's messenger bag. The sun had almost completely set, and the electro-current lamps along the campus paths began to flicker on.

"Look," said Hal, grabbing Bailey's arm.

Hal pointed at the darkened entrance to Treetop, where Tori and Lyle emerged. Lyle held a small bundle of black cloth. As Tori followed Lyle onto the path, a crow flew out of the dorm entrance and circled above their heads. Hal and Bailey ducked behind a hedge.

"Perfect timing," Hal whispered. Behind his glasses, his eyes were lit with excitement—or jealousy. Bailey wasn't certain which.

Just then, Bert jumped out of the messenger bag and began side-winding his way across the lawn.

"Hey!" whispered Bailey, trying not to attract Lyle's and Tori's attention. Bert was heading in the same direction as they were.

"What's he doing?" Hal asked.

"Exactly what I'd be doing," said Bailey, who stood up and began following the lizard.

Bailey caught up quickly. He could still see Lyle and Tori farther up on the path, heading toward the library and administration building. Bert trailed along after them.

The sun had set now, and the sky quickly shifted from a bluish gray to complete darkness, dotted with stars. Bailey and Hal hung back outside the entrance to the library as Tori and Lyle entered.

"So, what's our plan?" Bailey asked Hal.

"I'm thinking. . . ."

"You don't have a plan?" Bailey nearly laughed. Hal *always* had a plan.

"I do," said Hal, defensively. "Just figuring out how to execute it! For now, stay hidden and follow me. We don't know what Lyle's up to."

"Lead the way," Bailey said. He doubted that Lyle was "up to" anything more than making Hal jealous, but he followed Hal into the library atrium all the same.

As they walked past the bookcase that held the Loon's book of prophecies, Bailey paused to make sure it was still there. It was, camouflaged by the other bound volumes flanking it. A thin layer of dust had even settled on the shelf, ensuring that no one had touched it since the Midwinter break.

Hal stood at the end of the hallway, facing the entrance to the Science section. Across the room, light shone from underneath a closed door.

"Well?" said Bailey, catching up.

Hal's eyes were closed. Bailey looked around, and didn't see the bat that had come with them from the dorms.

A moment later, Hal opened his eyes and looked at Bailey, determined. "That door leads to a set of stairs, and at the bottom there's a wide room with a low ceiling. That's where Lyle and Tori are—with others. We can go into the stairwell and listen from there."

"You saw all that?" Bailey asked.

"No, not quite," said Hal. "But the bat was reading the sound vibrations in the room, and I could feel them too. My sight is never very good," he said, putting his glasses back on. "No matter how you define 'sight.'"

The boys walked silently to the door, which did lead to a set of curved stairs. Just around a corner they heard voices. Bailey peeked quickly around the wall.

Several students and animals were gathered in a low-ceilinged study room, with windows at the top of the walls that looked out to metal grates. They were in the basement level of the library. A fire had been lit in the stone fireplace, and the threadbare armchairs were all turned toward one corner of the room, where Lyle stood unwrapping something from the bundle he'd been carrying. Shadows obscured the back wall of the room, where a few squat bookcases flanked a cushioned love seat. Bailey gestured to Hal, and together they crept from the doorway to hide behind the shadowed seat.

Bailey recognized many of the students gathered in the room—a handful of other Year Ones, a smattering of students from his homeroom, and even one or two of his Scavage teammates. Tori sat close to the fire, at the front of the room. Bailey could see the black outline of one of her snakes settled into its usual place near her collarbone. A pair of squirrels huddled together on a bookshelf, their tails twitching.

"My dad just sent this," Lyle said to the gathered group. "I've been excited to see what it can do! He's a high-level tinkerer and this was a prototype made for Viviana *herself*."

Bailey straightened up—Lyle was more than Tori's new love interest, for sure.

Lyle gingerly lifted up a small, round object about the size of an egg, and turned it so the room could see. It was made of a shining metal. Bailey caught himself before he gasped out loud—it was almost identical to the centerpiece from Tremelo's blueprint.

Lyle's crow squawked—it perched on a tall shelf that held a number of glass jars, and looked in Hal and Bailey's direction. But it turned away, and Lyle continued speaking as though nothing had happened.

"Not sure exactly what's inside, but the metal is special—my dad's been helping the Dominae, and this is his new top secret project—the Catalyst!"

"But what does it *do*?" someone asked.

"It traps electro-current inside," Lyle said. "It basically absorbs any energy that you put into it. Here," he said. He folded his hands over the egg, pressing hard. Then he breathed between his hands as if he were trying to warm his fingers. When he opened them again, the egg glowed bright red, and Lyle had to quickly transfer it back onto its black cloth.

"Hot!" he said, laughing.

One boy sitting closest to Lyle reached forward and touched the egg with a finger. Bailey recognized him as Evan, from his Latin class.

"What do you do with it?" he asked.

"I'm not sure," admitted Lyle. "But they've made more of them,

I think—even bigger ones! My dad sent me this because they don't need it anymore."

Several students rose from the seats to get a better look. The orb had cooled down, and returned to its silvery hue.

"Can you open it?" someone asked.

"No," said Lyle. He ran his finger over a seam up the middle. "It's sealed shut. Plus, if you *could* open it, it would just dissipate."

"Huh?" someone asked.

"The energy would dissolve into the air," Lyle explained. "I think, anyway."

Bailey looked over at Tori. She wasn't one of the students who'd gone up to crowd around Lyle. Instead, she sat in the armchair by the fire, playing with a thin black snake. Her expression was completely blank, and Bailey wondered what she was doing here, with Lyle.

The boy from Bailey's Latin class, Evan, was now holding the metal orb.

"Whoa," Evan said. "I just got a really powerful feeling."

"What do you mean?" asked Lyle.

Evan gestured to his front jacket pocket, which seemed to be moving. A brown mouse popped its head out from the top.

"I could see exactly what the mouse was seeing," he said. "I could see all of us, through the fabric of my pocket. I've *never* felt the bond that strongly."

But the mouse was less enthused. It crawled out of Evan's pocket and scurried down his pant leg. Once it hit the cold stone floor, it began to dart away. Bailey instinctively ducked down—the mouse was headed straight for them! But Evan put up his free hand, and the mouse immediately stopped as though frozen in place.

The mouse turned around and began walking slowly back to him.

"Wow, cool," breathed Alice, the Year One girl from Bailey's Scavage team. Curious murmurs rose from the crowd. It was common for human and kin to understand each other, but for animals to act on command? It was eerie, and while the other kids were obviously fascinated, Bailey grimaced in disgust. This was Dominance, Viviana's sickening philosophy of controlling animals. He looked over at Hal, whose fists were clenched.

Evan smiled nervously at the onlookers, uncertain of what to do next.

Lyle stood at Evan's side. Together, they stared down at the mouse.

"Tell it to do something again," he said. His mouth stayed open in a strange, awed smile.

"Okay..." said Evan nervously. He looked from student to student, as if he couldn't think of what to do. Then he shook his head slightly, as if something had come into focus in his mind.

"Um...lift your right paw," he blurted out.

The mouse lifted its right paw.

Someone in the group squealed with excitement—the others simply gasped and whispered with astonishment.

"Another one!" said Lyle.

"I...I don't know, what should I make him do?" Evan asked.

"Do a backflip!" someone suggested.

Bailey looked at Tori. She sat stone-faced and silent in the front of the group, like she was watching a boring play onstage. Bailey felt a little sick.

"Okay, do a backflip," said Evan. The mouse jumped and twisted oddly in the air—hardly a perfect flip, but its tiny body obeyed. The students clapped and laughed.

"Would it bite itself if you asked?" someone said.

Evan looked at Lyle as though he could answer this question. Lyle merely shrugged. As Evan fixed his gaze on the mouse, it suddenly lifted its left back paw into its mouth and bit. A spot of blood appeared on its white foot.

"I didn't even say anything," Evan exclaimed, looking frightened. He backed away, unnerved.

"Whoa!" exclaimed Lyle. "All it takes is a thought! It's like it does anything you want it to!"

Chaos erupted over the group. The students were fascinated, and they kept shouting different suggestions.

"Make it chase its tail!"

"Make it dance on its hind legs!"

Evan seemed to hear and envision every suggestion—he couldn't help it. The mouse, powerless and under his complete control, performed every action that Evan thought of, in a sickeningly fast-paced sequence of jumps, chomps, and twists. The mouse moved so quickly that its body could barely keep up.

"This is heinous," whispered Hal.

"It's awful," agreed Bailey. "We have to stop them."

But he didn't need to.

"Okay—okay, stop!" Lyle said. Evan's eyes had grown wide and panicked. Lyle reached out and grabbed the Catalyst from him.

"I said, stop!" he shouted.

The mouse went still. Bailey held his breath, and many of the students gasped.

Then the little mouse began twitching and shaking uncontrollably. Lyle, holding the orb in his left hand, moved forward to pick it up. But before he could reach it, the mouse dropped, lifeless, to its side.

The students became very quiet. Soon, the only sound in the room was Evan's muffled whimpering.

"Oh, no," breathed Bailey.

"Oh, no," said Lyle. He nudged the mouse with a careful finger. The crow on the high shelves squawked.

Evan broke out in a sob.

"You *killed* it," he said.

"Maybe it had a bad heart," said Lyle. The color had drained from his face. He stood up and looked at Evan, unsure of what to say. "I didn't think that would happen—I'm sorry. . . ."

"Why would you bring that thing here?" Evan sobbed. "It killed my kin!" He stood. He looked like he might step forward and punch Lyle. But he didn't—instead, he crumpled, and began to cry harder.

Bailey didn't realize that he had begun to rise from a crouch until Hal placed a firm hand on his shoulder.

"*Don't*," Hal said. "We'll only get ourselves into trouble."

Bailey nudged his hand away, but Hal grabbed his arm with a force that Bailey didn't expect.

"Come on, Evan, let's go," said another boy, who put his arm protectively around Evan's shoulder. "This is your fault," he said to Lyle.

Lyle looked on, shocked, as one by one the other students filed out of the room. Their faces were cast downward, and an air of shame and confusion remained behind them in the room. Bailey and Hal stayed in the shadows as everyone left—even Tori. When they were sure they'd be the last to leave, they finally crept toward the door.

Bailey glanced back once more at Lyle. He stood over the body of the mouse with the orb held in both his hands. He looked thoughtful.

"What's he doing now?" Hal asked, peering over Bailey's shoulder.

Lyle watched the mouse closely, then stepped back, a look of awe on his face.

The mouse had lifted its right paw.

Seventeen

THE CHEERY GLOW OF the candles and the shouts of the boys playing Rabbit Flash were gone by the time Hal and Bailey returned to the Towers common room. The last cracklings of a fire still spat in the grate. The two boys collapsed into armchairs, and Hal covered his face with one hand.

"Nature's eyes, Bailey," he said. "What are we going to tell Tremelo?"

Bailey shook his head numbly; he didn't understand what he'd just seen.

"We have to talk to Tori first," he said. "We don't know what she was doing there."

"Wasn't it obvious?" said Hal, gesturing to the door and beyond, toward the library and its basement study room. "Her boyfriend's a card-carrying Dominae! 'Looove' has blinded her! She's not our friend anymore. I don't even know *who* she is."

"She's still our friend," said Bailey firmly. But he felt a little sick to his stomach, thinking of the mouse. Evan's cries echoed in his mind. And Tori had just sat there the entire time, with that strange, vacant look in her eyes. What had she been thinking?

"She knows everything, about you and about Sucrette. Let's not forget that," Hal continued. "How do we know she hasn't told Lyle something that could get you killed?"

"There's no way she's buying into that Dominae stuff," Bailey answered. But he couldn't think clearly, and hearing Hal's argument made him feel uneasy. Tori had defended them, had fought by their side—but he had to admit, there was a lot about her that he didn't know.

A slinking movement down on the floor caught Bailey's eye. Something slithered along the floorboard—he rushed to grab it. A small black snake writhed in his hand.

"Hey!" said Hal.

Bailey, keeping hold of the snake, walked over to the door of the common room and opened it. Tori leaned against the wall of the hallway, her arms crossed and her eyes piercing.

"How long have you been listening?" he asked her.

"How long have you been following me around?" she countered.

"We weren't," Bailey lied.

"Like ants, you weren't," said Tori, storming into the room. "You two are about as covert as a rhino. I wanted to die right there in that study room from embarrassment."

Bailey and Hal both straightened their shoulders defensively.

"You knew we were there?" asked Bailey.

"The snakes knew, the second you crawled into the room,"

she said. She held out her hand for the black snake. After plopping into her palm, it disappeared inside the cuff of her sleeve.

"Did you rat us out to your new friend Lyle?" asked Hal.

"No," snapped Tori. "And the *reason* I haven't is because I'm doing the same thing *you* are—except I'm better at it. I'm *spying* on him." She paused, eyeing the boys' shocked expressions.

"You're spying on Lyle?" Bailey asked. "We thought you liked him!"

Tori rolled her eyes.

"He's not actually that bad—for a Dominae-loving freak," she said. "He just doesn't realize what he's doing. His father is a high-level tinkerer for Viviana—that blueprint Tremelo copied was his! He sends Lyle old prototypes like they're toys! I had to check it out. Science Club is just Lyle's excuse to show off, and the perfect way for us to get more information about Viviana's Reckoning! What do you think that Catalyst machine is *for*?"

"But why didn't you tell us you were spying on him?" asked Hal.

Tori went quiet for a moment, and shrugged.

"It felt nice to have my own mission, for once. I was going to tell you once I'd seen the orb, but I wanted to be sure first."

Bailey believed her, but he was bothered by her insistence that Lyle wasn't "that bad."

"I don't understand how you can stand being near him—after that poor mouse," Hal said, adjusting his glasses, the better to glare at her.

"He felt terrible about that!"

"You mean the fact that someone's kin was murdered?" Bailey said, not bothering to hide the sting from his voice. What he'd seen in that basement made him seethe. Whatever Lyle was playing with, it was dangerous. "You don't even know what happened afterward." But Bailey wasn't sure that *he* knew what had happened—had the mouse come back to life? Lyle had seemed just as surprised as they had been, and had quickly dropped the orb, causing it to clang on the stone floor. Then he'd wrapped it in its black fabric and hurried out of the room, leaving the dead mouse behind.

"He has no idea what he's even doing," Tori said.

"That's for sure," breathed Hal.

"I'm not defending him—but he's just some kid playing around."

"But he sides with the Dominae!" said Bailey. "You've seen the things they do. What if he's working with them?"

"I've been watching him closely," said Tori. "He doesn't know anything about the prophecies or the Child of War. It's his dad I'd worry about—he's the one who's gotten Lyle into all this stuff."

"Tori, this is dangerous!" Bailey said.

"You're right," said Tori. As she spoke, the small black snake emerged from her collar and settled around her neck. "And that's why you have to trust me. Lyle can't know, or even suspect, that I'm not his happy little Science partner. And if you two are always sneaking around, we'll only get caught. One thing's for sure, though: we'll need to tell Tremelo about the Catalyst first thing tomorrow."

Bailey went to bed that night somewhat relieved—he knew Tori wasn't a traitor. But his imagination raced when he thought about Lyle and his orb. It had to be the missing piece from Viviana's Reckoning machine. And now that he'd seen what Lyle had been able to do with it, he knew that Viviana was planning something terrifying. Her power, fed through that orb, could control countless animals. He wondered what Tremelo would say when they told him in the morning—hopefully, that he knew how they could stop it from happening.

Bailey couldn't sleep. Every time he closed his eyes, he saw the shuddering right paw of the dead mouse, and Lyle's shocked face above it. But finally, after what felt like hours, he drifted into dreams.

He woke to the sensation of rough hands holding his chest down, trapping him against his bed. He felt a heavy, cold metal around his neck—choking him. He cried out, but the metal chain tightened as he kicked and flailed. Total darkness cloaked him, hiding his vision. He opened his mouth, bared his teeth, and roared.

Then Bailey sat up in bed. His heart raced. He was sure someone was here, in his room, and had tried to tie him down. He tossed his covers off. There were no chains on him, and no one else in the room but Hal, asleep. But it had been no dream—he'd felt the heavy, cold chain squeezing around his neck. And even how, sitting up in bed, he felt the strange sensation of being pressed to the ground. He could hardly breathe. Taleth was in danger. Someone had taken her, someone who meant them both harm.

All of Tremelo's advice about lying low left his head like dried leaves in a harsh wind. He hurried to put on a pair of pants and his boots, and left Hal snoring behind him. He rushed down the front stairs of the Towers, not caring who heard or saw.

He knew he couldn't rescue Taleth alone. He needed help, immediately. He ran to Tremelo's quarters.

The night was bitterly cold; Bailey could see his breath

streaming from his nose and mouth. A light shone from Tremelo's sitting room window. Bailey ran to the door of the carriage house and rushed up the narrow wooden stairs. He stopped, out of breath, on the landing and pounded on the apartment door.

"Tremelo! Tremelo, I need your help!"

There was no answer from inside, though Bailey could smell myrgwood smoke. He stopped knocking and cried out as a fresh pain overtook him: he felt heavy sticks pummeling his sides and legs. His vision swam, and he could almost see the shapes of two tall men standing over him, kicking him—but they weren't there, not in the hall outside Tremelo's door. They were standing over Taleth, subduing her. Bailey felt the pain of welts forming on his sides and back. Catching his breath, he called out again to Tremelo. When he didn't hear an answer, he leaned heavily on the latch and thrust his whole weight onto the door, breaking the flimsy lock. The door swung open.

Tremelo was not there.

On its side, on top of a porcelain dish speckled with ash, was Tremelo's myrgwood pipe.

"Sir?" Bailey said to no one. He collapsed against the closest bookshelf, doubling over in pain as another blow struck Taleth's flank. He looked around the apartment, hoping that Tremelo would emerge from behind a doorway—but the apartment was empty. Taleth needed them. "Where *are* you?" he wondered out loud, but whether he meant Taleth or Tremelo, even he wasn't sure.

He felt a strong hand on his back, and straightened up, terrified. In the doorway stood Dr. Graves.

"Now, Mr. Walker," he said. "What do you know of the Child of War?"

Eighteen

RUN, BAILEY THOUGHT.

He pushed past Graves, but a sudden pain in his right leg caused him to stumble. He crashed against a bookcase and knocked over a heap of papers. A gray cat leapt out of the way, hissing.

Graves bent to catch Bailey's arm, but Bailey pulled it away.

"Get away from me!" he shouted, fighting through Taleth's pain to stand. He hoped someone would hear him. His showdown with Sucrette was the last time he'd been caught alone with a Dominae spy, and it would've killed him if his friends hadn't come.

"There's too much at stake," Graves hissed, grabbing for Bailey again. He was too weak to dodge Graves a second time; the teacher took Bailey's arm and bent it at an awkward angle behind his back. Bailey was marched down the stairs like a prisoner, barely able to walk or even think through the acute pain that throbbed in his leg. He felt nauseated but tried to clear his mind—where were they going? He needed to break free of Graves's grip, but timing would be crucial.

"What did you do with Tremelo? What do you want?" Bailey said.

"Information," Graves said, and pushed Bailey along across the empty campus. They walked in silence to the classrooms.

When they reached Graves's office, he hurriedly shoved Bailey through the door and into a chair. The gray cat skittered in too, and rubbed its face against Graves's leg.

"The Dominae will not be denied their prize, Mr. Walker, so think carefully about your answers. Again, what do you know about the Child of War?"

"I don't know anything," Bailey said.

Graves crossed his arms over his patched velour dressing gown.

"You're lying," he said. "Perhaps because you underestimate how much I know already."

What *does* he know? Bailey wondered. Sucrette hadn't gotten a chance to pass along the information from the Loon's book of prophecies before she'd died . . . or had she? Panic began to rumble in his belly and chest. He didn't have time for this—Taleth was being dragged farther and farther away. Graves stared at him with his dark, beady eyes. Bailey looked away, trying to think of how to escape.

His eyes fell on something on Graves's desk that sent a shiver down his already aching back: it was a list of names.

Sophia Castling, Harold Quindley, Victoria Colubride, Bailey Walker.

"Your 'Bert,' as you call him, is not your real kin—that much is obvious." Graves leaned closer to Bailey, his voice lowering. "I've been watching you since I arrived, and you're hiding something. So what is it, Bailey? Tell me, and I'll—"

"I won't!" said Bailey. Though his body throbbed from Taleth's injuries, he kicked upward from the chair, sending Graves reeling.

"Mr. Walker! You must—"

A shrill chatter cut him off, and a tall stack of books in the corner collapsed. Two squirrels stood on a pile of books fanned out across the floor. The gray cat scrambled across the room and swatted at them.

"Stop that!" Graves said.

The cat began biting at the squirrels, its tail lashing. Two against one, the squirrels retaliated, with one latching on to the cat's back, and the other scratching at its face and ears. Yowls, chittering, and hissing filled the room.

"Stop. This. At. Once!" yelled Graves, though neither the cat nor the squirrels paid him any attention. The cat shrieked and hissed as one of the squirrels bit its ear, and Graves cursed, holding the side of his head. Annoyed, in pain, and nearly out of breath, Graves bent and attempted to pull the squirrels and cat apart. One of the squirrels leapt up onto a bookshelf, causing a heavy Latin textbook to tumble down from where it had been hastily stowed on the edge. It landed with a thud on Graves's head. Crying out, the teacher stumbled forward against the wall. Bailey took his chance. He slipped out of the chair and grabbed the list from Graves's desk. Then he ran. Behind him, he heard Graves yell something indistinguishable.

Bailey didn't look back; the longer he stayed on campus, the more likely Graves would come after him again. There was no time to try to find Tremelo, and he knew now what he had to do. He had to go after Taleth alone.

As he ran down the corridor of classrooms, Taleth's consciousness washed over him. His vision blurred, and he saw dark shapes moving around him. She was being hustled onto a boat—the unsteadiness beneath her feet transferred to Bailey, making him dizzy. He saw the moon through her eyes—she, and the boat too, were facing north. He heard a voice speaking close by, but he had to strain to make sense of the words. "Reach the Red . . . days, maybe less."

As soon as the wave had come over him, it receded, and he was once more aware of the long hallway around him, with photos and paintings of Fairmount's past lining the walls. All was quiet.

So the kidnappers were taking Taleth up the Fluvian, to the Red Hills. They weren't too far yet, and he could still track them if he could only continue to bond with Taleth as he just had—but he didn't know how.

When he returned to the Towers, Hal was sitting alone in the study room. He'd wrapped a tasseled scarf over his striped pajamas, and his coat was draped over the chair next to him, as though he was getting ready to leave. He stood up as Bailey entered, and his eyes were heavy with worry.

"What's going on?" he said. "I heard you leave, and then a whole flurry of bats was at the window. They were scared for you. What happened?"

"Graves," Bailey said, not sure where to begin. "Taleth was kidnapped, and Graves—he knows about the Child of War."

"Bailey, what happened?" Hal asked.

"I went to Tremelo's office, looking for help, but Tremelo is gone—I don't know where—but Graves showed up and he asked me all these questions. He knows about me. Which means the Dominae know too."

Hal listened silently. Bailey could almost see the whirring of gears and cogs behind Hal's thick glasses.

"Something doesn't add up here," said Hal. "You said Taleth's been kidnapped? By who? Did Graves have something to do with it?"

"I don't know, but I do know that Graves has been watching us." Bailey took Graves's list from his coat pocket, and waved it at Hal. "I found this on his desk. There's no doubt now—look! He has a list of our names. He knows one of us is the Child of War!"

Hal looked over the paper closely.

"And you said Tremelo is gone too?"

"His apartment was empty, but I can't wait. Taleth is in danger, and they're taking her north, on the river. I have to follow her."

Hal nodded.

"We'd better get packing, then," he said.

Bailey leaned on the back of one of the wooden chairs around the study table. He still felt a little weak.

"You can't come," he said. "It's too dangerous."

"More dangerous than staying here, with Graves?" Hal asked.

"Find Tremelo," Bailey said. "He'll take care of Graves, and then you'll all be safe here. What I find out there might be even worse than one spy. I'll be better off on my own."

"You're wrong," Hal said. His tone wasn't argumentative or even defensive. It was clear and to the point. "It's too dangerous for you to travel alone. You need me; you need my help. How will you find Taleth by yourself? And how will you travel? On foot or by train? Have you thought about getting money, so you can eat—or whether you'll be able to scavenge? Who'll watch your back?"

Bailey had to admit he hadn't considered any of this.

"But who will find Tremelo?" Bailey said. "You need to warn him. If the Dominae knows about me, then they could know about him too."

"The Dominae wouldn't send Graves after you if they already had him," Hal said. "If they don't know who the Child of War is, then they don't know about him being the True King. He's probably hiding out. Listen, Tremelo can take care of himself," Hal continued. "And *your* kin was kidnapped, meaning *you're* the one who needs the most protection. Tori's not safe here either—her name's on that list as well. Let us come with you. Let us help."

Within five minutes, Hal and Bailey had made their way through the darkness to Treetop, with rucksacks packed with warm clothes, some food, and Bailey's only weapon: the Velyn tiger claw. A bleary-eyed Tori met them.

"Are you insane?" she asked, as Hal laid out their plan to follow Taleth. "We can't all go disappearing. How will *that* look?" She raised an eyebrow at Hal. "It makes more sense for me to stay here. Someone will have to fill Tremelo in on everything once he reappears—we can't all leave without him knowing about that orb. And I can help him keep tabs on Graves."

"But what if Graves comes after you?" Hal asked.

"I can handle myself," she said. "And besides, what did you think you were going to do with *him*?" Tori pointed at Bert, who sat cradled in Bailey's arm.

"We figured we'd just bring him with us," said Hal.

Tori reached out her hands.

"Give him here," she said. "He'd die out there with you two. Honestly. He's *cold-blooded*. He can't keep himself warm!"

"As soon as Tremelo comes back, stick with him," Bailey said, after handing over Bert. He felt relieved that the lizard would be safe with Tori. "Tremelo won't let anything happen to you. That is, if he's okay."

"*I* won't let anything happen to *Tremelo*," Tori corrected him. "I'll watch his quarters tonight. Bet you a snailback he comes home full of rootwort rum. But be careful. For all you know, this could just be a big trap. Send word as soon as you can. . . ." But she was looking at Hal, not at him.

Hal managed a nervous smile, and the two boys took to the woods, out of sight of the sleeping campus. Bailey could see the moon reflecting off the grand windows of the library as they walked quickly into the trees. He thought once more about the Loon's book, safe—he hoped—in its hiding place. Because of that book, he knew he had a role to play in what would come: as the Child of War. But he hardly knew what that foretold for him, except that now it meant he had to run.

Nineteen

TREMELO ALSO RAN, SEARCHING for something lost. He'd set out late that afternoon, and now had already passed the divide between the campus and the Dark Woods. He had nearly reached the rocky hills that led toward the southern mountains. It was the path the Velyn had taken away from Fairmount, led by Eneas Fourclaw. Tremelo had questions for him—most of which were contained in the leather-bound book tucked safely in his traveling bag.

The Loon's book, written in the Velyn's language, was much like the Loon himself: it asked more riddles than it answered. *The Child is both the reflection and the opposite of evil?* What was he meant to understand by that? The Equinox was only a few weeks away; without knowing what to make of the strange orb in the center of the blueprint or what role Bailey would play at the Reckoning as the Child of War, Tremelo had decided to seek out assistance. Perhaps the Loon's prophecies contained some hint that would help him. Eneas, he wagered, could give him some sort of advice—but in truth the prophecy was not the only mystery that occupied Tremelo's mind.

He stopped to catch his breath, and Fennel, trotting alongside him, jumped ahead. The Velyn moved quickly, and they'd had several weeks' head start. He hoped to come upon them camping over the ridge.

He fished the worn photograph of Elen Whitehill from his coat pocket, though he knew it by heart: her strawberry-blond hair, and her sharp Velyn features. She had been his first love—murdered during the Jackal's massacre.

In the dozen or so years since her death, he'd become obsessed with finding anyone who had known her. He ached when he remembered her smile, and he wanted desperately to fuel that pain with more stories of her life. But the only people who could know of her were now miles away, doing their best not to be found.

He still remembered taking the photo. Elen hadn't known what to do in front of a camera. She had lived her entire life in the mountains, traveling the Unreachable Road with her father, Luca. A photograph was a luxury she was unfamiliar with. She'd laughed when he arranged her furs around her, and told her to sit very, very still.

"Why do you ask the impossible?" she'd said. "Sitting still for five whole minutes! I'll turn to stone! *You* couldn't do it, I'd bet a set of claws."

"That's why I'm *here*," his nineteen-year-old self had said from his place behind the camera. It was a pity, he thought now, that she hadn't smiled. But then, a smile was hard to keep for five whole minutes while the image set into the film. It was almost as hard to keep a smile in one's memory for over a decade, but somehow Tremelo had managed to do it.

His fingers grew cold. He placed the photograph back in his pocket. A few yards ahead, Fennel stood as still as a statue. She crouched, and the fur along her back stood on end. Her nose sniffed the air. Tremelo tightened his grip on his walking stick and moved toward her, climbing over a large boulder that reflected the full moon overhead. When he arrived at Fennel's side, Tremelo could sense it too—something had happened here. The snow up ahead showed signs of a struggle: scattered footprints and what looked like a large animal dragged on its back and side. Tremelo's heart began to pound. Fennel circled the area, her ears twitching back and forth.

There were claw marks in the nearby trees: so deep they tore through the bark and exposed the raw wood of the trunk under-neath, and as wide as a grown man's hands—even wider.

"Taleth," Tremelo breathed. He looked again at the snow-covered ground, and saw the huge cat's paw prints.

Fennel whimpered. Tremelo looked to the nearby slope of the southern hills, just once. Then he ran back toward the school.

Twenty

ON THE OTHER SIDE of the spiderweb bridge, the terrain quickly became rockier. Gwen's shoes slipped on the stones, and she had to crawl across sharp formations jutting up from the ground. Without her pack, she missed something soft to lay her head on at night, as well as her dry socks and packaged food inside. She'd had a few loose matches in her coat pocket, but they wouldn't even last her a week, and she'd never learned how to start a campfire using only stones and tinder. She was hungry and cold, and she agonized over the bird flying away with the Seers' Glass.

After two more days of climbing, she decided to take shelter for the night against a stone wall. Although she was high in the mountains, the land had flattened here into a rocky plain, with patches of wild thistles. The sun began to set, and the color of the rocks deepened to purple, then finally to dark, midnight blue. The landscape was bleak and empty, and Gwen felt lonelier than she ever had in her life. She wished she could have stayed at Fairmount, with her new friends. She wished the Elder still lived. She wished to feel the weight of the heavy Seers' Glass in her hands.

But wishing would not bring anything back. Tremelo had given her one task: to keep the Glass safe. And she had failed. The prophecies in the Loon's book could only be read by using it. What if now they were lost forever, undeciphered?

If only she had gotten a closer look at the bird that had swooped in and grabbed the Glass, she thought. It might have been a vulture, like Sucrette's—or even worse, one of Viviana's horrifying Clamoribus birds, all clockwork and menace. But she knew better than to follow it and risk running into its kin. Her only choice was to continue to the highest peak, as the Elder had instructed her, and find the Instrument of Change.

At least the wild thistles were familiar to her. They were similar to the cast-off roots she'd cull from the market sidewalks as a child, and she remembered how to boil them down into a gruel that was filling, if not very tasty. She used one of her precious matches to light a fire and cooked herself a small supper of thistle-root gruel in the small metal bowl she'd tied to her belt.

The gruel was warm, at least—though she wished she had a pinch of sugar or something sweet to liven up the tastelessness of the thistle root.

The sun set over the mountains, and a bitter cold set in quickly—a harsh reminder that winter was not over, though Gwen had noticed some early-blooming berries at the edge of the plain. As she walked over to the bushes, the smallest of the owls half hopped, half flew to the berry bushes and hooted.

Gwen plucked one of the small red berries from its branch and sniffed it. She hoped they were sweet. She squeezed it carefully, splitting its red skin. Orange-pink flesh burst from it and trickled down her fingers. The small owl screeched, surprising her.

"What was that for?" she asked. She looked around the grove nervously. For the last two days she'd sensed she was being followed, but nothing stirred around her camp.

She lifted her hand to her mouth to taste the liquid from the berry. The owl suddenly leapt from the ground and batted its wings in her face.

"What are you doing?" she cried.

Then something extraordinary happened. Her vision clouded, and was replaced by an image of herself—but not as she was now, standing in the mountain plain, holding a burst berry on her fingertips. She saw herself lying on the ground, motionless, with traces of red juice on her lower lip. She realized that she was looking at herself from the owl's perspective as it hopped around her face, trying to revive her. The berries, the owl knew—and now Gwen knew as well—were poisonous.

Gwen gasped as the vision disappeared. The little owl, who was still sitting on the ground between her and the berry bush, hooted at her.

"How did you do that?" she whispered. Her hands shook. She had never been so connected to her kin that she could see through their eyes. Even stranger, she saw something in her kin's eyes that had not yet happened. Frightened and awed, she threw the crushed berry to the ground and carefully wiped her hand on her pant leg. She wrapped herself in her cloak and waited, unsleeping, for the dawn.

Twenty~one

THE BOYS TRUDGED THROUGH the forest, making a wide loop away from the school. Taking the rigimotive from Fairmount was far too dangerous, Hal had decided—they'd immediately be recognized as students. Also, Hal's pocket money would only take them so far. Their plan was to board the rigi in the village of Stillfall, midway between Fairmount and the Gray City. A colony of bats rallied around them for most of the night, emitting a constant buzz of flapping wings. Occasionally, a few would dive down to alight on Hal's shoulders and head.

In the morning, they hiked down the side of a cliff to the village, carefully negotiating the series of switchback trails that led to the low river valley. Once there, they boarded a cramped rigimotive departing for the city that afternoon.

On board, Bailey tried to catch an hour's sleep, but he could see that Hal, who sat alert and staring out the window, was agitated.

"What are we going to do, once we find Taleth?" Hal whispered when Bailey asked what was wrong. "We're just a couple of kids. The people who have her . . . They might be like Sucrette."

"We'll just have to be smart," said Bailey. "We'll try to sneak her away—and if that doesn't work, we might have to fight. But if we can free her first . . ."

"We don't know who's got her," said Hal. "Or where. Do you think we'll just come up on her tied to a tree? I doubt it'll be that easy."

"We'll figure it out once we find her," said Bailey.

Hal frowned and went back to staring out the window at the Fluvian rushing past.

Bailey thought to say more, but instead he rubbed his eyes. He craved sleep.

By the time they disembarked at a shambling platform in the Gudgeons, next to the shipping docks, Bailey was exhausted and more than a little worried. He hadn't felt a connection to Taleth since they'd left Fairmount.

"This is perfect," said Hal as they stepped down from the ramshackle rigi platform. He gestured to the docks. A few ships and barges floated motionless and unmanned in the deep river.

"If Taleth's going east through the Red Hills, then the rigi will take us too far north," explained Hal. "We'd have to backtrack south. But these barges go to the south side of the hills. Much closer, and much faster. We just need to figure out which one of these is going in our direction."

Bailey scanned the harbor. Several docks stretched out into the river, connected by a wooden pier covered with ropes, crates, and cast-off buoys. A commotion brewed next to one empty dock—Bailey heard the sound of baying dogs echoing above the shouts of the men who stood gathered in a circle.

Hal's dark eyebrows furrowed. "I'm going to find the shipping master's office, and see if I can learn anything useful—will you survey the ships in port? We'll need a list of their names."

"Sure," said Bailey, though he was distracted by the hurly-burly on the pier.

"Don't attract attention," ordered Hal.

"Of course not," Bailey answered.

As Hal took off toward a clapboard building with windows facing the port, Bailey scrambled over the mess of ropes and sea-worn boards that made up the docks. He heard growling and snarling as he drew closer to the huddled group of men, and what he saw made his stomach turn.

Two dogs circled each other in the middle of the crowd. An old sailor with a face full of gray stubble sat off to the side, holding his fingers to his temples.

"That's right, get 'im!" shouted a man.

"Go on, Macon! I've got two snailbacks on the black one," yelled another man, who patted the bristly sailor on the back. The dogs fought, howling as their sharp teeth and claws tore into each other. There was blood everywhere—matted in their fur and streaked across the ground below them. With each wave of aggression from the dogs, Bailey could see that the man, Macon, concentrated harder.

"He's *making* them fight!" he whispered to himself, wishing that Hal was still by his side to witness this. He knew that this was the work of the Dominae. The students in Lyle's Science Club were just experimenting, but these men along the pier were using Dominance for fun, which made it even more sickening.

One of the two dogs, a slim, light brown mutt with short, smooth hair, yipped pitifully as the other dog bit fiercely into its ear. The men hollered. Some cheered, while others, who were clearly Animas Dog as well, groaned.

"Ninnies!" yelled the man, Macon, at those who looked like they might be ill. "If you're feeling the pain, then you ain't doing it right! It's all in your head! See, watch—"

Bailey felt like he needed to sit down—or to scream at someone. Fury built inside him.

The short-haired brown dog attacked, sinking its teeth into the other dog's glossy black hide. They both yelped and barked in pain. Bailey couldn't take it anymore. He fought his way into the crowd with his fists clenched.

"STOP IT!" he shouted. The circle of men turned to look at him. "You're hurting them," he continued, looking at the man they called Macon. He hoped he'd kept his voice even.

The men grumbled. One shouted: "Whose boy is this? Get him out of here!"

Macon rose from his seat, and the two dogs slunk away, whimpering. The men, watching them go, became even more angry.

"I had five snailbacks on that terrier!" shouted one sailor.

"What's this? Can't handle a little game?" Macon said, approaching Bailey until the man towered over him. He was very tall and broad-shouldered, and the lines on his weathered face and his gray hair showed him to be fairly old. He could still knock me flat, Bailey thought.

"It's not a game," Bailey said.

"Oh, no?" said the sailor. "*We* were all having a fine time, before you barged in here."

"Maybe the boy'd like to take their place in the ring, eh?" someone shouted, prompting uproarious laughter from the seamen.

"Two snailbacks he's out in the first round!" another man continued.

"I wouldn't even wager *one* on that," said Macon darkly. "Little shrimp of a thing, thinks he can rumble with real men. Go home to your mother, boy, or to whatever soft furry you're bound to." The sailor turned around. "Now, who wants to see my dogs in a *real* fight? Got two more in yon crate ready for a licking!"

"Those animals don't understand why you're hurting them!" Bailey yelled.

Macon turned back to Bailey and regarded him like he was a cockroach who'd just crawled across his dinner table. Then he swung up with a heavy right fist, and punched Bailey right under the chin. Bailey fell backward, splayed on the wooden planks of the dock. He could hear the other men laughing and exchanging bets now—it really *was* all a game to them.

"Little boy—don't think you can come onto my dock and tell me what's good in the eyes of the world," Macon growled. "Unless you want worse next time."

Bailey groaned and lay back on the dock. The men stepped around him, spitting mockingly in his direction as they dispersed to their posts.

Suddenly, Bailey saw Hal's concerned face looming over him, upside down.

"Are you all right?!" Hal asked.

"Don't say 'That was stupid,'" Bailey said.

Hal shook his head. He bent down, put both of his arms under Bailey's, and helped him to his feet.

"I wouldn't dare," Hal said, "because you already knew that. Anything broken?"

Bailey shook his head.

"I don't think so . . . just sore." He thanked Nature that Macon and the other men had decided to leave him alone when they did. He could have gotten worse.

Hal smiled sympathetically and put a hand on Bailey's shoulder.

"Look, you can't just rush into fights like that. Who knows whether the people who took Taleth are watching for us? We start pulling tails, and we're liable to get bit."

"You're starting to sound like Tremelo," said Bailey.

"I'll take that as a compliment," said Hal. "Now, while you were busy getting the ants beat out of you, I listened in on two of the men there talking about their next shipment going out tonight—on the *Sly Lobster*, headed up to The Maze by special order of Viviana Melore."

"What's The Maze?" asked Bailey. He leaned against a lobster crate as a fresh jolt of pain flashed down his side.

"It's the last city before the Red Hills and the Dust Plains! We can find out more about the Dominae's plans *and* follow Taleth."

Bailey nodded at the plan as he breathed in deeply, which caused a thudding ache in his ribs. The thought of being so close to Viviana's operations made his blood speed up in his veins. This was what he'd hoped being the Child of War would bring: the chance to make a difference against the Dominae.

"So, we'll be traveling by boat, then?" he asked.

"Just us, a bargeload of Dominae goods, and what are sure to be some pretty nasty-tempered guards," Hal said. "But it beats another day on the rigimotive!"

Bailey scouted the *Sly Lobster* at its mooring as Hal ventured to a nearby market for some food. As he waited for Hal to return, Bailey thought about what would be said back at Fairmount. Was Tremelo back? What would happen when the teachers and students noticed he and Hal were missing? Tori couldn't tell Shonfield or Finch. Or Bailey's parents, for that matter. At this thought, Bailey felt an immense guilt settle in his stomach. The school would notify the Walkers that he was missing, and they'd be worried sick. But they'd be *more* worried if they knew where Bailey had actually gone. He wondered if Tremelo—when he returned, *if* he returned—would tell Hal's uncle Roger where he and Hal were. Roger sold myrgwood, and he might even have connections in the Red Hills who could help them. But Bailey wasn't sure whether he could truly be trusted. On top of all that, Bailey couldn't help but worry about Tori. Could he be sure that Graves wouldn't go after her, with Tremelo not there to help her? And what would Phi think when she returned from her trip home to find that he had left on an adventure without her?

Hal returned from the market with some dried slices of apple and pear. The sun had nearly finished setting, and the Fluvian river seemed to glow orange and red in the last light.

"There wasn't anything heartier at the market," Hal said, joining Bailey behind a stack of shipping crates. "But this will have to tide us over until The Maze."

Bailey bit into one of the thin slices of dried apple, a snack his mother used to pack when he and his dad would load up the wagon with grain for a long delivery ride. *Make them last,* she'd say. *It's a long road.* He savored the second bite, finishing the slice.

"We need to get a note to our families," Bailey said. "Otherwise they'll come looking for us."

"I hope Roger won't be too mad," Hal said. "My mom and dad hardly keep track of me as it is, but I guess Roger would have to tell them. He'd go crazy if he knew what we were really doing the past few months."

"Can we use a bat to fly a note home?" Bailey asked.

Hal pursed his lips, thinking.

"Maybe," he said. "But what will it say? 'Decided to run off to the Red Hills. Promise not to get captured by traders. Much love!'"

"I don't know," said Bailey. "Tremelo would know what to do. But we don't even know where he is!"

"But what if Tori's right about him just being out on his own? He could be back already," said Hal. "It's our best shot."

They scrounged a piece of paper—an old cargo boat schedule—and a pen from the shipping master's office, and composed a short note.

We're okay—please let our parents and Roger know. B & H

Hal managed to coax a fuzzy brown bat down from the eaves of the shipping office. Squinting behind his glasses, he held it carefully in one hand, and tied the note to its delicate foot. Bailey watched with awe—the little bat was so patient and unafraid in Hal's hand. Nothing like communing with Taleth: overwhelming emotions, but little understanding. It would take practice for him and the tiger to truly be able to communicate if he managed to find her. He couldn't bear to think of how empty he'd feel if he never saw her again.

"That was amazing," Bailey said as the bat took off from the dock, along with a cloud of about thirty of its fellows. They fluttered across the river and south toward Fairmount. "I remember last fall, when Taylor had me come to the clock tower, you weren't nearly as connected."

"Maybe you all have rubbed off on me," Hal said. "Phi and Carin, Tori and her snakes. And now that you've Awakened... I've got to keep up!"

They set their sights on the *Sly Lobster*. They would spend the night hidden among the cargo on the covered barge as it floated upriver to The Maze—that is, if they managed to board without being seen. Several men stood posted where the barge was tied to the dock. An open space about as long as a classroom stretched between them.

"Maybe we could dive in farther up the dock and swim to the other side, where they wouldn't see," Bailey suggested. "Stay hidden under the boards until the coast is clear."

"Dive into that?" Hal motioned to the Fluvian, which was a light shade of green with a layer of debris and oil on the surface. "I'd rather stay up here. But what we need is a diversion." He dug into his vest pocket, and produced two small, stonelike objects, each the size of a snail. The stunners.

"How did you get those back?" Bailey asked, impressed.

"Taylor's not the only sneaky one in the family," Hal said. "I nicked them from his jacket pocket one day while he was at lunch. I don't have your throwing arm, though." He handed the stunners to Bailey. Together, they peeked over the side of the crate to find the best place to launch them.

"There," said Hal, pointing to the end of the barge where the steerage cabin sat. Three of the five guards were clustered in that space. "If we get them all to the front, maybe we can get up the gangplank before—"

Bailey didn't let Hal finish; he stood up and hurled the first stunner toward the front of the barge. A blinding flash of light exploded in front of the steerage cabin, causing Bailey to shield his eyes with the back of his hand. Hal grabbed Bailey's elbow and yanked him down so they were both crouching behind a crate. It was just in time—they could hear the guards running past them along the pier to investigate.

"What were you saying?" Bailey asked Hal.

"That we need to run along the dock to the barge's shipment-loading end, but *all* the guards were supposed to be occupied!" Hal had peeked over the crate and pointed at the one man who remained at his post, craning his neck to see what the commotion was instead of joining the others.

"Ants," muttered Bailey. He held the last stunner in his hand. At the front of the barge, the other men were talking loudly with a sailor who'd been on board when the stunner hit.

"Don't know what it was—I couldn't see a thing!" the sailor exclaimed.

Bailey readied himself to make another throw.

"As soon as I throw this, run as fast as you can to the cargo hold," he said. "We need to be up that gangplank before any of the other guards make it off the front of the barge, okay?"

Hal looked carefully at the distance between them and the gangplank.

"All right," he said. The two boys crept behind the crates, closer to the other end of the barge, knowing that the longer Bailey waited to throw the last stunner meant more time for the other guards to return to their posts. As they neared the final crate, Bailey rose and threw the stunner. It was just like Flicking a blob of paint at an opponent in Scavage—the stunner whizzed through the air and hit the final guard on the shoulder. The sun had set completely by this time, and the burst of light was so intense that Bailey's eyes stung. He blinked hard and saw stars, and when he reopened them he saw Hal make a run for it; Bailey raced behind him to the covered cargo hold. Together, they ducked under the thick canvas stretched over the back end of the barge, and slid into the darkness among the boxes and crates underneath.

They lay flat behind a large wooden box, waiting to make sure no one had seen them. Hal turned onto his back, took off his glasses, and rubbed his eyes.

"It's a good thing I'm nearly blind already," he whispered, "or those things would have done the job for me."

As Bailey's eyes adjusted, he saw a dark shape atop the crate take form. It made no movement, and neither did Bailey. What seemed like entire minutes passed, and finally Bailey could see that the figure—a giant metal bird—was not going to strike. Its slick, black-painted wings folded behind it as it stared forward, unseeing and unblinking.

"Nature's ears, that's creepy," said Hal.

"It's Viviana's," said Bailey. "One of those Clamor-birds Gwen told us about. Doesn't look like it's on, though."

It was then that he noticed the box underneath the metal bird. It was a shipping crate as tall as Hal, and blazoned diagonally across its wooden side in red were the words RECKON, INC.

"Look! That's what the note said!" Bailey said, shaking Hal's shoulder and pointing. "*Reckon, Inc.*—not *Reckoning*; it's the name of a company or something."

The barge shuddered underneath them, groaning into motion. The sound of lapping water beat rhythmically outside the cargo hold. They were on their way to The Maze.

Twenty~two

BAILEY SHIFTED AMONG STRIPS of newspaper packing and some very uncomfortable cooking pots; he couldn't sleep, despite the fact that he'd gotten no rest on the rigimotive the night before, either. They'd found a crate with a loose top that made a good hiding place, but despite his exhaustion, Bailey was afraid to shut his eyes. He thought of Taleth, who he knew was frightened and somewhere in the hills, and the mysterious crate that shared the barge with them. After seeing the name RECKON, INC. stamped onto the side, Bailey had wanted to pry it open on the spot. It was Hal, as usual, who'd held him back.

"There's a whole night's ride to go! If we open up a crate now, what happens if someone walks in?" Hal had asked. "I'll tell you what—they won't have far to look before they find whoever opened it. Let's wait until we dock in The Maze, break it open, and hopefully get off this barge before they find us."

And so Bailey sat awake in the cramped crate while Hal slept, looking through a hole in the boards at the red letters, only a few feet away, that spelled out the answer to a mystery. The hours seemed to slide by at a slug's pace.

Finally, the canvas cover over the barge lightened, and the sun rose outside. The barge began to slow, and Bailey crawled out of the crate toward the edge of the cargo hold. Looking out, he saw a pier ahead of them. A small city of low stone buildings stretched from the river up into a range of wide hills covered in crags and weathered trees.

"Hal," he said, shaking him awake. "We're here."

"*Oof*," said Hal, stirring out of sleep. "Not the most comfortable pots I've ever slept on...." He shifted up into a crouch to peer out the side of the crate. "You're sure no one's around?"

Bailey nodded. "Now's our chance," he said. His heart thumped in his chest as he and Hal approached the Reckon, Inc. crate.

"We've got to move this bird," Hal said, pointing up to the Clamoribus.

The two of them climbed on top of the crates neighboring the Dominae shipment. Bailey's hands shook as he took ahold of one wing of the metal crow and Hal took the other. The bird was lighter than he'd imagined it would be, and the metal was cool under his fingers. They eased it over the side of the Reckon box and set it down atop another crate.

Just as they were about to pry open the lid of the Reckon, Inc. crate, they heard a noise from the far end of the cargo hold. Three men entered, talking and joking loudly to one another.

"Quick," Hal said, pulling Bailey back to the crate where they'd slept. They tried to slip back inside without making a noise.

Bailey pulled the top closed, praying that the men hadn't heard them.

"So, this lot's going straight to factory row," said a thin-voiced sailor. "And the rest stays in the storehouse to be picked up later. Got it?"

Two other voices sounded their assent, and Bailey heard the scrapes, grunts, and footsteps. The cargo was being unloaded. He squeezed his hands into fists, hoping with his whole body that the crate he and Hal sat in was going to the same place as the crate from Reckon, Inc. The sound of heavy footsteps drew closer to the crate.

"Ants, another Reckon shipment. These give me the creeps," said one of the laborers.

"Why? What's in it?" asked the other.

Bailey strained to listen as the two men heaved the Reckon, Inc. crate onto a large, flat dolly.

"Haven't a clue," said the first man. "But it's not about what's in it as much as where it's going. You haven't heard about the factory?"

"Only that they've been offering jobs."

"Don't take one," said the first man. "My neighbor tried for one of those jobs. Miriam. Animas Sparrow. Always had birds flying around her."

"What about her?" asked the second man.

The two men grunted as they straightened the crate on the dolly.

"I saw her when she came back—she was only supposed to take a day job, but she came wandering back home after being gone for three days. Couldn't tell us what had happened. Her words didn't make any sense; she just whispered to herself. . . ."

"Went nutty, eh?"

Bailey held his breath. The two men had stopped to catch their own. The crate stood solidly on the dolly, towering and ominous.

"*Their wings, their claws.* That's what she was whispering, over and over," the man said. "*Their wings, their claws.* There weren't a sparrow who'd go near her after that."

Bailey heard the other man let out a low whistle.

"Ants alive. You've got me shuddering," said the second man. "Don't want to touch this thing now."

The first man sighed.

"Think of it this way—we move the boxes down here on time, we won't find ourselves having to look for work up the hill. So let's get a move on."

The men went silent, except for a few grunts as they rolled the dolly with the Reckon, Inc. crate off the barge.

Bailey breathed out heavily as they left.

"Bailey," whispered Hal. "It must have been something to do with those machines. What do they *do*?"

Bailey didn't have time to answer—footsteps echoed on the boards.

"This one's for the storehouse, then?" said a voice.

The next thing Bailey knew, he was jostling around in the crate as the two men lifted it onto another dolly. They were wheeled out of the cargo hold, down the gangplank, and into the cold, dark interior of a shoreside warehouse. The men dropped the crate without ceremony or care, and Bailey felt a fresh bruise form on his rear end where he'd collided with one of the cast-iron cooking pots packaged in the box along with them.

The boys waited until long after they heard the door of the

storehouse clank shut to make sure no one would see them emerge. Bailey lifted the top of the crate just an inch, and looked around. They were alone in the warehouse—but he didn't see the giant metal bird anymore. It, along with the Reckon, Inc. crate, had been taken to the factory, wherever that was.

"Come on." He gestured to Hal. The storehouse was a long, metal room. Cutouts in its rusty roof let in shafts of light, but inside was as silent and cold as a cave. Together, they crept to the door, and carefully peered out. The serpentine streets of The Maze lay before them. The shipyard was empty except for a flock of river birds, circling and cawing above the docks. A weed-patched alley led away into the city. Beyond the red roofs of The Maze, Bailey could see the crest of the hills, covered in dead, leaf-bare trees.

The boys set off into the alley. They saw barely anyone on the streets as they walked to the hills beyond the town. Bailey felt a stirring in his chest that he hadn't felt since they'd left Fairmount—Taleth was not far away. In fact, the streets they walked through seemed so uncannily familiar, and he knew she had seen them too.

"Taleth was here," he said to Hal. "It's like the bond is telling me where to go."

Hal smiled. "It's like that sometimes," he said. "Can you tell where she is now?"

Bailey shook his head. He wished he knew how to bring on a more intense connection—if he could only see through her eyes right then, he might know where he was headed. He'd go whichever direction he needed to save her.

From the path up the hill, they could look behind them and see The Maze spreading out over the Fluvian harbor like a rust stain. It wasn't until they'd reached the peak of the first hill and begun their descent into a narrow valley that the vegetation grew taller and thicker. The trees were just as stark as they had been in The Maze, but Bailey was relieved that they did not have to trudge through snow. They kept to the path that led down into the valley and slept under the cover of some low-bending branches as the temperature plummeted that night.

The next day they woke to a cloud-hazy sunrise and ate a handful each of pear slices before they set off again. The path wound them into the heart of the valley and up the other side.

Hours had passed when Bailey finally felt a desperate pull from Taleth. Her fear overcame his mind, and his heart rate rose. Taleth could sense that he was near. She was confined to a cage or cell. He could feel the cool metal of the bars as she pressed her head and flanks against them. At the sound of footsteps on stone, she began to growl.

"Who are you thinking of, my pretty beast?" came a deep, threatening voice. Then Bailey snapped to, back to the valley.

"What's the matter?" asked Hal.

"I can feel Taleth—she's afraid. It's almost like she knows we're coming, but she doesn't want us to." He wished he could have stayed in her thoughts longer, to see who was speaking to her, and to comfort her. Did she know that he sensed her? He'd ask Tremelo someday if that was what it felt like to be life-bonded . . . if he and Taleth made it back to Fairmount safely, and if his teacher decided to return.

Hal steadied his glasses on his nose and pinched his lip between his teeth.

"We have to keep going," said Bailey, sensing Hal's hesitation. "We can't just leave her."

Hal nodded. "I know—I just wish I knew what we're going to do when we find her. This could be a trap."

"There isn't another way," Bailey said, and pushed past Hal to continue on the path.

As the sun set that night, the boys had reached the other side of the valley. The Dust Plains stretched out beyond the next hill, flat and spotted with patches of dried, dead grass poking up through the crusty dirt. Bailey's chest thudded with knowledge of Taleth's presence. Standing on the crest of the last of the Red Hills, he felt pulled to her as he looked out over the moonlit plain.

"She's somewhere close," he told Hal. "If we keep going, we can find her by morning."

"We're not going down the side of the hill in the dark." Hal said. "We'd be safer setting up camp. We can head into the Plains at daybreak."

"But we're so close," said Bailey. "And I have the claw."

"We're *not* close—not by a long shot. We're still half a day from the Plains if we follow the path!" Hal exclaimed. "And the point is to stay safe so we don't *have* to use weapons. What exactly do you propose to do? Lunge at an assassin with a single tiger claw?"

Bailey tossed his knapsack down.

"We're going to have to be ready for a fight at some point, Hal," he said. "Like you said, it won't be easy."

"But you're so eager for a fight all the time," said Hal. "We don't know what's going to happen, so that's all the more reason not to go looking for trouble *now*. Seriously, you've almost been killed how many times in the last six months?"

Bailey clenched his fists.

"If that's how you feel, then why bother coming with me?"

"Because you need someone to protect you—" Hal began.

"And that's *you*?" scoffed Bailey.

"I mean, someone to protect you from getting yourself in trouble!" said Hal. "You're going to wind up getting killed unless you start thinking things through!"

"*I* follow my instincts," snapped Bailey. "Maybe you should try it. Who wants to be around someone who's afraid of everything? I bet Tori doesn't. In fact, I *know* she doesn't."

Hal was silent for a moment, and Bailey could almost feel the workings of Hal's rational brain trying to come up with the perfect comeback.

"Do whatever you want" was all Hal said. Then he turned and walked heavily over to a tree to set up camp.

Bailey didn't follow. He felt tired in more ways than one. He was tired of worrying and feeling watched, tired of being told what to do—*be careful, stay hidden, be on guard*. Of course, it had been sound advice—but he wondered how much longer he could go on like this, hiding and ducking attention, only to end up in more trouble.

Bailey began to walk down the path. He kept an eye on the stars to the northeast, trying to memorize them in case he needed to cut away from the trail to get to Taleth. Still, his mind wandered back to Hal. Bailey never would've made it this far—or still be alive—if not for his friend. He stopped, took a deep breath, and turned back toward his camp.

At first, he thought that the faint whispering sound he heard was the wind—but he'd soon realized that the noise was the beating of small leathery wings. The hillside was full of lively bats. Bailey reached the top of the hill, and from there, he could just make out the fluttering shapes that flew from branch to branch across the treetops. Up in a gnarled old oak in the middle was Hal, hanging upside down.

Quietly, Bailey hiked a little ways over the hill. Hal watched as he climbed up to his branch and awkwardly hooked his knees over it.

"What do you want?" asked Hal.

Hanging upside down, Bailey felt his blood run down—or rather, up—his whole body.

"Why are you hanging like this?" he asked. "Doesn't it make your head hurt?"

"No, it helps me think," Hal said curtly. He wouldn't look at Bailey. Bailey sighed. They had enough to worry about already without him saying things he didn't mean.

"I'm sorry I said that about Tori," he confessed. "It isn't true. Tori really cares about you."

"Now I know you're just trying to make me feel better," said Hal.

"She does!" said Bailey. "In her way."

The two boys hung there for a moment in silence, looking up at the moon.

"You did mean part of it, though," Hal said, not unkindly. "I don't follow my instincts. I think about every angle, calculate every possibility—and then the moment passes. I never take action. Not like you."

"That's not true," said Bailey. "You're the one who found Lyle's secret meeting—and you always stand up to Taylor when he's being a jerk. And besides, you're here, aren't you? You packed your bags, got me on a boat, and led me to the Dust Plains. . . ."

Hal laughed. "I guess so."

Just then, Bailey felt a sensation different from just the rush of blood coursing upside through his body—he felt a twinge in his chest and a heightened sense of alertness.

He swung himself up and hopped into a crouching position on the tree branch.

"Someone's here," he said quickly. Whoever it was, was close by, dangerously close.

"*Shh,*" said Hal, putting a finger to his lips. "I hear them, over by that tree."

Bailey bent down to follow where Hal pointed. A branch moved a few yards away.

Hal did as Bailey had done and swung himself up. Bailey gripped the tiger claw tucked in his belt.

The branch moved again, and a deer—a dark-eyed doe—ran out from behind the bushes.

Bailey relaxed until he realized the doe was followed by a man in shabby, dark clothing. He carried a crossbow, ready to shoot. A poacher.

A young coyote prowled behind the man, and its ears perked in Bailey and Hal's direction. The man, distracted from his prey, turned and searched the trees where the boys were hidden. Bailey felt his entire body go numb as the poacher's eyes met his own. The poacher, surprised, swung his crossbow around and took aim. Hal's grip on Bailey's arm tightened.

The valley was suddenly filled with the sound of baying and yipping—at least five doglike animals bounded out of the trees and attacked the hunter. He dropped the crossbow and yelled as the beasts bit and tore at him. Shocked, Bailey looked in the direction the doe had run. A pack of dogs huddled around the fallen deer. They weren't like any dogs Bailey had seen in the Lowlands or at Fairmount. But he'd seen pictures of them, with their long snouts and ragged yellow-brown fur—in his History textbook, he'd seen these same dogs at the side of a False King. Jackals.

Out of the trees walked a man—older, with broad, imposing shoulders. He wore a peaked cap with a black visor, and what looked like a military coat covered in shiny buttons; a metal cane swung at his side. He surveyed the jackals, who continued attacking the hunter and the deer ravenously. Then he lifted a silver whistle to his lips. Bailey heard nothing, but the jackals rolled their heads as though in pain, and backed away from their prey like dutiful beasts.

"Bailey..." Hal gasped. "Is that...?"

"Yes," Bailey whispered. He had assumed that this man was dead, but it was clear Bailey had been wrong. He was looking at the man who'd ordered his real parents, along with the rest of the Velyn, killed. He'd murdered King Melore, sending Tremelo and Viviana into the night. The kingdom had endured nearly thirty years of chaos because of this man.

The Jackal pulled back his coat and dropped the whistle into an inside pocket. Two attendants followed him up the hill, and lifted the wounded poacher between them.

"Get rid of him," the Jackal said. As the attendants carried the poacher down the hill, back into the bristly foliage of the valley, the Jackal stood and sniffed the crisp night air. The moonlight shone on the buttons of his uniform as he straightened his shoulders. He caressed the top of his metal cane with his thumb, and lightly licked his lips. Bailey noticed a scar running in a menacing curve across his cheek and down to his chin.

The Jackal breathed in deeply, as though savoring the night chill.

"You can come down from that tree now, boys," he said.

Twenty~three

THAT SAME NIGHT, GWEN made her campfire on a wide, flat rock. She was closer to the tallest peak, the place where the Elder had told her to seek the Instrument of Change, but she felt sure someone was pursuing her—and that they were very close behind. She knew she was exposed out here, with no place to hide—but the open space made it impossible for anyone to sneak up on her. She stayed awake, sitting cross-legged with her bow in her hand.

Sure enough, just after sunset, she saw the figure of a large bird flying low over the trees. This was it. Her hand closed tightly over the bow as she stood to get a better look. The tawny owlet hopped on its branch behind Gwen, shuffling its feathers with anticipation. As the bird swooped closer, Gwen felt jittery.

Whit whit whoo came a call from the trees, and Gwen recognized Carin the falcon as she landed on the edge of the flat rock.

Gwen echoed the call, and saw the silhouette of someone

climbing over the rocks in the waning light: someone with a small, delicate frame and a head full of curly, windswept hair.

"Phi!" Gwen cried, dropping the bow and rushing forward to meet her friend.

Phi rushed forward as well, and the two girls hugged.

"You're fast!" said Phi. "It's taken me ages to catch up to you!" Phi looked tired and flushed, and a little cold under her thin second-hand coat. She dropped her pack and reached around her shoulder—she carried Gwen's pack too. Gwen laughed with relief as Phi handed her the rucksack: inside, safe, was the Seers' Glass.

"Carin sensed how worried I was about the Glass. She brought it back to me. . . ." Phi said apologetically. "I wanted her to leave it with you, but I can't communicate with her perfectly. It meant I had to catch up even more quickly!"

"How did you find me?" Gwen asked.

They reached the glow of the campfire, and Phi sat down, leaning on her pack with a tired sigh. Gwen held the Seers' Glass, wrapped in its piece of wolf pelt, tightly in her hands.

"I sent Carin to look for you after you disappeared," she said. "We saw you heading from the Gray to the Velyn Peaks."

"But why? What are you doing here?"

Phi looked away and folded her hands inside her long coat sleeves.

"I wanted to help," she said. "You had the Seers' Glass, and that meant you'd be in danger. I left Fairmount as soon as I knew where you were. The others wouldn't have understood."

Gwen studied Phi as she gazed into the campfire. She wondered if Phi was telling the entire truth, but she pushed aside the thought for now. She was only glad to have a companion.

The girls relocated their camp under the overhang of a large boulder, facing the open mountain field. They relit their campfire as the sun set completely, and cooked a meal of grains, flavored with wild hackleberries.

After supper, Phi and Gwen curled near each other with their rucksacks as pillows, pulling their coats around themselves for warmth.

"Why'd you come out here?" asked Phi. "Did the RATS send you to hide?"

"No, it was the Elder who sent me here, to find something called the Instrument of Change. He left a message for me with the RATS before he died. I don't know what I'm actually looking for, but it must be something that can help convince Tremelo that his rightful place is on the throne." *Without its help, our True King cannot find the strength in his heart to lead.* Whatever this Instrument was, Tremelo needed her to find it.

"The Elder—that reminds me, I have something else for you," said Phi. She fished in her coat pocket, then placed Melore's harmonica, in its worn leather box, in Gwen's open hand. "I figured you'd want this back someday."

Gwen closed her fingers over the familiar gift.

"Thank you," she said. "I sort of missed it." She smiled, remembering how the Elder had grinned when he'd first presented it to her.

Phi continued to look up at the stars, as if studying them.

"I wish school were like this," she said. "Having adventures, being in the mountains . . . Sometimes I feel like I'm going to crawl out of my skin at Fairmount."

"It doesn't feel like an adventure, does it? Sometimes I wish things could go back to the way they were before," said Gwen. Her eyes stung as she thought of the Elder. "Now I'm always afraid."

"We're going to be okay," said Phi firmly, pulling the collar of her coat up close to her face.

Gwen was glad to have her friend here, but the feeling of being watched hadn't gone away. She took the Seers' Glass out of her pack. After believing she'd lost it forever, she couldn't resist the urge to hold it in her hands and feel its smoothness. As she unfolded the wolf pelt around the Glass, she felt a sliver of fear stab at her heart—the Glass was glowing. It emitted a faint shimmer, like rippling water.

"Phi," Gwen whispered. "Phi, how long has it been like this?"

But Phi's eyes were closed and her mouth had fallen softly open. She was asleep.

Gwen stared at the Glass for another moment. The light unnerved her, as though the Glass itself were watching her. She shivered, then wrapped it up and stowed it deep in her rucksack. She eventually fell asleep, into fitful dreams.

Twenty~four

"GENTLEMEN," SAID THE JACKAL, grinning at both boys. "I believe I've just saved your lives."

Through the trees, Bailey could see the attendants pushing the poacher into a polished metal motorcar, and the glint of the moon reflected off its black hood. The Jackal must have been waiting for them.

It felt like a strange, awful dream. He had only heard people talk of the Jackal as though he were a ghost. And now he stood right in front of them, tapping at the roots of the gnarled tree with the metal tip of his cane, politely asking them to come down from their tree as if inviting them to a formal supper.

"We're fine up here, thanks," Bailey said, trying to sound brave, but his voice cracked. He and Hal knelt together on the branch, too high for the Jackal to reach them—but not high enough to feel safe.

"Ah, but you see, if you do not come down there's a very good chance that you'll never see your dear white tiger again."

Bailey's blood froze in his veins. His muscles tensed, and he wanted to roar, to spring from the branch and attack. But Hal shook his head quickly, telling Bailey without words to ignore those dangerous instincts and stay calm.

"How do we know you're telling the truth?" Hal said. "Taleth could be anywhere."

The Jackal looked from Hal to Bailey, and raised one eyebrow.

"*He* knows I'm telling the truth," he said. "What does your kin tell you, boy?"

Bailey said nothing. He remembered the flash he'd felt earlier that morning of Taleth's consciousness. He didn't need to hear that menacing voice again—*my pretty beast*—to know that the man standing in front of him was the one who had taken her.

"She's been getting more and more anxious, the closer you've come," the Jackal said. "My men have watched the docks, and every pathway out of The Maze since first capturing her. I knew it would only be a matter of days before her kin arrived in my valley, and here you are."

The two guards returned. They were burly men dressed in dark uniforms and boots, like soldiers. One had a bow and quiver of metal arrows strapped to his back; the other, a long, imposing blunderbuss. They joined the Jackal at the trunk of the gnarled tree.

"So come on down now, boys," the Jackal said again. "And let's have a nice chat."

Hal and Bailey looked at each other. Bailey imagined bringing his claw up swift and sharp across the man's already-scarred face—but Hal was right. He was too eager to start a fight, and this time, the risk was too great. His hands shook from terror, and he nearly slipped from the branch on his way down. He tried not to take his eyes off the Jackal's amused smirk.

At the base of the tree, the guards searched their knapsacks, and took away both Hal's knife and Bailey's tiger claw. Then they marched the boys through the underbrush to the gleaming car, its engine growling like a waiting wolf. The Jackal had done well for himself in exile. The guards shoved Hal and Bailey into the backseat. The Jackal slid into the opposite seat facing them.

"I've had men canvassing the Fairmount woods since Midwinter," said the Jackal. "I knew the Velyn were still lurking about, but they couldn't stop me from finding her—the last white beast, just like the prophecy said." He met Bailey's eyes. "But she's no use to me at all without you."

"What do you want?" Bailey asked. The car was moving now, with the shadowy mountain-shapes of the two guards looming in the front seat.

"The people believe in the symbol of the tiger, even after all these years," the Jackal began. "My time in exile has shown me my error: prophecies have a way of coming true, don't they? Instead of fighting the prophecy, I should just make it work in my favor."

"But you're not the True King!" Bailey spat.

"Why wouldn't I be? I have the Child of War and his rare white tiger! You should thank me—Viviana wants you dead, but I won't let that happen, because I'm smarter." The Jackal grinned. "Her clanking ravens are far too easy to intercept. Imagine my surprise when I coaxed that charming voice out of its parts—*Joan? What happened with the Child of War? Confirm that the child is dead, and the prophecy is no longer a concern!*—Ha! She's been so preoccupied trying to kill *you* that she didn't think to find the tiger first, as I have. And won't she be surprised when I arrive at her fair with both prizes?" He laughed and leaned forward with his hands folded on his cane.

"Tell me, how did you overcome Joan Sucrette? She was a ruthless one, from what news I receive out here. Did you slit her throat? Poison her?"

Bailey stiffened at the mention of Sucrette's name. The Jackal seemed excited about the death that haunted Bailey still. He wished he could simply grab Hal and tumble out of the car to safety. But where would they go, and how would they ever rescue Taleth? The Jackal's amused stare was still fixed on him, waiting for him to speak.

"I didn't kill her," Bailey admitted. "The animals she'd been dominating did, once we set them free."

"Poetic," spat the Jackal, "but hardly as interesting."

Soon the car stopped, and the guards opened the door for the Jackal to step out. Bailey and Hal followed, and found themselves standing at the entrance of a bunker set into a low, grassy hill. Flat plains surrounded them, stretching into the darkness. They were marched into the bunker and down a long hallway with rooms on either side. Gas lamps hung at intervals on the ceiling, emitting a faint yellow glow.

As they passed one of the heavy closed doors, Bailey felt his pulse quicken and a buzzing in his chest. It was Taleth—her consciousness washed over him. He sensed the cold floor under her paws as she leapt up onto all fours; he felt her whiskers twitch, and her massive heart begin to thrum faster. She knew that Bailey was nearby.

They turned a bend and arrived at a meeting hall of sorts, with a wooden table and metal chairs, and thick bars clamped onto a set of high windows. A lone jackal sat in the corner of the room near a small fire grate, its bushy tail swatting the floor as it watched the men enter.

"Welcome to my prison," said the Jackal. "I am prisoner and warden both."

The Jackal pulled up a metal chair, and its legs screeched against the cold stone floor. He sat facing the boys, who stood across the table side by side, the guards at their elbows. The Jackal thrust his thick hand into the pocket of his uniform and took out a cut of raw, red meat wrapped in a piece of oilcloth. He dangled the meat in the direction of the jackal in the corner, holding it by his thigh as the dog came closer, sniffing. It dutifully lifted its paw and set it on the Jackal's leg, the very image of devotion and tender admiration. Then the Jackal tossed the meat away, and the animal went snarling after it. The Jackal didn't have a life-bonded kin at all; he manipulated his kin into looking adoring. He was nothing but vile appearances.

Hal was peering off to the side, toward the end of the long wooden table. On it, Bailey recognized one of Viviana's metal birds—a Clamoribus—but this one was in pieces, scattered. He knew it wasn't a real animal, but still the sight of the detached wings and head unsettled him.

"I thought I'd killed all the Velyn, until I got word of that white beast lurking outside the school. And now here *you* are. I hope you do not hold the death of your people against me," the Jackal said. "Men who seek power must be willing to get blood on their hands."

"Sounds like something a killer would say," said Bailey.

"I *am* a killer!" shouted the Jackal, slamming his fist down on the wooden table. The furry jackal in the corner yipped, frightened. "And it would serve you well to listen. Leave the past where it is, and align yourself with real power. The kingdom is ready for my return. Join me at Viviana's fair, and help me prove to Aldermere that I am the True King."

"I'll never join you," said Bailey. His whole body shook.

The Jackal pursed his lips as though he were chewing his next words before spitting them out. He stood, and walked around the table toward them. Bailey's skin began to crawl with gooseflesh, and he had trouble distinguishing his own fear from Taleth's— wherever she was, she could sense his dismay.

"A shame," the Jackal said. "Your refusal makes me upset, and I often like to hurt things when I'm upset. But you and your beast— you're too valuable to kill outright."

The Jackal reached his thick hand out and grabbed Hal fiercely by the shoulder.

"I'll just have to kill this one instead."

Twenty~five

"NO!" CRIED BAILEY AS he lunged forward. The guard to his left grabbed Bailey's arm and twisted it behind his back. Pain radiated from his shoulder socket.

The Jackal shoved Hal over to the other guard, who dragged him toward the table.

"It's going to be all right," Hal called over his shoulder.

"You're a coward!" Bailey yelled at the Jackal, who slapped him hard across the face. Bailey tasted blood in his mouth.

"And all you are is a little pup," the Jackal replied, "barking at a dog with much sharper teeth than yours." Bailey struggled in the guard's grip.

"Stop! You can't do this!" he yelled. Neither the guards nor the Jackal answered him.

"Hal!" Bailey yelled. "Hal!" He didn't know what else to do.

Hal didn't even look at him—his eyes were shut tight behind

his glasses. Bailey could hardly breathe. All he could think to do was yell and kick—all he wanted was to protect Hal. Hal had never been anything but loyal and wise—and all Bailey brought him was trouble. If Hal died here, in this filthy bunker, he'd never forgive himself.

"What are you going to do?" asked Bailey. "What do you want?"

"A simple yes," said the Jackal. "Will you do as I ask of you, when the time comes?"

Hal opened his eyes and shook his head.

"Don't," Hal said. "Don't say yes!"

One of the guards grabbed Hal's glasses off his nose and crushed them in his fist in a single motion. He let them drop to the floor, a broken mess of metal and glass.

"Make him watch," said the Jackal to the man gripping Bailey's arm. The guard, a man with almost no chin and drooping, cold eyes, twisted Bailey's arms behind his back. As Bailey tried to free his hands, he felt sharp pains in his shoulders.

"No—no!" Bailey yelled.

The Jackal walked over to Hal and unsheathed a small dagger from a holster at his hip.

"I remember being young and foolish just like you," the Jackal said to Bailey. "I felt indestructible. But we all have our weaknesses. Our friendships, for instance . . ."

The Jackal grabbed Hal by the shoulder and held the dagger's edge to the side of Hal's neck.

"Stop!" Bailey cried.

The Jackal moved the knife in his hand ever so slightly, and Hal flinched, shutting his eyes tightly again.

"Let him go!" Bailey yelled.

Bailey heard another sound over his own anguish—a roar, muffled by a stone wall.

"Oh, very good," murmured the Jackal. "Now everyone's joined us."

The roar echoed in Bailey's ears, loud and pulsing. Taleth was in the next room, and as surely as he could feel her terror, she could feel his.

"Bailey," said Hal quietly. "Don't listen to him."

The Jackal's smile faded, and he tightened his grip on Hal.

"What's your answer, boy?" the Jackal demanded, his cold eyes set on Bailey's.

Bailey was silent. His whole body radiated with fear and panic. Hal met his eyes, and shook his head. *No,* he mouthed.

"No? Nothing?" said the Jackal. "Then you leave me no choice." He made to press the knife's edge against Hal's skin.

"Stop! I'll do it!" Bailey cried.

The Jackal released his grip.

Bailey looked at the Jackal and squared his jaw. "I'll do whatever you want."

The Jackal smiled, running a callused finger along his blunt chin.

"I'm pleased to hear that." He nodded to one of the guards, and the man grabbed Hal under his arm and dragged him to the door. The two boys' eyes met as Hal left the room.

The Jackal paced.

"I've been following this 'Dominae' movement of Viviana's with much curiosity," he said. "Since you've been so kind as to pledge your service to me, I'll tell you a secret: I've never bonded with an animal. But I have other ways of making animals fear and obey me. There's a word for what I am, which I despise. You're under orders never to speak it."

Bailey glanced at the whimpering jackal in the corner of the room. Its hackles were raised, and it guarded the remnants of the meat that the Jackal had given it like a beggar would a shiny snail-back found in the street.

"An Absence..." Bailey whispered to himself.

"I must admit, Viviana impresses me," the Jackal continued. "My spies in the city tell me that she doesn't only control *her* kin—already a feat for any normal citizen—but the kin of *others* as well! Alas, I am not so talented. I cannot control your tiger, which is why I need *you*."

Bailey began to understand what the Jackal wanted him to do, and the idea sickened him.

"You and your tiger will accompany me to Viviana Melore's Progress Fair, and there we will use this 'Dominance' to our advantage. You will force Taleth to bow down to me, in front of Viviana, and the whole of the kingdom. The people will see that the white tiger is under my control—and Viviana will see the Child of War name *me* the True King."

Bailey recoiled as the Jackal reached out to him. The Jackal grabbed Bailey's jaw, forcing Bailey to look at him straight on.

"The Child of War," said the Jackal softly, searching Bailey's face. "I imagine you and your lonely kin must have a very strong bond. She is the last, after all. That's because of me. But I did not kill *you*, all those years ago, and that's worth something—isn't it? Perhaps you can repay me now." Bailey clenched his jaw, trying not to scoff.

The Jackal straightened up and adjusted his hold on his metal cane. Grinning, he pointed the end in Bailey's face, as if to warn him not to step out of line. In the light of the fire, Bailey saw the carved image in the metal tip: the head of a wild laughing dog. A jackal.

Twenty~six

THE NEXT MORNING, BAILEY woke on the cold stone floor of a cell. The Jackal stood just past the bars, leaning forward on his cane. His smirk caused the scar across his nose and cheek to curve into a puckered half-moon.

Bailey pulled himself up and leaned against the wall. He listened for Hal, in the cell next to him, but all he heard was silence.

"Have a restful sleep?" asked the Jackal. He still wore his gray uniform, and had slicked back his dark brown hair.

"I slept fine," Bailey said, though he hadn't, not for more than a few minutes at a time. But he took care to keep his tone flat, calm, and agreeable.

The Jackal's smirk became a grin.

"A good night's sleep and you're practically a new Bailey!"

In the next cell, Hal stirred. Bailey released a breath of relief.

"Yes, sir," said Bailey. "I'm ready to cooperate." The words tasted like stinging acid in his mouth, but he knew that his only chance to save himself and Hal was to do as the Jackal wished—for now.

"But you have to let Hal go," he said.

The Jackal stiffened his shoulders.

"And risk him soliciting help for your rescue? I'm not stupid," the Jackal began. "But I am not heartless, either. I will let him live."

"Thank you," said Bailey. The Jackal blinked his cold eyes, and beckoned to a guard out of Bailey's sight.

"Mr. Walker is now a guest, not a prisoner. Bring him upstairs."

"What about Hal?" asked Bailey.

The Jackal had already turned his shadowy back on the cells.

"He's alive," he said.

The guard, the same droopy-eyed behemoth who'd held Bailey yesterday, led him upstairs to the Jackal's meeting room. The remnants of a hearty breakfast—smeared egg yolk and a scrap of wilted greens over a few last bites of ham—sat abandoned on the table. In the corner, two jackals munched on leftover slices of fried hog fat. The smell turned Bailey's stomach.

The Jackal took his seat. He jabbed his large fingers in the egg yolk and licked them before pushing the used plate away from him with a satisfied hum.

The guard herded Bailey forward to stand at the edge of the wooden table.

"We'll begin today by seeing how you use your bond with that beast down the hall," the Jackal said. "And try anything foolish, like escaping, I will find you both. The throats of your kin *and* your friend will be slit—and *you* can look forward to a much slower death."

Bailey hid his shaking hands behind his back. If he only knew how to control his bond and somehow explain to Taleth how she could help him, perhaps she would do what he asked of her. . . . But he didn't know whether he would be able to channel his intentions like that—and the thought of forcing her to do something against her will was too terrible. The Jackal might do something extreme once he saw how inexperienced Bailey was. If he and Taleth weren't useful to the Jackal, what would happen then?

The Jackal drummed his fingers on the table edge, watching Bailey curiously.

"Viviana is planning her Progress Fair for the Spring Equinox—that doesn't give us much time," the Jackal said. "Though I doubt the prophesied 'Child of War' will need much time at all. Otherwise, what are prophecies for?! And Viviana"— he waved dismissively—"she's nothing but an angry little girl. She'll be so surprised to see us—not to mention the soldiers I've gathered—that she'll surrender on the spot!"

"Soldiers?" Bailey asked. He hadn't seen anyone in the bunker but the Jackal and a handful of guards.

"I use the term loosely, I grant you. There are many thieves in the Dust Plains who'll carry a weapon," said the Jackal. "Let's just say I'm not without resources."

"Very clever, sir," said Bailey, taking care to keep his voice even. Inside, his mind raced. How could he possibly help Tremelo contend with both the Dominae and an army of Dust Plains mercenaries? If he made it out of the Jackal's clutches at all, stopping Viviana's Reckoning would be even more difficult.

"Indeed," said the Jackal. He leaned forward, with his fingers laced around the top of his cane. "But a simple surrender is hardly enough. *You* will lead the charge into war, young Bailey, just as the prophecy says! After your tiger bows before me, she will kill Viviana Melore in my name!"

Bailey's instincts were wrangling inside him. He wanted to recoil from this man who demanded he use Dominance. Of course he wanted to stop Viviana . . . but not if it meant murder, and not to put the Jackal in her place.

"Don't look so shaken, Bailey!" said the Jackal, leaning back in his chair. "What did you think being the Child of War would mean, eh?" he asked. "Sounds like you don't care for the job description."

"Just . . . getting used to the idea, sir," said Bailey.

"Let's get started, then," said the Jackal, standing up from the table. He led Bailey down the hall to a wide, open room. As they neared the door, Bailey could hear Taleth growling and pulling against the chained collar that bound her to the wall. Bailey feared his heart would burst, it was beating so quickly. At the sight of him entering the room, Taleth strained angrily against the chains and roared. The guards stationed at either side of the door took a cautious step backward.

"Not very pleased to see you, is she?" the Jackal joked. But Bailey knew she was afraid for both of them. Bailey was too.

Taleth roared again, this time in the Jackal's direction. The Jackal took one quick step forward and brandished his metal cane.

"No!" Bailey shouted, before he could stop himself.

Taleth slunk away and paced along the stone wall, her bright blue eyes never leaving the Jackal. Her whiskers shuddered, and her tail twitched.

"Not an impossible creature to train," said the Jackal. "It's your turn now, boy."

The guard shoved Bailey forward.

"Okay," Bailey said. He wasn't sure where to start. He tried to imagine Taleth bowing to the Jackal—her enormous bulk bending elegantly, her nose just touching the cold floor. The image disgusted him.

Taleth bared her teeth and let out a small growl. Bailey tried to find the same humming energy in himself that he'd felt back at Fairmount and crossing the Red Hills. Instead, he felt nothing but fear and the cold stare of the Jackal's eyes on him. Taleth paced back and forth, growling. She didn't seem to Bailey to be his kin at all—just a trapped, dangerous animal who could strike at any moment. He breathed deeply and closed his eyes.

As soon as he did, confusion and pain overwhelmed him. He was trapped, and his friends were in danger. He missed the smells of the woods and the feel of soft earth beneath his feet and hands. He would die here—they would all die here—and no one could help them.

He opened his eyes, reeling. Taleth rubbed her flank against the wall, as if she were trying to burrow her way out of the Jackal's sight. She met Bailey's eyes and roared once more.

"I'm sorry," Bailey said. *If you can just do this, we have a chance,* he thought. *He'll kill us if we don't. Do this and we live.* He concentrated on the image of her bowing again, fighting his way through the waves of fury. For a moment, she seemed to become calm, and Bailey was sure she understood him. He didn't even dare to breathe as Taleth, still as a statue, met his gaze. He wouldn't have to force her—he wouldn't have to figure out how.

Then Taleth lunged forward, straining against the chain. Paws outstretched, she tried to claw at the Jackal. Her eyes grew wide as the chain around her neck pulled her backward.

Bailey stumbled back, nearly running into the guard.

"This is more tedious than I'd thought," said the Jackal. "Where's your bond? Where's your strength?"

He waved his hand in Bailey's direction.

"We'll try again tomorrow," the Jackal said. "And you'd better have something to show me, or you can say farewell to your near-sighted friend downstairs."

With that, the Jackal walked past Bailey to the door.

The guard led Bailey back down the hall to the dining room and pushed him into one of the metal chairs. An old man hobbled in to place a plate of overcooked greens on the table, which Bailey gulped down. After, the guard hoisted him up and led him to an adjoining room with only one small window.

"Your new room," the guard said. "You'll come out only for meals and when the Jackal wants you." Then he shut the squeaking metal door.

Bailey leaned back against the stone wall and sank to the floor. He had never felt so hopeless. He'd put Taleth and Hal in danger. He longed for Tremelo, Phi, Gwen, and Tori. He wished he were back in the Lowlands, setting the table for the Midwinter feast. He wished he'd never left. The lingering sensation of Taleth's anger was still fresh. She was the last of her kind, and she might die here unless he could somehow make her understand. And if she couldn't, then Bailey had only one choice to save Hal: to become like the Dominae themselves.

Twenty~seven

TREMELO STEPPED OFF THE path from the Applied Sciences building to let pass a line of students on their way to the dorms for evening curfew. By the looks of the fading sunlight, the students had mere minutes to get to their dorms.

In the wake of Bailey and Hal's disappearance, the school was on lockdown. Ms. Shonfield had spoken to the boys' families, doing her best to keep them calm. Dr. Graves had also gone missing, and had not been seen since the night the boys had left to follow Taleth's kidnappers.

Tremelo had wanted to track Hal and Bailey immediately; he blamed himself for Bailey's recklessness. He'd failed the boy by taking off that night, but leaving the school now would only attract more questions. Tremelo was glad for the little bat who'd delivered a note a few nights after the boys' disappearance: they were safe. If Graves had gone after them, he was doing a poor job of keeping up.

Unlocking the workshop door, Tremelo grimaced at the familiar sight of the Halcyon. The machine had seen countless iterations since he'd first shown it to Bailey. He and Tori had been working nonstop—as much as the strict lockdown schedule would allow—and Tori's report about her friend Lyle's mysterious technology had been invaluable. Tonight, Tremelo hoped, they would finally see results.

As he lit the gas lamp that hung over the workbench, he heard a light tapping on the workshop's door. Tori entered, with Fennel behind her.

"Is it finished?" Tori asked.

"Just this morning," he answered, removing the fabric cover from a metal, egg-shaped orb nestled on the workbench next to the Halcyon. "I shaped the silver according to your specifications."

Tori stood on her tiptoes to see.

"It's almost exactly like Lyle's!" she said.

"Almost?"

"There's something different about the sheen," Tori said. "I'm still not sure this is the right metal—but even Lyle doesn't know what the original orb is made out of. And I didn't want to pry more than I already have."

"Worth a try, anyway," said Tremelo. "Want to do the honors?"

He moved aside so that Tori could maneuver the silver orb into a nest of wires in the middle of the Halcyon.

"There, now just attach that wire, there," he said, pointing.

Fennel trotted over to the bench, and with a hop, positioned herself next to the machine. Her white-and-red tail swished on the worn wood. Tremelo placed his hands on the orb.

"All right," he said. "Throw the switch."

Tori pressed a brass lever on the top of the machine, next to the gramophone horns. Tremelo breathed deeply. He did feel a tingling in his hands—but his connection with Fennel seemed as steady as ever. Nothing remarkable.

"Should we—" Tori faltered. "Should we try to make Fennel *do* something?"

Fennel cocked her head and then, losing interest, began to lick her paw.

"No, we shouldn't," said Tremelo, disheartened. "And we don't need to. This isn't right."

"What if I tried?" said Tori.

"We can't copy this," Tremelo said, shaking his head. "It was made by a far more clever tinkerer than myself."

"We need Lyle's orb," said Tori.

Tremelo sighed. "Yes."

"Lyle trusts me," Tori said. "I could figure out some way...."

"No," said Tremelo. "You'd be easy for Lyle to identify to the Dominae if they suspected foul play. We'll think of something, but in the meantime, get some sleep."

"So soon?" Tori asked.

"Our experiment is at a standstill," he said. "Back to your dorm with you. Take Fennel as lookout."

"Yes, I know," said Tori. "And take the woodland path, not the main path, and don't talk to strangers...."

"I shouldn't be letting you come here, with the curfews," Tremelo reminded her.

"Yep. You're a very bad influence," said Tori. "But who else would I spend time with these days?"

As the door closed quietly behind Tori, Tremelo leaned against the workbench, trying to avoid his beckoning myrgwood pipe upstairs. Since the night he'd almost abandoned the school for the mountains, he hadn't touched it. He'd even refused a fresh supply from Roger Quindley; they had exchanged letters about Hal's whereabouts. Roger had sounded equal parts distressed and proud, referring to his nephew as "a revolutionary." He promised to speak to both Hal's parents and Bailey's, and convince them that the two boys had merely snuck off the grounds on a lark, and would return as soon as they'd had their fun. Tremelo was glad that the Walkers and the Quindleys wouldn't fret—and for now, Tremelo was the one to shoulder all the worry. It was a role he didn't feel he fit into very well.

He rose from his workbench—a walk in the chilly air would do him as much good as a myrgwood pipe until he could get his hands on the Dominae's orb.

Twenty~eight

BAILEY ESTIMATED THAT A week had gone by—he'd begun to lose count of the sunrises and sunsets that lit the rectangular hole cut high into the wall of his room. The window taunted him; Bailey couldn't reach it, and he couldn't see outside.

Since that first disappointing morning, the Jackal had kept him on a steady routine: sleep in his lonely room, meals in the dining room, and hours each day of "practice."

On this morning, Bailey was awake with the dawn, huddled in the corner and rubbing his arms to keep warm. He heard the guard approach his door, and steeled himself for what was to come.

"Let's go," said the guard gruffly. Bailey followed him down a hallway, to the room where the Jackal waited.

"Good morning." The Jackal smiled as Bailey entered the room. He was sitting in a wooden chair by a small metal table, which held a beaker of liquid and a few maps. He leaned back in the chair, twisting the metal tip of his cane against the floor. "Ready for another try?"

Bailey moved his head in the smallest suggestion of a nod. In the corner, Taleth lay with her head on the floor, exhausted.

"All right, then, let's begin," the Jackal said coldly. "You know what I want—just make the tiger bow to me. Then I may decide *not* to kill you and your friend tonight."

It was the same speech he gave Bailey every morning, yet he was sure that Hal was alive—he hadn't seen him since that first night in the compound, but he'd heard the cook shuffling down to the basement with food. But Bailey wasn't sure how long either of them could hold out. The Jackal demanded he use Dominance on Taleth, and with every day that passed he grew more and more irate.

Without a word, Bailey stood facing Taleth. He felt trapped. He hoped Taleth understood. He wouldn't use Dominance on her— he wasn't even sure that he could—but he'd need her help to keep the Jackal at bay, at least until the Fair, when they'd have a better chance of escape.

"What are you waiting for?" the Jackal demanded, hitting a fist against the table. His cup rattled. "A week of this nonsense! What's stopping you?"

"Sorry," mumbled Bailey. He said it to appease the Jackal, but he was most sorry for Taleth. For what he needed her to do. It was too much to ask.

Just bow. Just once. He'll keep us alive. Please.

As he did each time, he pictured her bowing to the Jackal, hoping that she would understand. He imagined the Jackal's pleased sneer and the way his scar would curve up above the corner of his mouth. He felt like he might throw up. Taleth rubbed the side of her face against the stone, and then dragged herself to her feet. Bailey held his breath. Their eyes met.

Please, he thought. Please.

Taleth growled, and lay back down.

"Mangy beast!" the Jackal shouted. "I'm tired of this—you disappoint me, boy. It happens today, happens *now*, or you *all* die, and the prophecy dies with you."

Bailey's desperation felt like a small animal clawing its way up his arms. He didn't know what to do. He was exhausted and frightened. They couldn't keep on like this, or they'd never make it out of the compound with their lives.

"Do it, boy!" the Jackal snarled, mere inches from Bailey's ear.

I'm sorry, I'm sorry, Bailey thought. Taleth's fur shuddered. I'm sorry, Bailey thought again, deliberately forming each word in his mind as though he were carefully writing her a letter. I'm *asking* you. Please do this. It's the only way we'll survive.

He tried a new tactic—he imagined the mountains where Taleth had come from, where Bailey's people, the Velyn, still lived. He pictured the soft, stately pines and the craggy rocks covered with rust-colored moss. He visualized his bond with Taleth as a ball of light, growing brighter. He concentrated harder on his memories of the woods outside Fairmount. The sound of damp leaves underfoot. The smell of clean, cold air. *We can go back there, but I need your help. Please . . .*

Taleth turned her massive head from side to side as though protesting, and Bailey felt his heart sink. But then she got back to her feet and growled. Bailey felt his concentration falter. He squeezed his eyes shut, refusing to let the humming he felt inside of himself die again.

"Do it," he said out loud, his teeth gritted. The energy grew in intensity, so that Bailey felt as though his skin were vibrating. He opened his eyes. "Do it," he pleaded.

Taleth growled again, but then she backed away, never taking her eyes off Bailey. With a graceful arch of her back, she lowered her forehead to the floor in an unmistakable bow.

The Jackal clapped delightedly.

"Well done!" he cheered, slapping Bailey hard on the back.

Bailey watched, racked with shame and dizzy with relief, as Taleth padded to the corner of the room with her tail curled underneath. Her shoulders were hunched as she lay down, peering at him with tired eyes.

As the guard walked Bailey back to the dining room, Bailey tried desperately to make sense of what had just happened. But he'd never felt his bond become so intense, just by his own will. And he'd certainly never seen Taleth do anything that she so clearly did not want to do. He'd ask Tremelo, later, once they were free, how different the bond truly was from Dominance. Because he couldn't use Dominance. He would never . . .

He tried to concentrate instead on the one piece of hope he had: his secret.

Just as he had every day for the past week, Bailey finished his food and waited patiently, silently, for the cook to take his plate away. As soon as the door closed, Bailey knew he had mere seconds before it opened again, and a guard would enter to take Bailey back to his room.

Quickly, he dashed to the corner of the dining room, to the

pile of broken, discarded Clamoribus parts he'd seen on his first night in the compound. He grabbed whatever he could and stuck it into his pockets as he rushed back to his seat.

The door opened, and the guard shot him a blank, thuggish look.

Bailey stared at the table in front of him, taking care not to glance toward the pile of parts in the dim corner. It had grown smaller and smaller over the past week without any of the guards noticing.

After being led to his room, he eagerly emptied his pockets. Several small gears and springs came out—and a polished metal button that Bailey instantly knew was the starter. He rummaged in the darkest corner of his room and removed a loose stone from the bottom of the wall, then pulled out a scrap of fabric holding the other parts. The body of the bird was mostly reconstructed— one wing still lay on the floor of the mess hall, waiting for him. He placed the polished black button in a circular space in the metal bird's belly, and felt a satisfying click. The machine whirred, and with a burst of joy, Bailey heard the recording device inside the bird spin to life. Hope grew in his chest. He looked up at the window that mocked him, and, for the first time in many days, he smiled.

Twenty~nine

EACH DAY, THE SEERS' Glass glowed brighter.

"What do you think it means?" Gwen asked Phi as they hiked carefully along a steep ravine. The landscape had changed over the course of the last week, from steep but walkable mountainsides to narrow paths between jutting, angry rocks. Climbing had become painstakingly slow and treacherous.

"You would know better than I would," answered Phi. "Though I've noticed you don't like to look at it."

Gwen shook her head.

"It scares me," she said. "I'm sure it has something to do with the Instrument of Change, but each time I look at it, it only makes me nervous. My heart starts beating so wildly, and I almost feel like it's watching me or *calling* to me."

"I know that feeling," murmured Phi.

"You do?" asked Gwen.

Phi stopped walking and bent to adjust her boot.

"I know that sounds crazy," she said. "But I didn't just leave Fairmount because I wanted to help you—I do, of course. And I missed you too."

Gwen felt herself blushing.

"I *am* glad for the company," she admitted.

"I didn't tell Bailey this," Phi continued, "or Tremelo. They'd have only worried. But someone—something—was watching me at the school. I never saw them, but I heard rustling outside my dorm room almost every night. And I think someone was going through my things." She stood straight again and walked on. Gwen fell into step behind her.

"I made the decision to leave to protect the others," Phi said. "But I don't know if it did any good at all. The Dominae could still be watching *all* of us."

As they climbed, every sound on the mountain made Gwen jump. She wondered whether the Dominae was after the Instrument of Change too—and if it could be the key to ending Dominance once and for all.

"Why you?" Gwen asked her, as they edged along a cliff top overlooking the valley.

"I think I know," said Phi. "But you have to promise not to be mad."

"I promise," said Gwen, growing worried.

Phi leaned back against the rock face and opened the lapel of her coat. Pinned to the lining was a sparkling blue-and-green brooch in the shape of a blossoming flower.

"It belonged to Sucrette," said Phi.

Gwen gasped.

"You stole it?"

"No! I mean—yes, I did," Phi said. "But it's not why you think. . . ."

"Why, then?" asked Gwen.

"We were right there when she died," said Phi. "And I can't help but think: we *would* have killed her if those animals hadn't! It's so horrifying! I don't ever want to forget that. She was a person, and we were involved in her death. I can't pretend it never happened. So this reminds me."

Gwen breathed in deeply. She understood what Phi meant— the memory of Sucrette's grisly death upset her too. But she also remembered the Elder lying on the snowy forest ground, urging them to be brave. The kingdom needed them. Phi was sensitive; it made her vulnerable.

"You have to take it off," said Gwen. "Someone at Fairmount must have seen you wearing it."

Phi nodded.

"But I can't get rid of it," she replied. "Not yet. I—I can't explain it, but I don't want it lost in the mountains."

"Then you'll have to keep it hidden," Gwen insisted. She kicked at a rock, sad and angry all at once. But then, plunging her hands into her traveling coat pocket, she touched Melore's harmonica. Relics, reminders—they meant something, it was true. The Elder had known that.

"I will," Phi promised, pulling her coat tightly closed.

When they'd finally found each other, they had both assumed that the path would come to an end soon. But the air had grown much thinner in the last days of their journey, and the path had become so steep they climbed a cliff face that was nearly vertical.

Carin and the owls flew ahead each time, urging them with hoots and cries from the top of the rocks. Days came and went quickly, and each night Gwen lay awake, counting her sore muscles until she could count no higher.

And each morning, Gwen unwrapped the wolf pelt to check on the Glass, and found it glowing brighter and brighter.

Finally, on a foggy morning, Gwen and Phi ascended the highest peak, and pulled themselves over the edge of a black rock to find a desolate cave.

"This is it," Gwen whispered—the first words she'd spoken all day. They'd reached the mountaintop. She helped Phi to her feet, and together they faced the mouth of the cave. Gwen's heart raced at the sight of the cave—she feared the dark, enclosed space. Phi was scared too.

"Maybe there's a way around?" Phi asked.

Something moved toward them from the shadows. Gwen grabbed Phi's hand as a wolf the size of a bear padded out. It was all white, with blue eyes. It lowered its head and growled. Carin and the owls flew protectively low over the girls, and Gwen stepped in front of Phi in a useless attempt to shield her. Her mouth had gone completely dry. She frantically looked around the rocks for a means of escape.

To the girls' horror, another wolf followed the first out of the cave, this one just as large and just as angry. Gwen held her breath, hardly believing that this was their journey's end—to be attacked by vicious white wolves. Behind her and Phi, the rocks they'd just climbed dropped quickly down a steep ravine. There was nowhere to go.

Shhhh...

The noise was so quiet, so subtle, that when Gwen finally noticed it, she wasn't sure when it had begun.

The wolves stopped their growling, but they didn't take their light blue eyes off Gwen and Phi. Around their feet, the earth moved. At least, that was what Gwen thought she saw.

The hissing noise was the sound of the ground trembling and coming alive.

Phi gasped, and backed away a step.

"Spiders!"

Gwen could see them now, hundreds of them—tiny white spiders crawling along the stony bottom of the cave, glistening in the soft sunlight as they emerged to greet the girls. The wolves moved out of their way as the spiders massed forward eagerly.

"Oh, Nature!" breathed Gwen.

The white spiders clambered around the girls' boots and the hem of Gwen's traveling coat. Gwen stiffened as the spiders passed over and around her feet.

"Gwen, look!" said Phi, pointing to the mouth of the cave.

Walking behind the spiders like a queen at the end of a procession was a woman. She had white hair, piled wildly on top of her head, with wisps floating out behind her as she walked. She searched the rock for Gwen and Phi with eyes the color of fresh milk. She was blind.

"Come closer," the woman said, somehow knowing that they were there.

Gwen moved her right foot forward, looking down to see the spiders cascade away from her to make a path. She didn't know who this woman was, or what she wanted, but she felt compelled forward by a force very like the bond itself. She sensed comfort from this person. Gwen approached the woman, who was no taller than she was. The woman wore a long gray dress woven out of delicate fibers that shimmered in the light. Spiderwebs. She raised her hands and began to touch Gwen's cheeks and forehead, and the tip of her nose.

"My dear," she said, searching Gwen's face with her spindly fingers. "Here you are at last."

Thirty

GWEN SQUINTED AS THE woman led them into the mouth
of the cave, then stopped as though she'd forgotten something.
Reaching toward the stone wall, the Animas Spider felt around for
a metal lantern hanging on a hook. A flare of bluish light appeared.
Strands of silky spiderwebs glistened on the walls and rocks.

"That should make the way easier for you," the woman said
softly.

Gwen and Phi followed, with the blue light casting shadows
that danced and shone.

"Are you a Seer?" Gwen asked, though part of her didn't dare
believe. "An advisor to the old king sent me here. We called him
the Elder, and he told me I'd find something…" She trailed off,
wondering how much they could trust her.

The woman simply turned and beckoned with her bone-white
hand. Gwen remained silent.

They walked until the light from the mouth of the cave had disappeared, and then they walked even farther. The air remained chilly, and Gwen tugged the sleeves of her coat down over her fingers. Finally, the tunnel opened up, and the light from the woman's lamp illuminated a tall, rocky ceiling, full of downward-reaching stalactites. The room had been constructed by Nature herself, but it appeared as grand and solemn as any of the great halls of Parliament. Both Gwen and Phi craned their necks to gaze at the glistening ceiling.

"You live here?" asked Phi.

The woman nodded, and gestured to a table and chairs nearby. The furniture was made of crude, heavy wood. Gwen and Phi sat down.

"What's your name?" asked Gwen.

"We stopped using names long ago," said the woman. "They are of little use to us."

Gwen started—the old woman spoke firmly, and the sound of her voice echoed off the rocks.

"You asked if I am a Seer—that's what we are called, out there in Aldermere, yes. There are other Seers too, somewhere," the woman continued. "We do not visit one another often. The caves are deep."

"How many of you are left?" asked Gwen. Phi, sitting next to her, stared openmouthed at the lofty stone ceiling. The birds had not followed them inside.

"We do not make it our business to peer into one another's doings," she said. "But I believe there are others still alive. I would know if their lights had dimmed." She thought for a moment, and then smiled. "If you must call me something, you may call me Ama."

Ama knelt at a small fireplace in the rock, and after a moment, a small fire flared under her bony hands. Ama felt along the wall, then grabbed ahold of a metal arm affixed to the rock, and hung a copper teakettle on it.

"I am sorry if the wolves frightened you," Ama continued. "They are Velyn kin, lent to me for protection. While *I* may have known that you were expected guests, *they* did not." Gwen wondered how many guests a blind Seer entertained, alone under a mountain. Not many, she thought.

"Are you all alone here?" Gwen asked. "Does anyone live here with you?"

Ama shook her head. "Others cloud the sight. I have a visitor every—oh, year or so. More lately. But too much talk makes my light dim."

She walked over to the table with a small metal tray balanced on her hands. Three mismatched porcelain cups wobbled on it, filled with steaming tea. Ama set the tray down on the wooden table and gestured for the girls to take their pick. Dazed, Gwen gingerly picked a mug with an etched design of gold and yellow flowers. It was fine porcelain except for a chip in the handle. She wondered if the cups had come from the palace. A gift, maybe, from a long-dead king.

"You said we were expected," said Phi. "You knew that Gwen was coming to see you?"

"Oh, yes," said Ama. The light from the suspended lantern reflected in her milky eyes.

"Maybe you can tell me about the Instrument of Change," Gwen said, feeling her trust toward Ama growing. "The Elder—maybe you knew him—told me that I would find it here."

Ama nodded, and raised an eyebrow in recognition.

"The Elder, yes. He was a friend to the Seers. I was sorry to learn of his passing," she murmured. "And the Instrument of Change *is* here."

Gwen felt her heart jump.

"Please," she said, "tell me what I need to do. Tremelo—the king—he needs it, and I'm the one who has to bring it to him."

Ama leaned forward and pointed, unseeing, to Gwen's pack.

"Your Glass is calling to you, my dear," she said. "It's almost singing with joy, just for you to answer."

"What?" said Gwen. She brought her pack around to her front and dug in it for the fur-bound Glass. Carefully, she unfolded it and set it on the table in front of Ama. In the dimness of the cave, the stone still retained a soft glow, but it didn't emit a sound.

"I don't understand. Does it have something to do with the Instrument?" she asked.

Ama nodded.

"You can feel it beckoning to you, can't you?" she asked Gwen.

"It's glowing," Gwen admitted. "It has been for days. What does it mean? Is it—is it yours?"

Ama passed her hand over the Glass, but did not touch it.

"This does not belong to me," she said. She reached into her silvery spun dress, and took out a Glass identical to Gwen's. "Every Seer has their own. Your Glass belongs to you, just as this Glass belongs to me."

She set hers down on the table next to Gwen's.

"Every Seer has an instrument, Gwendolyn—that of true

sight. You cannot change what you are. *You* are a Seer, like me. How you use the instrument given to you is your choice. You have my guidance, if you want it. The Elder wished it so."

Gwen tried to take a deep breath, but found that she couldn't. The air seemed very thin. She turned to Phi.

"Are you all right?" Phi asked.

"I don't understand," said Gwen. "The Elder . . ."

"He saw the light in you years ago," Ama said. Gwen felt her heart fill will bittersweet joy. "He said that you would not believe him if he told you what you are. But he knew you would find me if he asked. He knew your love for him. Do not doubt that he treasured it."

Gwen felt a tear slide down her cheek. She looked down at the Glass, which pulsated a greenish-purple light. She felt dizzy.

"Gwen!" breathed Phi. "You're a Seer!"

Ama reached out and grabbed Gwen's hand. The Seer's fingers were dry and cool, and felt so delicate that Gwen was afraid of breaking them.

"The light grows, daughter," Ama whispered. Her white hair spilled over her face, obscuring one cloudy eye. "Don't be afraid."

And indeed, Gwen did see a growing light. At first, she thought that the Glass was becoming brighter, but it was filling her entire vision—almost too bright to bear. She wanted to hold her arm in front of her eyes.

"Don't be afraid," whispered the blind woman once more.

Her voice sounded very far away. The brightness took hold, and shapes began to form in the light.

The first image that Gwen saw was the tiny owl who had saved her life on the mountainside by showing her the poisoned berries. Melem. The owl's name manifested on her tongue as if the owl itself had placed it there.

Then came the screams.

Gwen stood in the middle of a crowd. All around her, animals lunged at their human kin with teeth, claws, and talons. The humans were confused and panicked, and began fighting back.

Suddenly, her vision was only Melem, her yellow eyes wide and steely, her talons aimed at Gwen's face. Gwen put up her arms to protect herself, all the while sending her intentions out into the air: *Don't hurt me; I am part of you.* But she felt no connection. Her chest ached with a feeling of being torn in two. Her bond was bending and wrenching itself into something terrible. Melem screeched, and bit at Gwen's hair and ears.

Then Gwen felt her bow secure in her hands; an arrow was firmly nocked against the string. She aimed the arrow's tip at Melem's feathered chest, and she shot. The owl shrieked and shuddered in front of her, falling from the sky to the muddy ground, where it lay staring at her with unseeing eyes. Gwen heard a pounding, like the ticking of a huge, awful clock. She covered her ears—it was so loud—and fell into darkness.

When she awoke, Phi knelt over her. Ama still sat in her chair with her back against the rock.

"It's all right," said Phi. "You're all right."

She'd fallen to the floor, and lay with her head propped on Phi's knapsack. At her feet lay her own rucksack, as well as the bow and quiver of arrows. She shuddered at the sight of them.

"Was that real?" she asked Ama of the nightmare she'd experienced. "Was that the future?"

Ama did not answer.

Gwen sat up, taking Phi's offered arm.

"What did you see?" Phi asked.

"It was terrible," said Gwen. "I was in the city, and there were so many people. They were all in pain. Everyone was gathered together, and the animals...they were attacking. It was Dominance, but stronger than I've ever seen it."

"The Fair," Phi whispered. "Viviana's Reckoning."

"Can I stop this?" Gwen looked to Ama. "It was only a vision, but the future can be changed, can't it?"

Ama stirred in her seat.

"'True sight is a light that grows—your sight is strengthened and made clear by true bonds. You see what lives unseen in the heart,'" Ama recited. Gwen felt calmed by those familiar words—though the Elder's note hadn't included the last line.

"What lives unseen in the heart..." repeated Gwen. "So, then, that wasn't the future, but what Viviana wants in her heart to happen?"

Ama reached for Gwen's hand. "It is a terrible thing to see the future," she said, clutching a chipped cup of pale orange tea in one hand, and Gwen's fingers in the other. "But altering it is not your task."

"But can it be done? Can I change it?" asked Gwen.

"I cannot stop you from trying," said Ama.

"I *will* change this," said Gwen. "I can't let it happen. If I reach the Gray in time and find Tremelo, we can stop her. We can destroy the machine. Can't you tell me how?"

Ama gazed at her sadly.

"The Elder spoke of your bravery," she said. "The Instrument of

Change, that is the name that *he* called you. But you cannot change everything, daughter. Some grief will come to pass, no matter your choice. I tried to tell the Elder this."

"I don't believe that," said Gwen. Her heart had filled with longing at Ama's mention of the Elder. He had led her here so that she could discover something remarkable, unbelievable, about herself—only to see that the way ahead would be just as hard, and full of doubt. "I have to change it. I have to *try*, or the Elder's death meant nothing."

Ama nodded.

The Glass's light had ebbed where it sat on Ama's table. Gwen picked it up, half expecting it to be hot to the touch. She still had so many questions.

"Will I . . ." She bit her tongue. Ama tilted her head, listening for the end of a question that, perhaps, she had already guessed.

"Will I become blind like you? Is it only by choice that you live here?" Gwen didn't think she could do it. She couldn't abandon the ones she loved.

Ama was quiet for a moment. Her fragile fingers wrapped themselves around her nearly empty cup of tea.

"The Instrument of Change. A new Seer, for a new time," she said. "Where you abide is your choice to make. Though you may find, once others know of your gift, that solitude is welcome. As for your worldly sight . . ." She pursed her lips in thought. "Take care of your eyes, when you can. The light takes its toll. Perhaps you'll find you need to look into your Glass less and less. For most of us, the temptation to look is too great, and we pay the price."

"When the Elder came last fall, it was you who told him that Viviana was coming, wasn't it?" Gwen said, the thought just occurring to her. "So you do try to change the future—through others."

Ama smiled again. "Each in her own way, I suppose. Now, if your intention is to reach the Gray before the Reckoning, then you cannot linger."

"I don't want to go," said Gwen. "I want to help my friends, but I have so many questions for you!"

"You would find my answers disappointing, child," said Ama. "You have everything you need to answer your own questions. You always have. Now, go. I must rest."

Gwen edged away from the table, shouldering her pack and her bow.

"Thank you for the tea," she said, though this seemed like a silly thing to say to someone like Ama. "Thank you for everything." Then she nodded at Phi, and started toward the dark uphill tunnel.

"Wait," said Ama, still sitting. She held her hand out to Phi, her white palm open. "Your secrets are safe here, Sophia Castling. We Seers never forget the dead."

Phi seemed to understand right away what Ama was asking of her. She unpinned Sucrette's brooch from the inside lapel of her coat, and placed it in Ama's bony hand.

"You dream of another form, Nature's child," Ama continued, as matter-of-factly as if she were reading a story out loud. "Your wings are possible. You will find them soon."

Ama stood, drawing her bent self up to her full height. She seemed much taller now to Gwen than when they had first seen her at the mouth of the cave.

"And when you do, Sophia, take care. You may give up too much, when you turn away from your true self."

The girls said good-bye and left the cavern, climbing the steep, pebble-laden path side by side.

"What was she talking about, turning away from your true self?" Gwen asked.

Phi shrugged. "Not sure..." she said, but her eyes were far away again.

The rest of the way through the cave was spent in silence. Gwen's hands still trembled at the thought of her vision. The screams, the terror—it was too much for her heart to bear. And that awful pounding sound that had echoed throughout the nightmare, like blood pumping through veins... It wouldn't leave her ears.

"How are we going to get all the way back to the city in such a short time?" asked Phi, finally.

Gwen remained silent, her thoughts turned inward. She was a Seer. *She* was the Instrument of Change. But what was she supposed to do to make change happen?

As they reached the mouth of the cave, she began to feel uneasy. The owls traveling with them were now swooping around the peak, excited by a new presence.

"Wait here," she said to Phi, gesturing for her to stay back. She edged along the cave wall to the entrance. Even before she peered around the rock, she could hear the sounds of animals breathing and pawing the ground.

"Hello?" called a voice from the clearing outside the cave. It was familiar.

With her arrow tight on the bowstring, Gwen emerged from the shadow of the cave. Before her was no Dominae spy at all, but the tall, fur-clad warrior, Eneas Fourclaw. On either side of him stood the snowy wolves who had menaced them earlier. Now they looked calm, almost docile. Behind Eneas were at least thirty Velyn men and women with their kin. They were laden with packs and cook pots, spears and bows and arrows and swords. They looked as though they had been traveling as long as she had—or for many years longer.

"The wolves tell us you're in need of an escort across the Peaks," Eneas said. "We would not let you travel alone."

Thirty~one

VIVIANA WATCHED AS HER chief tinkerer made a final inspection of the improved white tiger automaton. She stood in the doorframe of what had once been Parliament's assembly room. It made a rather spacious tinkering lab.

Viviana's mind churned—only a fortnight until the Fair, and none of her various traps had yet caught their prey. Just when her efforts at tracking Sophia Castling had begun, the girl's trail had gone cold. She had not, it seemed, been headed for the Dust Plains at all—and Viviana's contact at the school had either been too stupid or too slow to realize it. Viviana's hands clenched, as though to tighten themselves around a throat, whenever she thought of this failure; her spy would have much to answer for at the Fair. But even more distressing, and more immediate: she felt she could no longer trust the earnest efforts of the thin, long-faced man polishing the metal tiger in front of her very eyes.

"You have a son, Clarke?" Viviana asked, although she was already well aware of this fact.

"I do. His name is Lyle."

"A good student, I'm sure," she said. "Eager to learn from his father."

"I'd like to think so," answered Clarke. He stood back from the automaton. "There we are, completely reassembled. The tiger is ready for the Fair. Would you care for a demonstration, my lady?"

"Please," murmured Viviana, stepping forward into the room.

Clarke turned to fetch a small controller with a red-jeweled handle from his worktable. He handed the controller to Viviana, and, before he could even move his hand away, Viviana pressed a button.

The mechanical tiger's eyes lit up—a manufactured, glowing red. It growled, and turned its heavy metal head toward Clarke. Clarke went pale and backed up against the wall.

"My lady?" he asked, frightened.

Viviana's mind was a swarm of buzzing bees. The automaton crouched, then raised itself up on its hind legs.

It swiped at Clarke before he could duck. Clarke screamed as the tiger's steel claws left three deep slashes across his face. As the tiger backed away, Viviana stepped forward.

Clarke held his bleeding face in his palms.

"You've let some prototypes of the Catalyst go astray," Viviana said. "Sending them to a nest of children as though they were toys! You risk exposing us!"

She pushed Clarke's hands aside. The tiger had narrowly missed his left eye. Clarke whimpered in anguish as Viviana took his chin in her hand and forced him to look at her straight on.

"You're an arrogant man, Clarke," said Viviana. "And you need a reminder of whom you serve."

Clarke groaned; it sounded almost like an apology under layers of anguish. She let go of his hands, which he pressed against his face.

"It was just a test model, my lady—I didn't think any harm ... I'm sorry. . . ." he whimpered.

"You will live out the rest of your days with caution. No more prototypes sent to places where they can be found by meddling children. Your life, and that of your son, will last only until I decide you are no longer useful. Until then, you will be a shadow. Reckon, Inc. is under my command now."

Thirty~two

TREMELO SAT ON A stone bench outside the Fairmount library, smoking a pipeful of tobacco. To any passing student, he appeared to be enjoying the crisp March air. But in actuality, he kept a close watch on the entrance to the Mathematics and Medicine building. Viviana's Reckoning would take place in a little over one week, and he and Tori were about to add the last necessary piece to the Halcyon—if they could get their hands on it.

The bells in the Fairmount clock tower struck three. He rose from the bench and strode through the imposing marble archways of the building.

Students exiting their classrooms streamed past him as he climbed a set of large marble stairs to the second floor. Hal and Bailey were still missing, but the attitude of the Fairmount student body at large had shifted from fear to annoyance. Students whined openly about curfew, and more than one teacher had lately shirked their chaperone duties in favor of an early supper or warm fire. As he neared the large windows that looked out from the hall to the clock tower, Tremelo saw Tori standing in a recessed nook with a slim, black-haired boy—Lyle Clarke. Tremelo approached slowly, careful not to confront them too soon.

"Can I hold it?" he heard Tori ask. Lyle looked up to survey the hallway, and Tremelo quickly pretended to be reading a metal plaque on the wall next to him marking a room number.

"Just be quick," the boy said, so quietly that Tremelo barely heard him at all over the din of students.

When he turned, Tori cupped a metal, egglike orb in her hands. It appeared to be constructed of silver, with a seam through its middle that suggested another layer inside. Tremelo walked quickly over to the pair.

"And what's this, Miss Colubride?" he said loudly, employing his most authoritative, professorial tone. "You two aren't supposed to be on your own. And what's that?"

"It's for an experiment, Mr. Tremelo," Tori said. Lyle's eyes darted from Tremelo to the orb, but Tori was relishing her part in this little piece of theater. "For . . . Mr. Millstone's class." She looked at Lyle, who nodded fervently.

"Yes, for a class," he agreed.

Tremelo held out his hand for the orb.

"I happen to know that Millstone is only covering acids and bases in his Chemistry course this week," he said. "And I *don't* appreciate being lied to."

Tori's eyes met Tremelo's as she handed him the orb. This was going smoother than either of them could have hoped. Pretending to be sheepish, Tori folded her head and looked down at the floor. But Lyle stepped forward brashly.

"You can't take it," he said. "My father sent it to me, and he's very important...."

"Your father sent you a potent piece of machinery, which could do significant damage if used incorrectly. It has no place in a student's possession."

Tremelo turned the orb carefully, studying it. The metal seemed to tingle and grow warm against his fingers. Mr. Clarke, whoever he was, was tinkering with some dangerous energies.

"I'll need to take a close look at this before returning it by post to your father." He wrapped the orb up hastily and placed it in his blazer pocket. "Miss Colubride, Mr. Clarke. Be more careful in the future—this is no plaything."

He walked quickly away from the bright hallway windows, and reached his cluttered office with no trouble. Fennel waited patiently on his desk.

Several minutes passed before the door opened and Tori entered in a gust of adrenaline.

"Ants alive, he's upset!" she said.

"Let's just hope he doesn't contact his father right away," said Tremelo. "We'll need time to test this in the Halcyon."

"I don't think he *will* tell," said Tori. She lowered her voice and cast a sidelong glance at the workshop door. "As soon as you left, he went all shaky and said if anyone knew the orb was here, the Dominae would come after it."

"He might be right," said Tremelo.

"He's worried about his dad," she said. "Lyle's last letter to him was returned unopened. Lyle's afraid the Dominae found out that Mr. Clarke was sending prototypes to him. If we're found with this thing, promise me we won't tell anyone where we got it."

Tremelo placed a hand on her shoulder. The verve he'd witnessed in her earlier had given way to genuine worry for her friend.

"I promise," he said.

Tremelo unwrapped the orb. As he picked it up, the skin along his arm began to tingle, and his hair stood on end as he carefully inserted the orb into the Halcyon. The orb's potency struck him immediately: just touching it, he felt his senses heighten, and as soon as he threw the switch on the side of the Halcyon, the gramophone erupted in strains of beautiful music. Pure energy poured out of the machine.

"It's ingenious," Tremelo murmured, losing himself in the pull of new technology. "Kinetic electro-current contained within a highly conductive, yet virtually indestructible metal . . ."

"Tremelo," Tori said, folding her arms across her chest. "Slow down and explain."

He steeled himself and tried again.

"This metal is special. It's similar to silver, but with even stronger properties . . . I've never seen it," he began. "This little orb amplifies energy, even the bond itself. Amazing . . . and frightening."

Tori tilted her head and listened solemnly. Fennel sat on the desk, studying the machine along with them.

"My machine, in its original form, amplifies the energy of the Animas bond. When Fennel and I are connected to the machine, our souls communicate."

Tremelo smiled, thinking of the otherworldly music that it

created. Calming and beautiful—just as the bond was supposed to be.

"That energy leaves the machine as a wavelength you can hear, like music. It has the power to strengthen the bond, just the way Gwen's harmonica playing did before. But a machine fed by Dominance would create the opposite effect, spreading discord and mayhem.

"We saw what Sucrette was able to do with no assistance—it must have been twenty different animals she was controlling in the woods last fall. With something like this machine, a Dominae as strong as Sucrette could control fifty times that many, a hundred times, even! And we can be sure that Viviana is extremely powerful."

"What would she want to do with that many animals at once?" asked Tori.

"I don't know," said Tremelo. "I don't even want to imagine. But if the orb can be used to strengthen the bond as well as warp it, we can use our Halcyon to counteract Viviana's machine. I just hope that this prototype is as forceful as the one she'll have at the Fair."

Tori shrieked, and Tremelo jumped in his chair. He looked up from the Halcyon to see her gaping at the office window.

"It's one of those things," she said, leaving her chair and backing away to the far wall of the office. "One of those metal birds of hers—it's spying on us!"

Tremelo marched to the window, and immediately recoiled. Tori was right—a massive metal crow, easily four times the size of a real bird, perched ominously on the tree branch outside. It stared straight at Tremelo with cold black eyes. Something in the inner mechanics of the bird clicked and whirred, and its metal beak squeaked open.

Tremelo! the bird said, in a familiar voice.

It's me; it's Bailey! If this reaches you, then I actually put this thing back together right!

Tremelo leaned forward on the window ledge for support; the sound of Bailey's voice from this fearful contraption floored him. He was relieved, but he feared what would come next. Tori crept forward, and together they stood, listening.

We've been kidnapped, Hal and I, by the Jackal—he's got us in a compound in the Dust Plains, but he plans to take us to the Progress Fair.

Tori gasped, but remained quiet.

I can't talk long. But I needed to warn you—he'll be at the Fair, ready to start a war. It's time to act. You have to find the Velyn and convince Eneas to help you. Maybe if they know that the Jackal will be there, they'll be willing to fight. Please, find them, and the RATS too—bring everyone you can!

The machine stopped its whirring. Its eyes, which had been flickering red while the recorded voice had played, died like the last embers of a fire.

"The Jackal," breathed Tori. "I thought he was dead!"

Tremelo shook his head. Anger burbled inside him.

"Parliament imprisoned him in the Dust Plains," he said. "But it was only a matter of time before he gained influence out there, with so many outlaws who crave chaos instead of order."

"What can we do?" Tori asked. "We can't stop Viviana's machine if we have to fight the Dominae *and* the Jackal to do it. We'd need an army!"

Tremelo turned back to the desk. The Fair would take place the following Saturday. Time was slipping away too quickly.

"Bailey's right about the Velyn. If the Jackal will be there, they might return and fight with us," he said. "But they're far out in the Peaks. I don't know how I'd get word to them." He put his hand to his forehead, and tried to wish away the urge to retreat to his quarters, and into a pint of rootwort rum.

Tori sidled up to him.

"We couldn't get word to them by rigi or cable in time." She looked up at him with a hopeful smile on her face. "But Bailey didn't just send you a message. He sent you the perfect way to reach your army."

Thirty~three

THE FOLLOWING SATURDAY BROUGHT a blanket of heavy clouds with its arrival, casting a pallid glow over the Gray City. Just north of the capital, the Progress Fair bustled. Canvas tents lined the open field, each one housing a different tinkerer's inventions. At the far end of the space, the Scavage pitch had been cultivated with imported plants and shrubs from the southernmost tip of the kingdom, transforming it into a lush terrain. And between the exhibition tents and the field was a raised stage, where Viviana would make her speech to the crowds gathered in the stands that afternoon.

Citizens from all corners of Aldermere passed between vendors' tents, and in the corridors, children wearing paper crowns and collars made of garlands played tag with animals and munched happily on roasted seeds and candied apples. Outside one giant pavilion, a sign invited patrons in to SEE THE WONDERS OF THE FUTURE, while a scale model of an updated rigimotive engine looped on a track in and out of the tent's entrance.

Tremelo paced among the booths, studying each odd invention for any sign of Viviana's Reckoning machine, in case it was hidden in the crowd. But all he observed in the exhibition tents were too many automated knife sharpeners and one complicated electro-current device that would make a bed.

At the end of the row of tents was the area where the Science Competition would take place. Students stood proudly behind several tables showcasing their work. Among them was Tori with the Halcyon.

"Feeling confident, Miss Colubride?" Tremelo asked as he returned to the tables.

"Oh, yes, sir," said Tori, smiling widely for the benefit of the students and teachers gathered around the display area. "I think I've definitely got a winner here."

As it had for several weeks, the Halcyon appeared to be an elaborate music box, with gramophone horns reaching up from a square encasement. The orb—the final piece—was safe in Tremelo's coat pocket. He patted Tori on the shoulder and retreated behind the display area, where his motorbuggy was parked. He'd volunteered to chaperone some of the more delicate student competition entries up to the Gray from Fairmount, which allowed him to bring along a trunk that could hold any number of useful weaponry. He'd also brought Bert, who was napping on the passenger seat.

Tremelo's spot was barely visible from the central stage.

Viviana would be addressing the crowd in an hour. Only an hour to find Bailey, locate the Reckoning machine, and counteract its effects with their Halcyon.

A mechanical bird caw sounded over the hubbub of the fair-goers, and a flank of Dominae guards, all dressed in gray uniforms, marched down the main thoroughfare between the tents. Three Clamoribus birds perched on angled staffs held aloft by guards leading the march. Behind the solemn guards, a welcoming smile drawn wide across her all-too-familiar face, was Viviana. Tremelo took a deep, calming breath, which did not, in fact, calm him at all. Viviana was headed directly toward the Science Competition tables.

"Mr. Loren!" called a cheery voice. Jerri, Shonfield's assistant, approached him. His customary clipboard was held closely to his chest, and his brass spectacles were slightly askew on his angular nose. "Are you mentoring any of our entrants in today's competition?" he asked.

"Just observing," Tremelo said. He stood on his tiptoes, trying to keep one eye on Viviana.

"Ah, yes," murmured Jerri, following his gaze. "Commanding, isn't she?"

"*Hmm,*" hummed Tremelo, hardly listening.

Jerri waved—Ms. Shonfield was hustling over, squeezing her way through the mass of citizens and students jostling to get a look at Viviana.

"Here we are, Jerri," she said. "Viviana and the judges are coming 'round. Who's first on the list to present?"

Jerri consulted his clipboard.

"Colubride, Victoria."

"Tori? Now?" Tremelo asked. Out of the corner of his eye, he watched the procession surrounding Viviana draw closer to the students' tables.

"Certainly," said Jerri. "Best to start off strong when the quality's watching!" He cocked his head toward the oncoming Dominae, and followed Shonfield to Tori's table. Tremelo stayed close, trying to hide his shaking hands in his pockets. An older gentleman with a white goatee and a woman wearing a slightly askew purple cap approached from Viviana's party: the judges. As they, along with Shonfield and Jerri, admired the Halcyon, a worried Tremelo caught Tori's eye. To his surprise, she winked.

"The Halcyon plays randomly generated musical notes, depending on the listener's Animas, and the strength of their connection with their kin," said Tori. She'd expertly rehearsed what to say.

"How lovely," Shonfield said, eyeing the two sour-faced judges. "Could we hear a demonstration?"

"Of course!" Tori laid her beaded bag on the tabletop and two black snakes emerged. They nosed around the base of the Halcyon, then slid into a niche in the side of the machine. Here, where the interior metal connected to a series of sensitive wires, the snakes curled into sleek spirals. Tori fastened a metal cuff around her wrist. The Halcyon began to emit strains of music—in Tori's case, the chords were just slightly off-tone, but beautiful, almost mischievous. Tremelo smiled. The crowd in front of the tables parted, and he saw Viviana. Her eyes darted as though she was looking for the source of the strange sound. Then she placed a hand on her temple to shield her eyes, shook her head slightly, and walked on. Tremelo breathed out a gust of air that he hadn't even realized he'd been holding in.

"*Oof,*" exhaled Ms. Shonfield, as the judges moved to the next table. "Enough pressure for you, Miss Colubride? You did very well. I daresay they were fairly impressed."

"Thanks," said Tori, a little too nonchalantly. "But I had a little help." She placed her hand palm up on the table, and Shonfield laughed as the two black snakes left the machine and found their way back into Tori's bag.

"Yes, I see!" Shonfield smiled and moved to the next entry.

"Well done," Tremelo said to Tori, as soon as Shonfield and Jerri were out of earshot.

"All that fuss, and Viviana hardly even looked," said Tori, sounding almost disappointed.

"Just wait," said Tremelo. Once the orb was in place, he was sure they'd attract her attention.

They lifted the Halcyon off the table and carried it behind the row of canvas tents to Tremelo's motorcar. Tremelo carefully set Lyle's orb in the nest they'd made for it inside the Halcyon's frame.

"Let's try it," Tori said. "Where's Fennel?" She nearly had to shout over the noise of the bustling fair.

Tremelo looked around for his kin. He'd sent Fennel to find the RATS, with a message for both Digby Barnes and Gwen. He had not heard from Gwen since she left Fairmount, and the RATS were impossible to find, even for him. In the days since he'd sent the Clamoribus into the mountains in search of the Velyn, he'd gotten no word in return. He hadn't admitted as much to Tori, but he was worried help would not come.

"Tremelo—look!" Tori said. She pointed at the causeway mobbed with fairgoers—among them was the missing teacher, Dr. Graves. Half his face was hidden behind his bundled scarf, and he stood alone to the side of a tent bearing an advertisement for MADAME VICTROLA'S GENUINE SNAIL-SLIME FACE CREAM, looking about as comfortable as a hairless cat in a snowstorm. He snuck glances down the long alley of tents like he was expecting someone.

"Do you think he's looking for Bailey?" Tori asked.

"The sneaking cockroach," spat Tremelo. "Stay here." His blood boiled at the sight of Graves—he was the reason Bailey had left Fairmount and run straight into the clutches of the Jackal. Tremelo cursed himself again for not being there when the boy needed him.

Tremelo wove through the crowd. Barreling into the causeway, he was on Graves before the hook-nosed man had a chance to react. Tremelo grabbed him by the scarf and pulled him under the spectator stands.

"What are you doing here?" Tremelo snarled once they were out of sight. He backed Graves against a wooden post. "Who are you working for?"

"Madman! Let go of me, you don't have the slightest clue—" Graves sputtered, trying to pry off Tremelo's hands. Tremelo only held on tighter. Tori appeared behind him, a little out of breath. Alongside her trotted Fennel, tail swishing, back from her trek into the Gudgeons.

"Where's Bailey? Are you working with the Dominae or the Jackal?" Tremelo asked Graves.

Graves's jaw fell open in shock, and then his brows twisted downward angrily.

"The *Jackal*? You must be insane. Never mind, I *know* you're insane."

Tremelo wrenched Graves away from the post, and then

slammed the little man back again. Fennel yipped. Graves cried out and put up his hands in protest.

"Tell me what you know about Bailey, or so help me—"

"Get off me!" Graves said, shirking away from Tremelo's glare. "I'm not working with the Dominae!"

"Who, then?" growled Tremelo.

"The RATS, of course!" said Graves.

"What?" said Tremelo. "What do you know about the RATS?"

"I am *one* of them," hissed Graves. "From a nest north of the city."

Tremelo's hand shook, but he tightened his fist around Graves's collar.

"Prove it," he said.

"Barnes was against it—but Merritt Locksman and the northern RATS voted to send me to Fairmount. It was just after the Elder and the girl left to find you. We knew they went looking for something important, and that Viviana had spies there. I was able to keep an eye on you, and suss out Dominae infiltration in the school. We didn't know which side you'd be on."

"Which *side*?" scoffed Tori. "Do you even *know* who you're talking to?"

Graves regarded her as he might a cricket who had just landed on his sleeve.

"I knew your reputation when I arrived, Tremelo—as well as that of your father, the Loon. But your tinkering was suspicious. . . . Your experiments correlated with reports we'd received from the Red Hills of Dominae-engineered technology."

Tremelo let go of Graves's collar and stepped back in disgust.

"You thought *I* was tinkering for the Dominae?"

Graves's face turned redder than before, and he took the opportunity to huffily straighten his scarf and tweed cape.

"Is that really so preposterous? You've hardly been involved with our goings-on in the last decade—too busy smoking your pipe! And once I learned the Dominae were watching certain children"—he cast a glance at Tori, who stood behind Tremelo, fuming—"and saw *your* interest in them, I had to act. That's when I confronted young Mr. Walker. I only wanted to protect him!"

"Well, you mucked that one up, didn't you?" snapped Tori. "And now he and Hal have been kidnapped by the Jackal!"

"Nature's left ear," snarled Graves. "If that's true, why wouldn't you alert the RATS?" He faced Tremelo with an accusing stare.

"The RATS make themselves difficult to find," said Tremelo, matching Graves's ire. Tremelo glanced down at Fennel, who sat at his feet, but he did not have to focus long on her to understand that she had not had any luck in the Gudgeons.

"I knew there was something about that boy," said Graves. "*He's* the Animas Tiger, as I suspected—and you allowed him to vanish, at the mercy of who-knows-what!"

"Tremelo! Tori!"

The familiar voice jolted Tremelo out of his anger—it was Gwen, running across the causeway. To his amazement, Phi was at her side. Tori let out a yelp of surprise, and ran forward and hugged Phi as Fennel bounced toward them, ears happily perked. Gwen rushed to Tremelo.

"Thank Nature you two are all right!" he said, clasping Gwen's shoulders and grinning. "Where have you two been? Are you hurt? Where's the Glass? Is it safe?"

ANIMAS

"We're fine, and so is the Glass," she said. She patted her rucksack. "I have so much to tell you!"

Phi was looking around anxiously.

"Where is Bailey?" Phi asked. "And Hal?"

"They took off on their own, weeks ago, and were captured," Tremelo explained. "But they're here, somewhere, in need of help."

"Well, we've come with help of our own."

Gwen looked up into the sky, where Tremelo saw a huge black shape circling.

"Is that Carin?" he asked Phi, but even as he asked it, he knew that what he was seeing was too large, its movements too steady. This was no real bird—it was a Clamoribus.

"It's your messenger," Gwen said. "The Velyn received it, and they've answered."

She led them through the scaffolding and past the motorbuggy, where the fairgrounds backed up to the woods surrounding the Gray City. Here the sounds of the fair became muted, and the crowds seemed far away. Gwen pointed to the trees.

Men and women began to emerge from the shadows between those trees, and out into the light of the fairgrounds. The Velyn, led by Eneas Fourclaw, crossed the threshold of the forest and approached Tremelo.

"You came," Tremelo said, hardly believing what he saw. "I didn't know if I would reach you."

Eneas stepped forward and shook Tremelo's hand.

"Not all of us did, I'm afraid," he said. "There are many Velyn who aren't ready to be seen by the rest of the kingdom yet. But I was beckoned by the True King. We're ready to follow you."

Tremelo was dumbstruck; he was hardly ever at a loss for

words, but at this moment he could barely speak. His heart swelled with gratitude.

"I don't believe it," said Graves, who stood with his jaw hanging open. "The Velyn—they're *here*. They're alive!"

"Well, while you all are getting acquainted," Tori piped up, "some of us have friends to find!"

"We don't even know where to begin looking for the boys," said Tremelo.

"I think I can help with that," said Graves.

His nostrils flared as he breathed in. "*I* am not the Dominae spy you're after, but I just might know who *is*. We find them and we find the boy."

Thirty~four

BAILEY AND TALETH CROUCHED together in a metal cage
covered by a canvas tarp. Outside sat two of the Jackal's mercenaries from the Dust Plains. The Jackal had not exaggerated when
he'd described his army of outlaws; these men dressed in shabby
clothes and carried large knives for weapons. They'd been hired
to keep watch for members of the Dominae—or anyone else who
might try to take Bailey—while the Jackal and his usual guards
patrolled aboveground.

They had set out from the compound in a caravan of motorcars
a few days before. Bailey had caught his first glimpse of Hal since
the day they'd been taken: the Jackal's guards were strong-arming
him into a separate motorcar while he and Taleth had been shoved
into a trailer for livestock. Hal had looked thin and haggard, with
deep bags under his eyes.

They had arrived at the fair many hours ago, and Bailey sensed that he and Taleth were underground. From above came a steady rumble of music and footsteps, and he could smell damp earth all around. During several hours that morning, he could have sworn he heard the sounds of a Scavage match being played above him—running, and the sound of cheering. He curled against Taleth's side, feeling her breath in his ear. She hated being in the cage: every few minutes she would shudder and adjust her position, breathing out her apprehension in a wet huff. She jostled against Bailey, forgetting that she could easily crush him if she wasn't careful. For his part, Bailey had never been more exhausted or afraid.

But now everything was coming to a head: at any moment, Bailey and Taleth would be led from this tunnel to a stage. There, Taleth would bow before the Jackal, or they would both be killed, as well as Hal. He could see no way out for any of them. Even Taleth had become resigned to her part in it, though the sight of her bowing before the Jackal made Bailey feel guilty and sad. He'd wanted a close connection with her, his bond. But all he felt from Taleth as a result was confusion and fear. What worried him most, though, was the thought of what would happen once they'd done as the Jackal asked. He would have no use for them.

"Hello, chaps."

Bailey heard a cheerful voice enter the alcove where his cage was hidden. He lifted his head, and felt Taleth flex her muscles. This was it.

But then he heard one thud, and another, and then the sound of two large men falling to the floor. He held his breath, and pressed his body against Taleth. One footstep, two—and then the sheet that covered Bailey's cage was whipped away.

A thin man wearing a pair of brass spectacles smiled down

at him. It was Jerri, Shonfield's assistant. In his hand, he held an elaborately carved blunderbuss with a stag and a crow on the side. At his feet, two gray squirrels jittered and squeaked with fear at the sight of Taleth.

"Thank goodness," said Jerri, looking from Bailey to the tiger. "You're both safe!"

"Jerri?" said Bailey. "How did you find us?"

"It's a long story," said Jerri. "I'm just glad I did!"

He bent back the latch on the cage door and stood aside to let Bailey crawl out. Taleth followed, sliding her furry white side against the bars as she padded forward. Jerri stepped back as she passed, eyes widening as she showed her full size.

"This way," Jerri said, starting up the tunnel. The squirrels dashed ahead.

"Does Shonfield know you're here?" asked Bailey.

Jerri glanced over his shoulder at him. "Of course—she and Tremelo have been worried sick."

"How did you know I was here?" Bailey asked.

"Saw some sketchy types loitering near the stage—Dust Plains, from the looks of them."

"I don't understand," said Bailey. "What about Graves? He's been working with the Dominae—he tried to attack me at the school."

"I know," said Jerri. "I was there. I'm sorry I couldn't do more."

Jerri's squirrels jumped ahead of them; their chattering bounced off the walls of the tunnel.

"It was you, that night!" said Bailey. "Your squirrels kept Graves from kidnapping me!"

"Any good dean's assistant would do the same." Jerri smiled. "Unfortunately, I didn't catch him. He's still on the loose. But at least you're safe now!"

Bailey struggled to keep up as Jerri led him farther into the tunnel. At last, his nightmare was over—as long as Hal was all right too.

"Where's Hal?" Bailey asked. "I don't know where the Jackal put him. Are we going to find him?"

"He's safe and sound," Jerri assured him.

Bailey felt as though an anvil had been hoisted from his shoulders. Hal was safe, and soon he and Taleth would be too. He turned around to put his hand on Taleth's side, but she wasn't there. She was hanging back by the cage and the fallen guards, rubbing her flank nervously on the open door. A rumbling growl rose from her throat.

"Come on, Taleth," Bailey said.

"What's wrong?" asked Jerri, turning back.

"Taleth won't come; she's too nervous," Bailey said.

Taleth bared her teeth.

"Something's not right," Bailey said.

Jerri retraced his steps.

"There are Dominae soldiers all over this place," said Jerri. "We're beneath the fairgrounds. She probably senses how much danger we're in. We have to move fast."

Jerri reached out to Bailey as if to guide him forward. Taleth ran toward them and swung her left paw, claws extended, at Jerri. He jumped back and lifted the blunderbuss he'd been carrying.

"Nature's teeth," he cursed, aiming the weapon at Taleth.

"Don't!" shouted Bailey. "She didn't mean it." But as soon as he said this, he knew that Taleth *had* meant to attack. A terrible feeling began to grow inside him.

"Who sent you, Jerri?" Bailey asked, backing away. Taleth stayed at his side, growling and crouching, ready to attack again at any moment.

"Plan A clearly isn't going to work," Jerri said, still pointing the blunderbuss at Taleth. "But to spend all semester searching you out, just to *shoot* you? For Nature's sake!"

"*You're* the spy," Bailey whispered. Dread filled his mind. It had never been Graves.

"At your service." Jerri tipped his head. "Or rather, at the service of my lady. Viviana will be *very* happy to know I've found you; so happy that she'll forget I was mistaken, before, about which one of you truly *was* the Child of War. I'd been watching your friend Phi, until she disappeared. Once I'd figured out it was *you*, the school's lockdown made it impossible for me to send word. Viviana'd have my head for that mess-up, but now! Here *you* are. A welcome surprise to place me back in my lady's favor. Come along."

Bailey didn't move. His hands had formed into tight fists. Taleth could easily kill Jerri, he knew, with one swipe of her paw. But Jerri's weapon was pointed directly at her, at too close a range to miss. If she pounced, he would fire.

"If you won't come," said Jerri, "then I guess I don't have much of a choice but to dispose of you here and now." He cocked the blunderbuss. "A shame—I know Viviana would have wanted the honor all to herself."

Thirty~five

BAILEY SHRANK BACK AGAINST Taleth's flanks, searching the tunnel for a means to escape. There was nowhere to run—behind him was only the cage, and the two guards who would wake up at any moment. He felt Taleth arch her shoulders. She roared.

"Jerri, please. You don't need to—"

But Jerri suddenly jumped, looking down at his feet.

"What the—!"

A pair of black snakes were winding around Jerri's ankles and slithering up his pant legs. Jerri kicked his left foot, then his right, trying to throw the snakes off. Just then, a falcon—Carin—flew in front of Jerri and grabbed the blunderbuss. She hoisted it away from him, flapping hard to take it out of his reach.

"Hey!" Jerri stumbled after her, still trying to shake off the snakes. Bailey stepped back just as a pair of arms reached out of the darkness and caught Jerri from behind, tackling him to the ground.

"Gwen, get his legs!" yelled Phi, whose arms were wrapped tight around Jerri's middle. Gwen appeared and seized Jerri's kicking feet, quickly binding them with rope. Tori emerged from the shadows behind them and collected her snakes.

"You found me!" Bailey shouted. He joined them, holding Jerri down by his shoulders as Gwen fastened the knots. Taleth paced around the scene. As Jerri struggled, she purred.

"Let me go!" shouted Jerri.

"No way," muttered Bailey. He helped the girls drag Jerri into the cage, where he shut the door with a slam.

"You're only making things worse for yourselves," Jerri spat. "Viviana will be looking for me!"

"Won't you be embarrassed, then, when she finds you like this?" said Tori.

With Jerri out of the way, Bailey rushed forward, nearly tripping over his own feet, to greet his friends. Phi flung her arms around his neck, and Bailey hugged her back tightly. He laughed.

"How did you find me?" Bailey asked.

"It was Graves!" said Gwen. "He suspected Jerri all along. All we had to do was track him, and he led us right to you. Graves was never with the Dominae—he's with the RATS, and he's gone to find them now! They're going to come and help us!"

"Are you okay?" asked Tori.

"Depends on what you mean by okay," Bailey said.

"I should never have let you leave," Tori replied. "I might've known you boys would get yourself into this kind of mess."

Taleth stepped forward and touched her nose to Tori's hand.

"We've got to get you back to Tremelo," continued Tori. She paused. "Where's Hal?"

Bailey felt as if a heavy stone had just been dropped from his chest to his belly. Hal.

"The Jackal separated us," he said. "I don't know where he is."

"What?" Tori yelled. Around her wrist, a slender black snake coiled and stuck out its tongue. "We have to find him!"

"*I* have to find him. This is my fault," said Bailey. "He came to keep me safe, and I got him captured." He didn't want to tell them what Hal had been through. Part of him wanted them never to know just how close he'd let Hal come to death.

"When did you see him last?" Gwen asked.

"Yesterday, but only for a second," Bailey said. "We were separated, back at the Jackal's compound. Now he could be anywhere!"

Tori nodded. "I can ask the snakes to search for him," she said. "And maybe the falcons and owls!"

"The Reckoning is starting soon," Gwen said. She looked into the darkness of the tunnel. "We can't trust our kin to help us."

"What do you mean?" asked Bailey.

"The Reckoning..." Gwen trailed off. "I *saw* it. Viviana is going to set everyone's kin against them, using that machine. We need to send our kin away."

Bailey thought back to the conversation he'd overheard in his travels, about the poor Animas Swallow named Miriam. Didn't those men on the cargo ship say her kin wouldn't come near her? Was this the effect of Viviana's Reckon, Inc. machine—that it made people's kin turn against them? He knew that Viviana was capable of such hatred. And the Reckoning was set to begin at any moment.

"How do I get to the stage from here?" he asked.

"But what about Hal?!" Tori shouted. "You know, *Hal*, our friend?"

"The longer I play along, the longer Hal stays alive," said Bailey. "I'm going to show up onstage, just as the Jackal planned. Plus, it'll get me closer to Viviana. And I have a feeling she'll be keeping her Reckoning machine close. Maybe I can find it, and stop her."

"You can't, it's too dangerous!" said Phi. "Tremelo has the machine that will counteract it. Just come with us and you'll be safe!"

"I can't," Bailey said, pushing past the group and motioning for Taleth to follow. "The Jackal expects Taleth and me to join him. What will stop him from killing Hal if I don't show? And how else will we possibly get close enough to Viviana?"

All at once, the sound of applause and cheers came rolling over their heads from above ground.

Bailey felt Tori take his hand. Her eyes were brimming with tears. Phi too looked at him with worry and sadness written on her face.

"We don't want you to go," Tori said, looking down at the dusty floor. "But it's *Hal*. What can we do?"

"Go with Gwen, back to Tremelo," he said. "I'll find Hal."

"Viviana will find you first!" came Jerri's shrill voice from the cage. He was hunched against the bars, his bound arms at an awkward angle. His glasses hung, broken, from one ear. "You won't leave this Fair alive!"

Taleth retorted with a roar that reverberated through the tunnel. Jerri and his squirrels squeaked in fear.

"Maybe not," said Bailey. "But that'd be better than dying down here."

With that, he followed his friends out of the tunnel.

Thirty~six

VIVIANA OPENED HER ARMS as though she were preparing to embrace her audience all at once. Today, she would show them what real power was.

"This is for you," she said, indicating the sprawl of the Progress Fair around her. Behind the stage, three concrete pillars, just over four feet tall and topped with torchlike fires, provided a dramatic backdrop to her speech. "My father, King Lionel Melore, believed that with ingenuity and unity, we could build a brighter future— and that future is on display today."

She took a breath and smoothed her hands over her coat— black, with multicolored embroidery that depicted thorny vines. The crowd below was bubbling over with excited energy, though they had no clue what was about to occur. Behind her stood the clockwork tiger, flanked by two guards on either side in gray uniforms.

"Many of you remember the last time my father, King Melore,

stood on these grounds. His brutal assassination cast Aldermere into mourning, but it awakened an anger too—an anger that has been living in your hearts for over twenty-five years, as it has lived in mine!"

From the crowd came cheers and waves of applause. These people had loved her father. They'd suffered in his absence. But she knew what made her different from him: he had been weak. She had grown strong.

"Today I have prepared a special Military and Defense presentation in honor of him," she continued. "Never again will enemies of Aldermere overthrow the name of Melore. Never again will anyone be so foolish as to question the absolute power of your ruler."

This pronouncement was met with staggered clapping and whispers. Viviana breathed deeply and retrieved the brass, ruby-buttoned controller from her coat pocket, ready to show her kingdom how indestructible she truly was.

But then a collective gasp rose from the crowd, and more than one frightened scream. A troop of soldiers marched through the main thoroughfare, directly toward the stage. Viviana's fingers trembled with anger—whoever had organized this had clearly underestimated her. On either side of her, guards stood at attention, hands on their swords and rifles. Then the man leading the charge walked forward, and Viviana drew in her breath.

The very face of her nightmares—the man who had caused her years of terror, who had stolen her life by taking her father's— now stood in front of her, leading a company of ragtag bandits, all armed with swords, knives, clubs, and blunderbusses.

"No," she whispered.

"Surprised?" The Jackal grinned. "I had hoped so!"

"How dare you?" she hissed. She did not move from where she stood—she would not give him the satisfaction of seeing her afraid. She held her hand out, gesturing to her guards to stay where they were.

"You're not even the least bit amused to see me?" the Jackal said. His soldiers stayed in their ranks as he sauntered forward, swinging a metal cane. His voice rose, inviting the horrified onlookers to listen.

"Viviana Melore, your claim to the throne of Aldermere has very short legs—it can only run this far. I think after the people see what I have to show them, they will agree that I am the true ruler of this kingdom . . . and I always was."

He walked onto the stage, and Viviana stepped back before she could stop herself. The Jackal paced in front of her, crossing to the metal tiger. Viviana's nostrils flared as she watched him—so confident, so nonchalant. Oblivious to how powerful she truly was. Laughing, the Jackal tapped the tiger's metal head with his cane.

"Seize him!" Viviana shouted to her guards.

The Jackal simply smiled. Viviana heard gasps from the audience, and saw fingers pointed toward the stage, at something behind her. Her guards halted.

She turned.

Facing her head-on was a white tiger—a real one, with fangs bared. It stood staring at her with its snowy-blue eyes, ready to strike. She backed away from the beast.

"I believe you've been looking for this," the Jackal growled. "But as you can see, the white tiger, the herald of the true ruler of Aldermere, has chosen me."

"No," whispered Viviana. It seemed her body had begun to shrink. The tiger cocked its snowy head, fixed its eyes on her, and roared.

The Jackal stood in front of the white tiger for an unbearably long, silent moment. The tiger began to pace back and forth on the stage, whipping its tail in a menacing frenzy. Viviana's guards scattered.

"Do it." The Jackal was sneering through clenched teeth at the agitated tiger. "Do it, you filthy cur. . . ."

The tiger bared its teeth, clearly with no intention of doing anything the Jackal asked of it. Instead, it roared again.

Viviana steeled herself. This was nothing but a trick—an impressive one, but nothing she couldn't overcome. She snapped to her guards, who recovered from their stupor and caught hold of the Jackal's arms. She summoned her strength, and called her mechanical tiger to her. It arched its back, and echoed the real beast's roar. Viviana grasped the ruby controller and pressed a button, and the Reckoning began.

Thirty~seven

FROM HIS HIDING PLACE behind the platform, Bailey heard the two roars, one real and one mechanical. Confused shouts tore through the crowd. Animals began twitching and trembling, yelping and hissing. Then, all at once, every animal in the fairgrounds attacked the Jackal's men. With teeth gnashing and claws extended, the soldiers cried out in surprise. The people on the grounds did not understand what was happening: they tried to chase after their kin or restrain them, to no avail. But Bailey knew that, like the poor mouse in Lyle Clarke's Science Club, these animals had lost their own will. They were controlled by Viviana's murderous rage, now merely tools for the Dominae. Machines. He peered from behind the platform out into the crowd, hoping to hear the familiar clunking of Tremelo's motorbuggy, or see his friends running to help him. But all he saw were the shocked faces of the citizens as they watched their kin do battle.

Bailey returned his attention to the stage platform. Two Dominae guards held the Jackal, but Viviana herself was watching the two tigers: Taleth and the automaton circled each other on the stage, teeth bared. Bailey heard the sound of heavy boots clambering across the stage—a handful of the Jackal's mercenaries had broken through. They tangled with the guards, and the platform became a chaotic battleground.

Bailey closed his eyes and pressed his back against the side of the platform, hoping that, with enough effort, he could see the stage through Taleth's eyes. He needed to find Hal, and he needed to find the Reckon, Inc. machine. But he couldn't get a clear vision of anything—just a huge, catlike shadow that skulked in the corners of Taleth's vision. A constant, high-pitched whirring rang in his ears, accompanied by a strange thumping, like a drumbeat.

Behind him came a violent shout. He looked up just in time to see two Dust Plains mercenaries leap off the back of the stage with the Jackal, while others fought the tide of Dominae guards in pursuit. Bailey tried to crawl backward into the safety of the shadows under the platform, but it was too late.

"You!" said the Jackal, seeing him. Two pairs of arms seized him under his shoulders, and dragged him away from the stage. The mercenaries marched him behind the Jackal toward the concrete fire pillars behind the stage. Once there, the Jackal turned to face him; his eyes were narrowed, and his cheeks were blotched and red.

"What have you done, boy? We had a deal."

Up on the stage, the troop of the Jackal's soldiers beat back the Dominae who had been holding the Jackal only moments before. The Jackal grabbed Bailey's coat and pushed him against one of the pillars. These stood at Bailey's shoulder height, and he could feel the heat of the coals on his face and neck. The two soldiers from the tunnels stood there, as well as the Jackal's guards from the compound. One of the guards struggled with a barking jackal on a chain leash.

Bailey summoned up all his strength and pushed himself free of the Jackal, knocking them both off balance.

"Where's Hal?" Bailey demanded.

The man holding the barking jackal rushed forward to grab Bailey. The animal pulled on its chain, jumping like it had gone mad. Bailey backed away from the snarling beast and looked toward the stage, praying that Taleth would feel him and help him.

"Hold him, idiot!" the Jackal yelled at his guard.

The Jackal pressed a small button on the base of his cane. A hidden blade popped out from behind the carved metal dog head. Bailey stomped on the foot of the guard holding his arms and lurched out of his grasp. He looked up to the stage to see Taleth pacing the top of the platform. Neither she nor the mechanical tiger had lunged. The clash between Viviana's guards and the Jackal's soldiers on the stage was nearly finished, but out in the crowd, the bandits still struggled against the onslaught of attacking animals. A flock of owls, ravens, and other birds from the fairgrounds dive-bombed into the melee. Onstage, more of Viviana's guards approached Taleth cautiously, intent on corralling her. They had her surrounded, but not one of them could get close enough to strike without her immense claws slashing the air. Viviana herself circled the fighting, regarding Taleth with a hungry, wolfish stare. Bailey's blood froze as he watched several of the guards raise their guns at her.

"Don't shoot it, you idiots!" Viviana shouted to her guards. "We want it alive."

The Jackal lunged at Bailey, brandishing the knife end of the cane.

"Little sneak," he roared. His face was red with fury. He grabbed Bailey by the collar and pushed him against the concrete side of the nearest fire pillar. Bailey's head hit the lip of the column with a thud. The flames behind him were close enough to singe his hair. The Jackal kept his fist at Bailey's neck, holding his collar tightly.

"Where is Hal?" Bailey demanded again. "If you've killed him—"

"Ah, precious Hal," growled the Jackal. "You're in no place to bargain for lives anymore—not when you and your white beast ruined the plan."

"She'll never bow to you again," said Bailey.

"You don't think so?" the Jackal spat. "Look on the stage—look at your tiger." Bailey looked. Viviana stood at the edge of the stage with her own mechanical tiger, one eye on Taleth, and another on the bloody melee on the grounds. Taleth, in a frenzy of anger, was bearing down on Viviana and her guards.

"If Taleth kills Viviana, then I will have my throne back," said the Jackal. "You'll be of no use then. But don't worry—I'll spare your tiger and train her to bow then. Any beast can be trained with the right whip."

Bailey tried to wrench himself free, but the Jackal was too strong.

"Good-bye, Child of War," the Jackal said. The Jackal tightened his grip on Bailey's neck until Bailey could hardly breathe.

He kicked and grabbed at the Jackal's arms. His panicked mind flew between his own vision and Taleth's. One moment, he saw the Jackal leering at him, pressing him against the concrete column. The next moment, he was in Taleth's mind, watching a frightened guard jump away from her unfurled claws. Taleth could feel Viviana probing at her mind, like someone poking pins into her to test her reflexes. Bailey could feel it too, and it dizzied him.

But then he heard an angry snarl; the guard had lost his grip on the chain that held the vicious jackal. It leapt forward and clamped its teeth onto the human Jackal's leg. He shrieked and let go of Bailey. Bailey stumbled and pushed himself forward, away from the fire and into the dirt.

The animal leapt again, snapping, and the Jackal dropped his cane and held his arms up to protect his face. Bailey ran to the stage. Beyond the fire pillars was pandemonium—the fight between the animal army and the Jackal's men had escalated into a full-fledged battle, human against animal. The citizens watching screamed as their kin clashed with the soldiers.

Bailey looked up to the platform, and his heart seemed to stop in his chest—Taleth was running toward him. Her eyes were wild, their pupils just narrow black slits in a fire of blue. She breathed in heavy snorts through bared teeth. Bailey felt no connection to her, no vibration of emotion between them. She was beautiful, poised to attack, and she could kill him with one gnash of her teeth.

Please no, Bailey thought. Not you too. He felt paralyzed by fear, caught in a terrible decision: he could continue trying to reach Viviana, trying to stop what was happening. Or he could run. He hated Viviana even more then—she was forcing him to fear the one creature in the world whom he loved the most.

Suddenly, the automaton, controlled by Viviana, head-butted Taleth, knocking her onto her side. Bailey crouched at the edge of the stage. Above him, Taleth swung at the automaton with her heavy paw; her claws screeched against the metal. Bailey cried out and put his hands over his ears. He had to help her. No matter what, he couldn't leave her.

The Jackal appeared then, his meaty hands outstretched and his pant leg soaked with blood. Bailey, hardly thinking, scrambled backward.

"You little scab! You're a scheming locust, you are!" the Jackal screamed. He came closer, but the ferocious jackal leapt again. Its chain jangling, it knocked the Jackal to his knees. The Jackal's guard rushed to pry the dog off its master, but the animal was too strong. The Jackal's legs kicked into the air, and he screamed for help. Bailey hid his face, not wanting to watch. He heard a loud thud and moved his fingers to see the guard holding a wooden club, standing over the body of the canine.

"Nature's claws," the guard gasped, rattled. The animal lay still and lifeless—as did the Jackal. His face was a bloody mess of bites and gashes that extended down to his neck.

But then, as Bailey and the guard watched, the back left paw began to twitch. Its front right leg moved, and slowly, terrifyingly slowly, the jackal's body lifted itself up and stood facing the guard again.

"Ants," whispered Bailey.

"What in Nat . . ." whispered the guard.

Bailey's hands shook. He'd been certain the dog was dead, but it stood before the Jackal's guard, snarling. Its head was covered with blood. It reared its body back with its teeth bared, and the guard lifted the club to swing down once more. Bailey looked away and crawled quickly along the underside of the stage.

His whole body quivered. The Reckoning was happening all around him, and the violence was unimaginable. He had to stop it—but he needed help. Where was Tremelo? If he didn't appear soon, Bailey knew he would have to destroy Viviana's machine himself. But the only machine he'd seen on the stage was the mechanical tiger, and it was nothing at all like the blueprint Tremelo had copied. If he'd learned anything from Lyle's orb and Tremelo's music-making machine, then the Reckon, Inc. machine had to be near Viviana. His only chance to find it was to get close to her. Perhaps, with Taleth's help, he could restrain her ... if Taleth would still bond with him. He could see no other way. He took a deep breath, stood, and pulled himself up to the stage.

Thirty~eight

VIVIANA WATCHED AS THE two tigers fought head-to-head. The Dominance that she felt pulsed through her like stormy waves crashing onto a shore. And now the white tiger—the beast she'd been searching for—had all but lain down at her feet. Its resistance to Dominance was remarkable, she had to admit. But it was growing weaker minute by minute.

One of her guards ran onto the stage and approached her.

"The Jackal is dead, madam," he said. "Killed by one of his own dogs. The mercenaries have scattered."

Viviana smiled. Her demonstration had gone perfectly: her military power was terrifying. No enemy would dare stand up to her. After today, she'd never have to endure the protests of the RATS or any other naive uprising against her. The people had seen that she could command their kin whenever she needed to.

"Time to rein in the troops," she said, pressing the glowing red button on her controller.

Nothing happened. The light on the controller did not dim—instead, it began to glow more brightly. Viviana pressed the button again, and again. Still, nothing changed.

In the crowd, the screams of the people of Aldermere grew.

"What is happening?" she whispered. Her fingers buzzed with energy, almost as if the force she was sending through the Catalyst was flowing out of her without her control. The animals did not stop attacking—but now that the Jackal's soldiers had fled, the animals attacked indiscriminately, snarling and biting at the citizens in the fairgrounds. Viviana backed away from the platform edge. She threw the controller away from her. It bounced against the wooden boards under her feet and slid across the stage. The building intensity within her did not cease. Her skin seemed to grow warmer and warmer, like a kettle over slow-burning coals.

"Are you all right, madam?" the guard asked.

"Of course," she lied. On the fairgrounds, people fought off their own kin or tried to flee. She hadn't intended this—but she could not help the way her blood began to dance in her veins at the sight of so much chaos, or the way her heart thrilled to see the furthest limits of her strength. "They will hate me for this," she said, to no one but herself. *But at least they will know never to cross me.*

She looked at her fingers. They contained more power in them now than she had ever felt before. She smiled as she realized that, behind her, the automaton continued to fight, even without her pressing the controls on Clarke's flimsy remote. No wires, she thought. Nothing but me and my will.

She turned, and that was when she saw the boy.

Thirty~nine

BAILEY GROPED FOR THE Jackal's cane on the ground, fighting off the first of the Dominae guards to rush at him. He'd watched Viviana toss away the brass controller, and it had skidded to a stop only a few feet from where he stood. The whirring he'd heard earlier had grown into a terrible pounding that came from the mechanical tiger. He wasn't even sure it was sound at all—it felt more like a vibration or a heartbeat.

A feral cacophony rose from the fairgrounds: snarls and yips, screeches and hisses. People were fighting off their kin in shock. He saw a young girl, crying, protect her face with her arm as a ferret leapt at her, its teeth bared. It was just as Gwen had said. People were terrified and confused. So many had been wounded, while others fought back against their kin, sobbing all the while as they reluctantly defended themselves.

The automaton landed a severe blow to Taleth's right side, leaving four bleeding claw marks in her snowy fur. Bailey yelled out; he felt the splitting of her skin in his own side. He winced, but felt grateful—if he could feel Taleth's pain, then she wasn't lost to him. He focused on her, concentrating all his hope in her direction. *Don't give up,* he told her. *Don't lose yourself.* The energy of his bond radiated out from him—he could almost feel it. But with each blow from the automaton, he felt his connection waver.

One of the Dominae guards seized Bailey's arm. The Jackal's cane was knocked out of his grasp.

"Who are you? What are you doing?" shouted the guard.

"Taleth!" Bailey cried. She lifted her eyes away from the mechanical tiger to meet his own. The mechanical tiger rammed its forehead into her injured side; she staggered. Bailey felt his bond with her disappear, as though a cord had been snapped. She snarled and leapt at the automaton, and Bailey reeled backward into the guard, suddenly afraid.

The guard dragged Bailey toward Viviana. Like a bird of prey, Viviana swooped downward to him and took his face in her hand, forcing him to look into her eyes.

"The tiger is your kin, isn't she?" Viviana demanded.

Bailey said nothing. Viviana's violet eyes searched him, darting across his face with mad intensity.

"*You* killed Joan—you're the Child of War the Loon foretold."

Bailey couldn't answer; he could barely think. Behind him, Taleth continued to fight. Don't give in, he thought, but he knew she did not hear him. At any moment, she could abandon the automaton, and come after him. He looked around for the discarded controller—if only he could destroy it; perhaps that would stop all this.

"You die today," Viviana whispered, tightening her grip on his cheek. "Once the Child of War is dead, the prophecy will die with him. And the people will accept me as the true leader of Aldermere."

"But you aren't their leader," whispered Bailey, straining for air.

Viviana squeezed tighter.

"Oh, no?" she said, gazing out on the chaos she'd caused. "Then who will challenge me?"

Forty

GWEN GRIPPED HER SEAT as Tremelo's motorbuggy lurched through the fairgrounds. The battle among the soldiers, the Jackal's mercenaries, and the animals had made traversing the grounds impossible—but even now that the Jackal's mercenaries had dispersed, the crowds fleeing the grounds in the opposite direction did not make the way any easier.

"We need to go on foot!" Gwen shouted, leaning on the back of the front seat so Tremelo could hear her.

"Too easy to lose one another that way," Tremelo shouted back. "Too exposed!"

"But look," she said, pointing to the stage. "Viviana has Bailey!"

"Ants," growled Tremelo, peering over the mass of people and their kin. "Speed up!"

Tori sat on a thick book in the driver's seat; she pressed her hand down on the motorbuggy's horn and revved forward. In the vehicle's wake, Eneas and the Velyn marched as one mass.

All around them was a scene of blood and confusion. Gwen felt as though her bond with her kin was evaporating, diluted and sullied by the pain surrounding her. Terror caused her to look away from the stage, from Bailey's encounter with Viviana to the skies. For the first time in her life, she was afraid of her own kin. A woman began wailing as a snow-white rabbit bit at her neck and face. She flung the rabbit away from her, and it fell to the ground, its body twisted. It righted itself and attacked once more. All around her, Gwen saw humans fighting off their kin, uttering dismayed cries—these were their companions, their family. To hurt them was unconscionable, but they had no choice. Gwen did not feel like the Instrument of Change that the Elder believed her to be. Instead, she just felt helpless.

"We're too late!" Gwen cried. "We'll never be able to stop this!"

Tremelo sat in the passenger seat of the motorbuggy, both hands on the machine, aiming the Halcyon's sound-horn at the stage. Fennel, wearing a metal collar attached to the machine, sat next to him. A soft resonance issued from the machine, but the sound was too low, and not powerful enough to counteract the Reckoning from its position.

"Not too late!" shouted Tremelo, checking the round metal orb at the center of the Halcyon. "Just hasn't built up enough power to—"

"We have to help Bailey *now*," Gwen yelled back.

In the seat next to Gwen sat Phi, watching the skies.

"The Halcyon will work," Phi said, though her voice shook. "It has to."

In the driver's seat, Tori was struggling—her snakes were winding their way up her arms, distracting her from driving.

"Oh, ants—help!" shouted Tori. She took one hand from the wheel and flung a snake off her. The car swerved and nearly knocked over a candied-apple stand. Gwen reached forward and pitched away the other snake. She watched behind them as Tori drove on; the snakes coiled and uncoiled themselves in the muddy grass before slinking after them.

"Nature's teeth," Tori cursed. Gwen could hear a breathless fear in Tori's voice that she'd never heard before.

"Where's Bert?" Tori asked.

"In my rucksack!" cried Phi. "I know none of us are Animas Iguana, but I didn't want to take any chances!" On the floor of the motorbuggy, Phi's pack rustled.

They'd reached the center of the field between the exhibition tents and the stage. The ground below them was nothing but churned mud. The car stalled and lurched across the field.

Four Dominae guards appeared in the crowd, marching toward them. Tremelo rummaged at his feet, coming up with a crossbow.

"We need to get through this mob. Eneas!" He shouldered the crossbow, took aim, and shot at the approaching guards, skewering one's pant leg to the ground behind him. The guard struggled for a moment, then ripped himself free. Eneas, answering Tremelo's call, ran between the guards and the motorbuggy with a flank of other warriors, their weapons drawn. At the sight of the fur-clad fighters, the crowd became even more frenzied. Parents screamed and lifted their children out of the way, and many people who had been fighting gawked, and then took off running.

"It can't be!" Gwen heard someone exclaim. "The Velyn!"

As the motorbuggy sputtered to a start, the Velyn and the Dominae guards came together like colliding storm clouds, emitting lightning flashes of steel against repurposed claws. Two Dominae guards broke through the Velyn's defenses and lunged at the motorbuggy.

Tremelo grabbed a rusty scimitar from underneath his overcoat, and swung at the first guard. The man jumped back, but not before Tremelo sliced through his uniform, exposing the guard's skin.

"Tori, drive!" he ordered.

Gwen searched the motorbuggy for something she could use to fight. She would not watch the lost Prince Trent die at the hands of some Dominae underlings. She clasped a wooden staff from the pile of weaponry in the sidecar, and swung it hard toward the second guard. She felt a satisfying thud as the staff connected, hard, with the man's chest, knocking him backward.

Tori slammed on the clutch, and the motorbuggy jolted into action once more.

"Wait! Gwen, Phi, Tori!"

Gwen searched the crowd for the source of the familiar voice. At first, all she could see in the direction of the sound was a cloud of leathery black wings. A boy ran a few paces behind the motorbuggy, flailing his arms to fight away the colony of bats.

"It's Hal!" Gwen yelled to Tori.

Tori slammed on the brakes, causing them all to lurch forward. Then she spun around in her seat and tore off her driving goggles. "Hal!"

Gwen and Tori leapt out of the motorbuggy. Gwen took off her cloak and threw it over him to protect him from the bats.

"Come on!" shouted Tremelo, as he kicked a Dominae attacker off the sidecar. "Hurry!"

"How did you escape?" Tori asked. She put an arm around Hal so he could lean on her as they ran to the motorbuggy. "Are you okay?"

"I'm okay," said Hal, though his face and hands showed numerous bright red scratches.

They piled back into the motorbuggy, where Tremelo made room for Hal next to the Halcyon.

"Let's go!" said Tremelo. "Thank Nature *one* of you boys is safe."

Gwen and Phi squeezed into the sidecar as Tori jumped into the driver's seat, and they took off once more. The bats peeled away, flying higher above the field.

"I was held by two of the Jackal's men," Hal said. "But one of them had this." He opened his jacket, and took out Bailey's claw. "They'd taken it from us when we were captured. The bats came on fast, and attacked all of us. When neither of them was looking, I grabbed it and cut myself free. I ran as fast as I could."

He put his weight on Tori, clearly exhausted. He kept looking up, as if expecting the bats to appear again at any moment. Gwen followed his gaze, and her jaw dropped.

A small parliament of owls, Melem among them, circled closer and closer to the motorbuggy. Gwen screamed and covered her head. Hal swirled Gwen's cloak over her, doing his best to keep the owls at bay. But Gwen's vision was lost in a tangle of feathers as she felt talons tear at the skin of her arm—one owl had swooped out of the sky.

"No, no!" Gwen cried. Rattling at her feet, on the floor of the motorbuggy, was her walnut bow. No, please, she thought. I can't hurt my own kin. Melem's talons gripped the coat over Gwen's head, uncovering her. The others were shouting and trying to fight the owls off with stick and swords. Gwen reached down and grabbed the bow, along with one slim arrow. She turned and took aim.

Before she let the arrow slip from between her fingers, the owls surrounding her disappeared. She heard gasps of surprise from Tori and Phi, and the sound of flapping wings quickly quieted. She lowered her arms, bracing herself against the side of the moving car, and saw the owls struggling, on the ground, inside a tangled net. The motorbuggy lurched to a halt as several people ran in front of it and put up their hands.

"Come on now, girl," said a familiar voice, which was deep and comforting. Gwen looked up and met the eyes of Digby Barnes. He wore a makeshift piece of armor made from a metal keg, with the image of a mole hand-painted on it in white. Behind Digby stood a ragtag group of hundreds of men and women. They wore whatever protection they'd been able to make for themselves, and were armed with whatever weapons they could get their sly hands on. Many of them held nets that contained their squirming, possessed kin, while others had blood smeared across their armor. Gwen let the arrow fall from the bow; it clattered onto the floor of the motorbuggy. She began to cry at the thought of what she'd almost done.

"No time for tears," said Digby. "The RATS are here now. Come on—we've got a queen to stop."

Gwen gripped the bow tightly and nodded.

"RATS, move out!" Digby called. The RATS surrounded the motorbuggy and marched ahead of it, cutting a clear path to the stage through the swarming citizens.

Ahead, Bailey stood captive by Viviana's guards, and Taleth fought the automaton. The motorbuggy sputtered to a halt only a few yards from the platform. Gwen leapt out as Tremelo struggled to adjust the position of the orb in the Halcyon.

As she ran closer to the stage, Gwen could make out a pulse issuing from it—the drumbeat from her vision. Just as it had then, it pounded in her ears like the very blood in her veins. She repeated Ama's words to her, for guidance.

True sight is a light that grows—your sight is strengthened and made clear by true bonds. You see what lives unseen in the heart.

Onstage, Taleth and the mechanical tiger circled each other. With a hollow roar, the automaton rose on its haunches and prepared to swipe at Bailey's kin. The metal plates of the automaton's exposed chest seemed to glow.

"'What lives unseen in the heart,'" she repeated. Ama had added those words to the Elder's mantra—had she known?

"Bailey!" she yelled, as loudly as she could over the chaos around her. "It's *in* the tiger! Viviana's machine—it's the tiger's heart!"

Forty~one

BAILEY, AS WELL AS the two Dominae guards holding him, whirled toward the crowd at the sound of clinking weaponry rushing toward the stage. Bailey's eyes grew wide—he saw Eneas Fourclaw running in his direction, and the wide, friendly frame of Digby Barnes, leading a horde of fighters. Viviana's guards loosened their grip on him in surprise. Bailey lunged away. In the corner of his eye, he saw Gwen, shouting something at him with one hand cupped around her mouth, but the words were swallowed up by the fighting around him, and the rhythmic thudding. He thought he heard her say "cart" or "part," but he had no time to decipher her words—the automaton was upon him. He dashed across the stage, dropping into a crouch. Around him, heavy footsteps pounded the wooden boards. He looked up to see a dozen Dominae guards rushing past him to meet an advancing flank of fighters just offstage. Viviana stood at the back of the platform.

Her hands were rigid, fingers outstretched. The sound of wings and claws grew louder as almost every animal on the fairgrounds surged toward the oncoming fighters.

The incessant, mechanical pounding that Bailey had heard since returning to the platform grew louder as well—it vibrated directly behind him now. He scrambled around and came face-to-face with the mechanical tiger. It lunged; Bailey ducked and rolled away. As the automaton pivoted to leap again, Taleth appeared at Bailey's side. Bailey scrambled to get away from her, but he couldn't move quickly enough. With one step, she stood over him, her colossal paws on either side of him. Bailey put his arms over his head and squeezed his eyes shut.

He heard her roar, and then he felt her whiskers tickling the back of his neck. He opened his eyes—she stood between him and the automaton, protecting him from her false double. From somewhere close by, just offstage, Bailey heard faint echoes of music—long, sustained notes like choral chanting or the slow draw of a bow across a violin. The Halcyon. He looked out onto the field below the stage. In the midst of fighting among the Dominae and the Velyn and RATS, Tremelo was in his motorbuggy. He leaned over the passenger seat with Fennel the fox, directing the gramophone horn at the stage. Tori was with him, cranking a lever on the machine's side. At the sound of the haunting music the Halcyon created, Bailey felt a quivering in his chest, and he knew that Taleth felt it too.

The sound echoed over the fairgrounds, and Bailey could see that the kin of the Velyn and RATS were helping to fight the Dominae, not attacking like the other animals. The Halcyon was helping them resist Viviana's Dominance. Several animals on the outskirts stopped attacking their human kin as well—they paused, ears twitching, as though wondering where they were. The more wounded of the kin simply dropped to the ground, their bodies still at last. Viviana's hold on them had broken.

"Yes!" Bailey cried, but there was no time to celebrate. The rest of the fairgrounds was still in turmoil—the Halcyon wasn't strong enough to stop the Reckoning, not against Viviana's machine.

Suddenly, a roar and the shriek of claws on metal—the automaton leapt on Taleth, biting at her neck and shoulder. Bailey cried out as he felt the pain on his own body, just as two guards rushed at him, tackling him to the ground. He landed a hard kick to one's chest, but the other held him down, pinning him to the stage. Viviana appeared over him, her hands now clenched into fists.

"You feel her pain, her injuries—and look how pathetic you are because of it," she sneered. "You represent the old ways. Empathy is weakness! Dominance is progress. I can form an army at will. I can make animals serve humans for the betterment of the kingdom! And"—she beamed at him, as though she was sharing a wonderful secret—"I can control whatever I wish: animals, energy, perhaps one day even life itself."

"But you *can't* control it," said Bailey. "Just look at what's happening!"

Viviana did not answer him—instead, she raised her hand and gestured toward the automaton. It stopped, midlunge, in its fight with Taleth, and swung around to face Bailey. Its tail of metal lashed as it crouched. It was about to pounce.

The automaton opened its mouth, and Bailey stared up into the gleaming cavern of metal joints and wires within. It was a machine, an uncaring killer. Bailey regarded the subtle carvings in the metal plates that formed its face, and the painted copper made to appear like luminous fur. He could feel the waves of energy pouring out of its metal mouth and joints—Viviana's energy projected through it. Bailey concentrated on Taleth, and on the music emanating from the Halcyon. He could feel his own bond growing stronger. Bailey pushed back against Viviana's energy, focusing on his own. As though Viviana's Dominance was a tangible force, Bailey confronted it, his hands outstretched in front of him and his entire skin alive with sparks that only he could feel. He could feel Viviana's Dominance begin to fall back, its resistance wavering. The mechanical tiger stalled, its movements jerky and weak.

"What are you doing?" Bailey heard Viviana shout. "What have you done?"

The tiger stopped, as though it was jammed. It twisted its head to one side and lifted a paw, which remained frozen in midair like a statue. Its tail lashed in one direction, then the next, and grew still. The intense pounding that had echoed throughout the fairgrounds ceased, as though the tiger's heart had stopped. In its place, Bailey heard the battle behind him, and the shouts of familiar voices. His friends were coming, fighting their way to him through the Dominae.

Bailey looked back to the mechanical tiger standing over him. Viviana's own words echoed in Bailey's mind: *I can control whatever I wish: animals, energy... life itself.* But why control the *tiger* with the bond, and not the Catalyst? he wondered. Unless—

The realization came quickly, like an electro-current shock: the Catalyst was inside the tiger.

"It's the *heart*," he said aloud, understanding what Gwen had shouted earlier.

Viviana rushed toward him. Quickly, Bailey searched the tiger's body for weak points, wishing that he still had his claw, or even the Jackal's cane—anything that he could use to penetrate a seam in the machine's immaculate hide. He focused on Taleth. She paced around the automaton, growling. Bailey thought of the moment he'd first Awakened, imagining the crisp air of the mountains in her nostrils, the soft snow that had fallen around them as they looked at each other for the very first time. Then he pictured her heart, in its cage of bone and blood. He could feel it beating in rhythm with his own. Through Taleth's eyes, he pictured the automaton standing before her, and its rib cage of copper and steel. That's how we end this, he thought. The heart—that's what we need to destroy.

Taleth lifted her head in a victorious roar, and brought her claws down on the seam of the automaton's ribs. They wrenched open with a metallic screech. With her teeth, Taleth tore the wires holding the heart in place, lifted the Catalyst out of the automaton's chest, and spat it out. It bounced onstage, landing only a few feet away from Bailey. The orb throbbed, almost like a real heart, and the pounding that Bailey had heard before—which he now knew had been coming from the orb—had weakened to a low pulse.

Viviana shrieked.

Bailey reached for the orb, but it was too far. Viviana lunged at him and clutched at his leg—he could hear her calling to her guards to take him, to rescue the orb. He felt himself being pulled back, in the grip of the Dominae. Taleth, however, would not let him be taken. She leapt at the guards, forcing them away from Bailey.

At the edge of the stage, a thin figure appeared. Bailey's breath caught in his throat.

"Hal!" he cried. "Hal, you're all right!"

Hal waved, and Bailey saw that he had the claw in his hand. Bailey pointed to the orb.

"Help—it's the tiger's heart!" He wasn't sure whether he'd made any sense at all—but Hal seemed to know what needed to be done. With one powerful swing, Hal pierced the orb's metal shell with Bailey's own tiger claw.

The pulse died, and Bailey heard a pop as the last strains of energy left the orb. He stood, with Taleth positioned between himself and the Dominae, and watched as the Halcyon's soaring music reached not only the battlefield by the stage, but also the entire fairgrounds. The fighting stopped. Like a ripple radiating outward, Bailey could see the effect growing, reaching more and more animals and their human kin, as though each strengthened bond helped to fortify the next, until the entire field had attained a stunned, haunted peace.

Those who had covered their faces with their hands or crouched in the mud began to rise and look around, dismayed and bewildered. Heartbroken cries could be heard as the people regarded the aftermath—the bodies of their kin, and the wounded animals and humans.

Bailey ran to Hal, and threw his arms around him in a bear hug.

"You're okay! You're alive!" he said, holding his friend tight.

"So are you," said Hal, hugging him back.

"I'm sorry," Bailey said. "It's my fault that—"

He was cut off by a roar from Taleth: Viviana stood only a few feet away from them.

"You truly think you're able to stop me?" she seethed. "One fight—*one* destroyed piece of scrap—and it's over?" She stepped back and spoke loudly, addressing Bailey and Hal and the entire crowd all at once. Out on the field, the people held one another as they looked up to the stage.

"I am the queen of a New Age of Invention; I do not draw my power from one tiny machine. I have the means to control the entire kingdom at will, and my armies spring up whenever I choose."

"They'll never follow you now," Bailey shouted. "Not after what you've done today."

"After today?" Viviana repeated. "The people will fear me. Which is all the power I need."

She gestured to the grounds, where Bailey saw that indeed, the citizens of Aldermere were cowering. Families comforted one another, and those who weren't trying to run from the fairgrounds were hiding their faces, afraid to see what Viviana would do next. Bailey's heart broke to see so many animals fleeing the fairgrounds, skittering and flying and galloping to the woods, and their human kin watching them go with eyes filled with betrayal.

"That is what power looks like," Viviana said. "That is what my father never understood. And it killed him. But now the name of Melore is transformed! It lives on—"

"In his son," said Tremelo, as he stepped onto the stage. "Trent Melore."

Forty~two

TREMELO WALKED FORWARD TO face Viviana. At his feet, Fennel stood by him, her tail bristled.

The faces of every man, woman, and child in the Gray City were turned to him. Tremelo realized that if he had ever commanded this much attention before, it had been part of another life entirely, one he did not remember.

But when he laid eyes on the face of his sister, he remembered her all too well. He held his crossbow slack at his side and gazed at her—those familiar, fierce violet eyes, staring at him in shock. He remembered the sound of her young voice on the other side of a door as flames licked at the walls of his childhood chamber. *It's stuck—Trent! The door is stuck!*

"Viviana," he said. "Stop this. You must listen to reason."

He reached out his hand.

Viviana, his sister—his family—looked down at his open

palm as a skittish cat might regard a friendly dog. After a moment of silent recognition between him and his only living family, she straightened her back, and stepped away from him.

"Impostor," she spat.

"He's not!" shouted Bailey, running up behind Tremelo. "He's the True King! He should rule, not you, you—"

Tremelo held Bailey back and raised the crossbow.

"We are family," he said, "but I will not allow you to continue this plot you call Dominance. I will do everything in my power to stop you."

Viviana threw her head back and laughed. "You *have* no power," she said. "You are not my brother."

Beside Tremelo, Bailey shook with rage. The boy's knuckles were white from clenching.

Viviana looked from the Velyn to her own guards. The Dominae circled Viviana, inserting themselves between her and Tremelo. But Eneas and two of his men charged at them, fighting a clear path. As the guards drew back, Taleth opened her enormous mouth and roared. Viviana cringed.

"Surrender to us," said Tremelo calmly. "My sister—please. We are family."

The sound of whooshing wings echoed above, and Tremelo and his followers turned to see a colossal flying machine approaching the stage. It wasn't unlike Viviana's Clamoribus—Tremelo marveled at its birdlike design—but it was sleeker, with rigid wings. Its eyes were two curved, paned windows, looking coldly down at the crowd beneath it.

"The finale exhibit," smirked Viviana. As the enormous bird hovered above her, a polished set of metal steps folded down from its belly, and she stepped up. Tremelo came forward, mouth agape. The Dominae guards formed a circle around the strange bird, with their swords drawn. Out of reach, Viviana paused on the steps.

"My power is greater than yours," she said. Her gaze was on Tremelo, but she projected her voice out, addressing all who listened. The giant bird began to hum as it rose higher into the air. Viviana's voice amplified as she continued to speak, her words echoing throughout the arena. "I am not constrained by the bond. You would have me surrender to a False King, a *pretender*, when I have all of Nature under my control, past the bounds of life and death. *That* is true power."

Viviana Melore laughed, and Tremelo watched the woman who was once his sister fly away, forever beyond his reach.

Forty~three

OUTNUMBERED, THE DOMINAE GUARDS were no match for the RATS and the Velyn. With their help, Tremelo and Bailey fought their way off the stage and into the crowd. All around them, people comforted one another as they wrapped wounds in scraps of torn cloth.

Tremelo, Bailey, and the others followed Digby to the edge of the fairgrounds, while groups of fighters broke off to pursue Dominae guards. They ran to the thin forest between the fairgrounds and the first winding streets of the Gray.

Bailey and his friends dashed quickly into the trees, but a gray uniform appeared in the corner of Bailey's vision. A Dominae guard reached to tackle him, but Taleth reared back, and brought the full force of her claws down on the man's chest. Digby appeared at Bailey's side then, and sent a second man reeling backward with a blow from a heavy, blunt-ended wooden mallet.

"Never thought I'd live to see so much excitement," Digby joked. "Them Dominae keep comin' for us, we keep beatin' 'em back!"

A volley of arrows chased them into the woods as more Dominae soldiers appeared at the fairgrounds' edge. But the sound of whooshing arrows was quickly replaced by the flapping of wings and screeching of owls who ducked and swooped, confusing the archers. Together with the Velyn and his friends, Bailey plunged into the trees. Ahead, he saw the red-and-white tail of Fennel the fox leading the way. They ran until the sounds of the fairgrounds were far behind them, and he could see the first rows of tenement housing on the outskirts of the Gray.

After a trek through a series of underground tunnels and back alleys, the group finally reached The White Tiger. Bailey half expected Viviana to be there waiting for them—but instead, at least three dozen RATS fighters had beaten them to the cozy bar. They immediately helped themselves to Digby's taps. Several men and women used benches and stools as makeshift medical stations, washing and stitching up wounds while their patients dulled the pain with mugs of Digby's rootwort rum. Some of the RATS huddled in the corners, shaking their heads as they tallied the lives lost in Viviana's terrible experiment. But as Bailey entered the room with Taleth by his side, he felt their eyes and heard whispers echoing through the room: *the white beast . . . just like the Loon said . . . it was all true . . .* The whispers grew even more hushed when Tremelo entered, with Gwen behind him.

Bailey chose a spot on the floor next to the bar, and sank down gratefully into it. He felt proud, but also tired and a little self-conscious. He'd just stood in front of the entire kingdom and

ANIMAS

shown his true Animas. Everything would be different now—his life in the Lowlands seemed to have taken place long ago. He hoped his parents would be proud of him when he saw them again. When he finally told them everything that had happened in the last few months, he hoped they'd understand.

Taleth followed him, walked in two fastidious circles, and then settled on the floor too. Her enormous, bloodstained back was like a fortress between him and the world. Hal, Tori, and Phi sat behind Taleth, all in a huddled group. Gwen left Tremelo standing by the bar, and joined them.

"This is yours," Hal said to Bailey, digging in his vest. He pulled out Bailey's claw.

Bailey took it and turned it over in his hands in wonder.

"You were fierce up there," he said to Hal. "How did you get this back?"

"The guard who was holding me during the Fair had it tucked in his waistband," said Hal. "Like a trophy—I guess he was going to keep it. When the bats attacked, I grabbed it and ran like the anting wind."

Bailey looked up from the claw and met Hal's gaze.

"I'm glad you're okay," he said. His words fell short of the pride he felt for Hal's risky escape, and the sorrow that he'd ever put his friend in danger.

Hal lowered his head, and rolled up his shirtsleeves to reveal a crisscross pattern of deep, ragged scratches.

"I'm okay," he said. "At least, I will be. But when those bats came after me, I'd never been so afraid. A whole cloud of them. I didn't know what was happening. I was trying to find you, or anyone I knew, but all around me, wings were flapping and people were screaming...."

Tori reached out to him and examined the cuts on his exposed arms.

"I know," she said sadly. "It was horrible."

"But you stopped it," said Phi. "*We* stopped it." She gasped. "Ants! I almost forgot!" Phi dragged her rucksack to her and unbuckled its front flap. Bailey saw a familiar scaly nose poke its way free of the canvas.

"Bert!" he cried. Just as though they shared a real kinship, Bert scrambled out of Phi's bag and waddled across the floor to Bailey's lap. There he curled up and, true to form, fell asleep.

"You saved him," Bailey said to Phi. "Thanks."

"We had to send our own kin away," Phi said. "I think I saw Carin overhead as we ran through the Gudgeons, but I can't be sure. And Tori's snakes—"

"I don't think I want to even look at a snake right now," said Tori. "That's the worst part of all this. Viviana's made everyone afraid of their own kin. We stopped it, but the damage has been done."

"But now the kingdom knows that the prophecy is real," said Gwen. "And that Viviana will only use Dominance for her own power."

Digby busied himself behind the bar, opening more kegs that had not been destroyed in the previous raids. He poured a few mugs of sap milk and passed them down to Bailey, Hal, Gwen, Tori, and Phi. Bailey took a long, slow sip of the warm liquid. It seemed to him like the most delicious thing he'd ever tasted, especially after the horrors he'd witnessed that day. What Gwen had said was true, but they were still far from stopping Viviana. She'd gotten away.

Bailey thought about the dog who'd attacked the Jackal that day, and how it had continued to attack, ruthlessly. It made him shudder. He wondered too what else Dominance could be capable of. If, as Viviana said, she could make an army instantly from whatever beasts were nearby, then the battle ahead would be harder than any of them had anticipated. But there had to be a way to fight her. He had felt it, in his own body, when the mechanical tiger was bearing down on him.

"Somehow, if we could harness the goodness of the bond, in the same way that she twists it, we could overcome her," Bailey said. "Using the opposite of Dominance." He noticed Tremelo standing a few paces away with a funny look on his face.

"'Both the reflection and the opposite of evil,'" Tremelo said.

"Exactly," said Bailey, a little confused. "I think."

Tremelo walked over and crouched in front of Bailey. He gave Taleth a slow, respectful stroke along her spine, and then smiled wearily at the students.

"Even if Viviana does have infinite armies," Bailey continued, "and the people are scared, they know that *you're* alive." He nodded at Tremelo. "Trent Melore is alive! That has to mean something!"

"For some, it will," Tremelo said. "There are those who believe the rumors about a True King. But many will see me exactly as Viviana hoped they would—as an impostor."

He took a small jar of King's Finger salve from his pocket and handed it to Tori. She nodded, and held her hands out again to

Hal. Tenderly, she applied the healing salve to his cuts as Tremelo continued to speak.

"I don't see an impostor anymore," Tremelo said, looking directly at Bailey. "I wanted to hide from this—from my birthright and my true self. If I'd had my wish, I'd have ignored the real danger that the kingdom is in. But I can't, can I?"

Slowly, the entire room started paying attention. Everyone, RATS and Velyn, was looking at Tremelo. Fennel stood by his side, her furry chest puffed out proudly.

"I'm your king," he said, turning to face the entire room. "I didn't want it before. . . . I didn't think I could ever live up to it. But I know now that I have to try. If these kids—these brave kids—can face their enemies and their challenges with the courage and heart that I saw today, then I must try to do the same. I owe it to them."

Bailey smiled up at Tremelo. He petted Taleth's dirty, blood-matted fur, and he experienced a comforting moment of deep connection. He saw a flash of woodlands, and smelled mountain pine. Taleth was dreaming of the Peaks. He closed his eyes for a moment and joined her there, willing the memory of her nearly attacking him out of his mind. Viviana had tried to make them fear each other—hurt each other. But he wondered if, in fact, their ordeal had only made their bond stronger.

"Viviana claims to have created an army today—well, we have the seeds of an army too," Tremelo continued. "The greatest warriors in the kingdom are here together. The Velyn and the RATS."

Cheers sounded through the dingy room, filling its musty corners with hope and excitement. Digby Barnes and Eneas Fourclaw stood together in the corner. At Tremelo's word, Digby slapped Eneas's back, and Eneas nodded solemnly—but not unkindly.

"I still can't believe it," Digby said, overcome. "Bidin' your time all those years. Clever as old Loony always said you were. It's an honor, an honor."

"There are more of us, deeper in the mountains," said Eneas to Tremelo. "I can't promise you thousands, but those who still live will fight on your side. We're with you."

Bailey sat up a little straighter.

"More?" he said. "Are any of them my family? Are there more who are Animas White Tiger? Is Taleth really the last?"

Eneas and Tremelo regarded him seriously.

"That's not for me to answer," said Eneas. "I've known no humans with white tiger kin after the Jackal's reign other than you. But Aldermere is a larger place than some folks think. Over the mountains . . . one never knows."

Tremelo looked down at Bailey.

"You and Taleth together were the bravest fighters I've ever seen," he continued. "And your bond was able to overcome everything that Viviana tried to do to it. You have the Velyn to thank for that—and also your own hardships."

Behind the bar, one of the RATS pushed a foam-topped mug of rootwort rum toward Tremelo, who paused to take a sip. He continued to look at Bailey, with a small, tired smile showing under his mustache.

"You have enormous power, though it's not the kind that someone like Viviana treasures. You have an old soul, Bailey Walker. It stretches back to encompass those who loved you long ago, and those who paved the way for your life. They were with you today."

Tremelo raised his mug.

"To Bailey Walker," he said. "To the Child of War."

"To the Child of War!" echoed the RATS and Velyn.

Bailey raised his own mug of sap milk.

"To our king," he said, meeting Tremelo's gaze. "And to Aldermere."

"To Aldermere!"

Everyone in the room tipped back their glasses, eager to find the warm light at the end of a dark day. War was coming, whether they were prepared or not. Bailey knew that the next morning would bring more hardship—but now, with his friends, he counted himself among the luckiest in the kingdom. What he couldn't know was that at that same moment, in attics and alleys throughout the Gray, and even in the stone-walled homes of the nearby villages, others were whispering the very same words—*The True King! The Child of War!*—like a wish or prayer, like a flicker of hope in the darkness of a long, cold night.

Acknowledgments

I WOULD LIKE TO THANK the editorial team at Paper Lantern Lit: Lauren Oliver, Lexa Hillyer, Alexa Wejko, Tara Sonin, and especially Rhoda Belleza, as well as PLL alums Beth Scorzato, Angela Velez, and Adam Silvera, for their vision, guidance, and support. Thanks are again due to agent Stephen Barbara as well as Rotem Moscovich and Julie Moody at Disney Hyperion for their insight and dedication. I'm grateful to my good friends Jen Whitton and Michele McNally and to Judy, George, and David— my family—for their love and enthusiasm. I'd especially like to thank my husband, who keeps my oceans calm and blue.